AN ANTHOLOGY OF EROTI

KU-522-611

AN ANTHOLOGY OF
EROTIC PROSE

Edited by
Derek Parker

The Softback Preview

First published in Great Britain 1981
by Constable & Company Ltd
3 The Lanchesters,
162 Fulham Palace Road,
London W6 9ER

This edition published 1991 by
The Softback Preview
by special arrangement with
Derek Parker

Copyright © 1981 Derek Parker

Made and printed in Great Britain by
The Bath Press

To June and Robert

CONTENTS

CONTENTS

CONTENTS

[9]

CONTENTS

INTRODUCTION

'As for me, I see no deities that better suit together than Pallas and Venus. Whoever shall go about to remove amorous imaginations from the Muses, shall deprive them of the best entertainment they have, and of the noblest subjects of their work; and who shall debar Cupid the service and conversation of poesie, shall weaken him of his best weapons.'

Montaigne: *Upon some verses of Virgil*

This is an anthology of prose in which authors have recorded and described, for one reason or another, the human sexual impulse. Some, like Renoir, are trying very seriously to convey what the sexual instinct is *like* or about. Others, like the modern pornographic film-makers or photographers, fulfil A.P. Herbert's definition of the role of the pornographer – they are simply trying to make us as randy as possible as quickly as possible.

The analogy with the visual arts is an interesting one. For instance, it helps us to look disinterestedly at the relationship between the erotic and the pornographic. The erotic in painting is common enough; but it is sometimes overlooked that great artists have also created positively pornographic works, paintings or drawings that would be so regarded whatever definition of the word were accepted. Work, in fact, in which the purpose seems to have been to record or perhaps work out the artist's lust. Some of these paintings – Millet's peasants, for instance, certain works by Daumier and de Beaumont – are successful in that they very vividly convey the heights of sexual passion. Others – think of Achille Devéria's illustrations to *Don Juan* – are less successful, and for the same reason that most pornographic photography is unsuccessful: they are too selfconscious. But it is obviously not impossible to go a long way towards recording the full beauty and sensuality of coition, involving both body and spirit.

Should it then be represented? The fact that this anthology, which contains explicit accounts of love-making, has been completed, suggests my own attitude, reflecting that of the British Williams Committee on Obscenity and Film Censorship, and that of President Nixon's Commission on Obscenity and Pornography, perhaps even more exhaustive in its collation of available statistics and other data: that there is nothing wrong, intrinsically, with pornography, and that it does no more proven harm than any other pleasure may do if misused. The only argument which impresses me at all, and which (perhaps significantly) is relatively seldom put by the anti-pornography lobby, is that which suggests that the sexual act is so intimate, so close to the centre of our beings, if you like, that it is a kind of blasphemy to portray it.

But that argument is at least somewhat undermined by the loving reverence with which some writers have written with the utmost explicitness about love-making: Lawrence is an obvious example. Violette Leduc, too, writes about a young girl's first sexual experience with the most sensitive feeling.

However, most of the extracts included here were written to amuse, to entertain, to arouse the sexual appetite. In some of them, sexuality takes second place to narrative, in others to sheer charm. Elsewhere, charm and sensuality are brilliantly united – is there a better example of this than *Daphnis and Chloe* (which, incidentally, I have preserved in the original spelling of the seventeenth-century translation)? Even some works written entirely for pornographic purposes have passages of a loving intensity which, at least for a page or two, perfectly convey the full beauty of sexuality at its most caring: can anyone read unmoved Fanny Hill's description of waking, on the morning after losing her virginity, to see her lover lying at her side?

One of the witnesses at the American trial of a bookseller prosecuted for selling Cleland's novel pointed out to the judge that *Fanny Hill* had been almost solely responsible for the sexual education of generations of college boys. The educational value of erotic prose is not insignificant, though to the authors of, say, *L'Escholle des Filles*, titillation was doubtless more important than instruction. This however was certainly not the case either with the *Kama Sutra* or *The Perfumed Garden*, which can be read today possibly with as much profit as *The Joy of Sex*.

Comedy and sexuality are uneasy bedfellows, and when they are combined the result is generally anaphrodisiac. Nevertheless, the present century has somewhat reversed that rule, and Terry Southern, Philip Roth, Robert Gover and Gore Vidal are only four of the writers who have turned out novels which are both erotic and hilarious – the equivalent in art is, perhaps, the range of erotic cartoons drawn by Thomas Rowlandson. Elsewhere in this anthology, the humour is unconscious: I find the anonymous contributor to *The Exhibition of Female Flagellants* (p. 82) hilariously funny, and Restif de la Bretonne's account of the unfortunate effects of reading pornography (p. 67) only a little less so.

Autobiographical works such as Restif's are fascinating. Can they be true, or do all writers of sexual memoirs follow his example and 'do as engravers do when drawing an unfinished building, and put things down as they should have liked them to happen'? One can only guess, by their tone. Boswell, in his *London Journal*, giving an account of his affair with the actress Louisa (I have, alas, been refused permission to reprint this) is clearly entirely honest. And one suspects that 'Walter', whose *My Secret Life* is the most famous example in English of the purely sexual autobiography, is also probably being entirely truthful. Frank Harris, an inveterate liar where other matters are concerned, may have invented some incidents in *My Life and Loves* (his wife remarked that if Frank had indeed performed the amorous feats recorded on one journey through France, he must have done so on the running-board of their car, as far as she had observed). Others ring true. But one can only guess; writing erotica, one is not upon oath.

The really dull area of erotic prose is that which is entirely pornographic. Visual pornography can of course be beautiful – look at some of the eastern pillow books, or at Indian sculpture. Straightforward descriptions of copulation, often making use of extremely repetitive language, do not have much to commend them, however, and the Victorian pornographic novel, and more recently a great deal of the writing of Henry Miller, is undeniably tedious. Somehow, the imaginative faculty must be involved, as it is for instance in the otherwise extremely unpleasant modern classics *Story of O* and *The Image*. Pornography must stir the reader's imagination no less than the author's, if it is to be truly erotic, must absolutely convince him that however happy and complete his own sex-life may be, to quote the educationalist Lycaenium in *Daphnis and Chloe*, 'there are other leaps, there are other friskins than those, and far sweeter than them.'

I have naturally not gone out of my way to represent here writing which I believe to be unutterably boring; but the subject being one in which readers' tastes are liable to be extremely, perhaps excessively, varied, I have tried to keep the menu as catholic as possible. I find the literature of flagellation and sadism, for instance, entirely anti-erotic; but it is too common a theme in English erotica to be omitted.

A reviewer of the companion volume to this one, *An Anthology of Erotic Verse*, complained of a certain *ennui* after reading straight through that book. But of course only reviewers would do that: anthologies are meant to be tasted, dipped into, although I have been happily surprised at the wide variety of work which has suggested itself for inclusion here. Apart from any interest it may have for those interested in the history of pornography, or whatever, it is obviously in the first place the modern equivalent of a pillow book; the heroine of Barbara Pym's *Excellent Women* read cookery books before going to bed. Other people, other bedtime reading.

In the opening hours of the trial of the British publishers, Penguin, for publishing *Lady Chatterley's Lover* in full and in paperback, twenty years ago, the prosecutor, Mr Mervyn Griffith Jones, asked the jury: 'Is it a book you would even wish your wives and servants to read?' The question was, even then, recognised as ridiculous, and probably contributed much to the jury's eventual decision to acquit. And today, happily, the great majority of people would probably assent to the proposition that Mr Griffith Jones put forward as the central argument of Lawrence's novel – that 'it sets out to defend sensuality as a virtue.'

DEREK PARKER

ACKNOWLEDGEMENTS

The author is grateful to the following authors, authors' estates, agents and publishers in respect of passages listed:

Amatory Experiences of a Surgeon, The, extracted by permission of the British Library.

Balzac, Honoré de: Alec Brown and Granada Publishing Limited, for an extract from 'The Danger of being an Innocent', from *Droll Stories*.

Bretonne, Restif de la: Robert Baldick and Messrs Barrie & Rockliff for an extract from *Monsieur Nicolas*.

Burroughs, William: Messrs Calder & Boyars for an extract from *The Naked Lunch*.

Colette: Roger Senhouse and Messrs Martin Secker & Warburg for an extract from *Chérie*.

Coppens, Armand: Messrs Charles Skilton for an extract from *Memoirs of an Erotic Bookseller*.

de Berg, Jean: Messrs Georges Borschardt for an extract from *The Image*.

Genet, Jean: the author and Messrs Rosica Colin for an extract from *The Thieves' Journal*, c 1949 and 1965.

Gide, André: Messrs Martin Secker & Warburg for an extract from *Si le grain ne meurt*.

Glyn, Elinor: the author's estate and Messrs Gerald Duckworth for an extract from *Three Weeks*.

Harris' List of Covent Garden Ladies: extracted by permission of the British Library.

Harris, Frank: Grove Press Inc and Arthur Leonard Ross for the Frank Harris Estate, for an extract from *My Life and Loves*.

Jong, Erica: the author and Messrs Martin Secker & Warburg for an extract from *Fear of Flying*.

Leduc, Violette: the author's estate and Messrs Peter Owen for an extract from *La Batârde*.

Li Yu: Richard Martin and Messrs André Deutsch for an extract from *The Before Midnight Scholar*.

Miller, Henry: the author's estate and Messrs Calder & Boyars for an extract from *Sexus*.

Nabokov, Vladimir: Weidenfeld (Publishers) London for an extract from *Lolita*.

Nin, Anaïs: the author's estate and Messrs W. H. Allen for 'Saffron', from *Little Birds*.

Roth, Philip: the author and Messrs Jonathan Cape for an extract from *Portnoy's Complaint*.

Sacher-Masoch, Leopold von: Anthony Cheetham for an extract from *Venus in Furs*.

Southern, Terry: the author and Messrs Calder & Boyars for an extract from *Blue Movie*.

Strachey, Lytton: The Society of Authors as agents for the Strachey estate for an extract from *Ermyntrude and Esmeralda*.

Tabori, Paul: Peter Tabori for the author's estate, for 'The Glass Princess'.

Vidal, Gore: the author and Messrs Anthony Blond for an extract from *Myra Breckenridge*.

Welch, Denton: the author's estate and Messrs Hamish Hamilton for an extract from the *Journals*.

Wharton, Edith: the author's estate for an extract from Beatrice Palmato.

Whore's Catechism, The: extracted by permission of the British Library.

Despite his best endeavours, the editor has failed to discover the whereabouts of the copyright-holders of material by Xaviera Hollander, 'Pauline Réage', and Robert Gover. He would be pleased to hear from them, so that the proper acknowledgments might be made.

He is grateful to the staffs of the British Library, the London Library, Cambridge University Library and the Bodleian Library, Oxford; to Winston de Ville, of New Orleans and to William Blatchford, for their help in the matters of Mark Twain and Cora Pearl; and to his publisher for help, encouragement and at least one valuable suggestion for inclusion.

ANON

Harun al-Rashid and the Slavegirls; Mus'ab Bin al-Zubayr and Ayishah; and The Women and their Lovers

It was in the eighteenth century that Antoine Galland published in France the collection of Arabic anecdotes and tales known as the *Arabian Nights' Entertainments* or *The Thousand Nights and One Night*, in which Schehérezade, threatened with the fate of previous wives of a sultan who killed each one on the morning after their marriage, engaged his attention with a series of stories which were always unfinished as the sun set. There have been many English translations, but in many ways the earliest, by Sir Richard Burton, remains the best.

The Caliph Harun al-Rashid lay one night between two slave-girls, one from Al-Medinah and the other from Cufa, and the Cufite rubbed his hands, while the Medinite rubbed his feet and made his concern* stand up. Quoth the Cufite, 'I see thou wouldst keep the whole of the stock-in-trade to thyself; give me my share of it.' And the other answered, 'I have been told by Málik, on the authority of Hishám ibn Orwah, who had it of his grandfather, that the Prophet said, "Whoso quickeneth the dead, the dead belongeth to him and is his."' But the Cufite took her unawares and, pushing her away, seized it all in her own hand and said, 'Al-A'amash telleth us, on the authority of Khaysamah, who had it of Abdallah bin Mas'úd, that the Prophet declared, Game belongeth to him who taketh it, not to him who raiseth it.'

The Caliph Harun al-Rashid once slept with three slave-girls, a Meccan, a Medinite and an Irakite. The Medinah girl put her hand to his yard and handled it, whereupon it rose and the Meccan sprang up and drew it to herself. Quoth the other, 'What is this unjust aggression? A tradition was related to me by Málik after al-Zuhri, after Abdallah ibn Sálim, after Sa'íd bin Zayd, that the Apostle of Allah (whom Allah bless, and keep!) said: Whoso

---

* *concern*   the word used in the original means *capital*, or share in a business

enquickeneth a dead land, it is his.' And the Meccan answered, 'It is related to us by Sufyán, from Abu Zanád, from Al-A'araj, from Abu Horayrath, that the Apostle of Allah said: The quarry is his who catcheth it, not his who starteth it.' But the Irak girl pushed them both away and taking it to herself, said, 'This is mine, till your contention be decided.'

It is told of Mus'ab bin al-Zubayr that he met in Al-Medinah Izzah, who was one of the shrewdest of women, and said to her, 'I have a mind to marry Ayishah daughter of Talhah, and I should like thee to go herwards and spy out for me how she is made.' So she went away and returning to Mus'ab, said, 'I have seen her, and her face is fairer than health; she hath large and well-opened eyes and under them a nose straight and smooth as a cane; oval cheeks and a mouth like a cleft pomegranate, a neck as a silver ewer and below it a bosom with two breasts like twin-pomegranates and further down a slim waist and a slender stomach with a navel therein as it were a casket of ivory, and back parts like a hummock of sand; and plumply rounded thighs and calves like columns of alabaster; but I saw her feet to be large, and thou wilt fall short with her in time of need.' Upon this report he married her and went in to her. And presently Izzah invited Ayishah and the women of the tribe Kuraysh to her house, when Ayishah sang these two couplets with Mus'ab standing by:

> And the lips of girls, that are perfume sweet; so nice to kiss when with
> smiles they greet:
> Yet ne'er tasted I them, but in thought of him; and by thought the
> Ruler rules worldly seat.

The night of Mus'ab's going in unto her, he departed not from her, till after seven bouts; and on the morrow, a freedwoman of his met him and said to him, 'May I be thy sacrifice! Thou art perfect, even in this.' And a certain woman said, 'I was with Ayishah, when her husband came in to her, and she lusted for him; so he fell upon her, and she snarked and snorted and made use of all manner of wondrous movements and marvellous new inventions, and I the while within hearing. So, when he came out from her, I said to her, "How canst thou do thus with thy rank and nobility and condition, and I in thy house?" Quoth she, "Verily a woman should bring her husband all of which she is mistress, by way of excitement are rare buckings and wrigglings and motivations. What dislikest thou of this?" and I answered, "I would have this by nights." Rejoined she, "Thus it is by day and by night I do more than this; for when he seeth me, desire stirreth him up and he falleth in heat; so he putteth it out to me and I obey him, and it is as thou seeth."'

Quoth Abu al-Ayná: There were in our street two women, one of whom had for lover a man and the other a beardless youth, and they foregathered one night on the terrace-roof of a house adjoining mine, knowing not that I was near. Quoth the boy's lover to the other, 'O my sister, how canst thou bear with patience the harshness of thy lover's beard as it falleth on thy breast, when he busseth thee and his moustachios rub thy cheek and lips?' Replied the other, 'Silly that thou art, what decketh the tree save its leaves and the cucumber but its warts? Didst ever see in the world aught uglier than a scald-head bald of his beard? Knowest thou not that the beard is to men as the sidelocks to women; and what is the difference between chin and cheek? Knowest thou not that Allah (extolled and exalted be He!) hath created an angel in Heaven, who saith: Glory be to Him who ornamenteth men with beards and women with long hair? So, were not the beard even as the tresses in comeliness, it had not been coupled with them, O silly! How shall I spread-eagle myself under a boy, who will emit long before I can go off and forestall me in limpness of penis and clitoris; and leave a man who, when he taketh breath clippeth close and when he entereth goeth leisuredly, and when he hath done, repeateth, and when he pusheth poketh hard, and as often as he withdraweth, returneth?' The boy's leman[1] was edified by her speech, and said, 'I forswear my lover by the lord of the Ka'abah!'

---

[1] *leman*   a lover or sweetheart

APULEIUS
(c200 AD)

The Bending of the Bow

Apuleius, born at Madaura, a Roman colony in Morocco, went to Carthage University, became a priest of Isis, had a successful career at the bar, and later wrote *The Transformations of Lucius Apuleius* (more popularly known as *The Golden Ass*), which became immediately popular, and has never lost its popularity. In 1566, William Adlington published a translation of the book which, while inaccurate, is spirited and highly readable. Here is Apuleius' account of how, before being magically transformed into an ass, he has an affair with Fotis, a slave-girl in the house of Milo, his friend and host.

When I was within the house I found my dear and sweet love Fotis mincing of meat and making pottage for her master and mistress. The cupboard was all set with wines, and I thought I smelled the savour of some dainty meats. She had about her middle a white and clean apron, and she was girded about her body under the paps with a swathel of red silk, and she stirred the pot and turned the meat with her fair and white hands in such sort that with stirring and turning the same, her loins and hips did likewise move and shake, which was in my mind a comely sight to see.

These things when I saw I was half amazed, and stood musing with myself, and my courage then came upon me, which before was scant. And I spake unto Fotis merrily, and said, 'O Fotis, how trimly you can stir the pot, and how finely, with shaking your buttocks, you can make pottage. O happy and twice happy is he to whom you give leave and licence but to touch you there.' Then she being likewise merrily disposed, made answer, 'Depart, I say, miser, from me, depart from my fire, for if the flame thereof do never so little blaze forth it will burn thee extremely, and none can extinguish the heat thereof but I alone, who in stirring the pot and making the bed can so finely shake myself.' When she had said these words she cast her eyes upon me and laughed, but I did not depart from thence until such time as I had viewed her in every point. . . .

Then I, unable to sustain the broiling heat I was in, ran upon her and kissed the place where she had laid her hair. Whereat she turned her face, and cast her rolling eyes upon me, saying, 'O scholar, thou hast tasted now both honey and gall, take heed that thy pleasure do not turn into repentance.' 'Tush,' quoth I, 'my sweet heart, I am contented for such another kiss to be broiled here upon this fire.' Wherewithal I embraced and kissed her more often, and she embraced and kissed me likewise, and moreover her breath smelled like cinnamon, and the liquor of her tongue was like unto sweet nectar, wherewith when my mind was greatly delighted, I said, 'Behold, Fotis, I am yours, and shall presently die unless you take pity upon me.' Which when I had said she eftsoons kissed me, and bid me be of good courage, and 'I will,' quoth she, 'satisfy your whole desire, and it shall be no longer delayed than until night, when assure yourself I will come and lie with you; wherefore go your ways and prepare yourself, for I intend valiantly and courageously to encounter with you this night.' Thus when we had lovingly talked and reasoned together, we departed for that time. . . .

And when I was entering into the bed, behold my Fotis (who had brought her mistress to bed) came in and gave me roses and flowers which she had in her apron, and some she threw about the bed, and kissed me sweetly, and tied a garland about my head, and bespread the chamber with the residue. Which when she had done, she took a cup of wine and delayed it with hot water, and proffered it me to drink; and before I had drunk it off all, she pulled it from my mouth, and then gave it me again, and in this manner we emptied the pot twice or thrice together. Thus when I had well replenished myself with wine, and was now ready unto venery not only in mind but also in body, I removed my clothes, and showing to Fotis my great impatience I said, 'O my sweet heart, take pity upon me and help me, for as you see I am now prepared unto the battle which you yourself did appoint – for after that I felt the first arrow of cruel Cupid within my breast, I bent my bow very strong, and now fear (because it is bended so hard) lest my string should break; but that thou mayest the better please me, undress thy hair and come and embrace me lovingly.' Whereupon she made no long delay, but set aside all the meat and wine, and then she unapparelled herself, and unattired her hair, presenting her amiable body unto me in manner of fair Venus when she goeth under the waves of the sea. 'Now,' quoth she, 'is come the hour of jousting; now is come the time of war; wherefore show thyself like unto a man, for I will not retire, I will not fly the field. See then thou be valiant, see thou be courageous, since there is no time appointed when our skirmish shall cease.' In saying these words she came to me to bed, and embraced me sweetly, and so we passed all the night in pastime and pleasure, and never slept until it was day: but we would eftsoons refresh our weariness, and provoke our pleasure, and renew our venery by drinking of wine. In which sort we pleasantly passed away many other nights following.

GIOVANNI BOCCACCIO
(1313–1375)

Putting the Devil in Hell

Boccaccio, who spent most of his life in Florence, wrote a number of books
– a life of Dante, a prose romance called *Filocolo*, a poem on the story of
Troilus and Cressida, and another which Chaucer adapted as *The Knight's
Tale*. But he is best remembered for his *Decameron*, a collection of
anecdotes first published between 1347 and 1351, in which seven young
ladies flee from Florence at the onset of the plague, and spend part of each
of ten days telling each other anecdotes. The translation of the following
anecdote is anonymous.

Charming ladies, maybe you have never heard tell how one putteth
the devil in hell; wherefore, without much departing from the tenor
of that whereof you have discoursed all this day, I will e'en tell it
you. Belike, having learned it, you may catch the spirit thereof and
come to know that, albeit Love sojourneth liefer in jocund places
and luxurious chambers than in the hovels of the poor, yet none the
less doth he whiles make his power felt midmost thick forests and
rugged mountains and in desert caverns; whereby it may be
understood that all things are subject to his puissance.

To come, then, to the fact, I say that in the city of Capsa in
Barbary there was aforetime a very rich man, who, among his other
children, had a fair and winsome young daughter, by name Alibech.
She, not being a Christian and hearing many Christians who abode
in the town mightily extol the Christian faith and the service of
God, one day questioned one of them in what manner one might
avail to serve God with the least hindrance. The other answered
that they best served God who most strictly eschewed the things of
the world, as those did who had betaken themselves to the solitudes
of the deserts of Thebais. The girl, who was maybe fourteen years
old and very simple, moved by no ordered desire, but by some
childish fancy, set off next morning by stealth and all alone, to go to
the desert of Thebais, without letting any know her intent. After
some days, her desire persisting, she won, with no little toil, to the
deserts in question, and seeing a hut afar off, went thither and found
at the door a holy man, who marvelled to see her there and asked

her what she sought. She replied that, being inspired of God, she went seeking to enter into His service and was now in quest of one who should teach her how it behoved to serve Him.

The worthy man, seeing her young and very fair and fearing lest, an he entertained her, the devil should beguile him, commended her pious intent and giving her somewhat to eat of roots of herbs and wild apples and to drink of water, said to her: 'Daughter mine, not far hence is a holy man, who is a much better master than I of that which thou goest seeking; do thou betake thyself to him;' and put her in the way. However, when she reached the man in question, she had of him the same answer and faring farther, came to the cell of a young hermit, a very devout and good man, whose name was Rustico, and to whom she made the same request as she had done to the others. He, having a mind to make trial of his own constancy, sent her not away, as the others had done, but received her into his cell, and the night being come, he made her a little bed of palm-fronds and bade her lie down to rest thereon. This done, temptations tarried not to give battle to his powers of resistance and he, finding himself grossly deceived by these latter, turned tail, without awaiting many assaults, and confessed himself beaten; then, laying aside devout thoughts and orisons and mortifications, he fell to revolving in his memory the youth and beauty of the damsel, and bethinking himself what course he should take with her, so as to win that which he desired of her, without her taking him for a debauched fellow.

Accordingly, having sounded her with sundry questions, he found that she had never known man and was in truth as simple as she seemed, wherefore he bethought him how, under colour of the service of God, he might bring her to his pleasures. In the first place, he showed her with many words how great an enemy the Devil was of God the Lord and after gave her to understand that the most acceptable service that could be rendered to God was to put back the Devil into Hell, whereto He had condemned him. The girl asked how this might be done; and he, 'Thou shalt soon know that; do but as thou shalt see me do.' So saying, he proceeded to put off the two garments he had and abode stark naked, as likewise did the girl, whereupon he fell on his knees, as he would pray, and caused her to abide over against himself.

Matters standing thus and Rustico being more than ever

inflamed in his desires to see her so fair, there came the resurrection of the flesh, which Alibech observing and marvelling, 'Rustico,' quoth she, 'what is that I see on thee which thrusteth forth thus and which I have not?' 'Faith, daughter mine,' answered he, 'this is the devil whereof I bespoke thee; and see now, he giveth me such sore annoy that I can scarce put up with it.' Then said the girl, 'Now praised be God! I see I fare better than thou, in that I have none of yonder devil.' 'True,' rejoined Rustico; 'but thou hast otherwhat that I have not, and thou hast it instead of this.' 'What is that?' asked Alibech; and he, 'Thou hast hell, and I tell thee methinketh God hath sent thee hither for my soul's health, for that, whenas this devil doth me this annoy, an it please thee have so much compassion on me as to suffer me to put him back into hell, thou wilt give me the utmost solacement and wilt do God a very great pleasure and service, so indeed thou be come into these parts to do as thou sayest.'

The girl answered in good faith, 'Marry, father mine, since I have hell, be it whensoever it pleaseth thee;' whereupon quoth Rustico, 'Daughter, blessed be thou; let us go then and put him back there, so he may after leave me in peace.' So saying, he laid her on one of their little beds and taught her how she should do to imprison that accursed one of God. The girl, who had never yet put any devil in hell, for the first time felt some little pain; wherefore she said to Rustico, 'Certes, father mine, this same devil must be an ill thing and an enemy in very deed of God, for that it irketh hell itself, let be otherwhat when he is put back therein.' 'Daughter,' answered Rustico, 'it will not always happen thus;' and to the end that this should not happen, six times, or ever they stirred from the bed, they put him in hell again, insomuch that for the nonce they so took the conceit out of his head that he willingly abode at peace. But, it returning to him again and again the ensuing days and the obedient girl still lending herself to take it out of him, it befell that the sport began to please her, and she said to Rustico, 'I see now that those good people in Capsa spoke sooth, when they avouched that it was so sweet a thing to serve God; for, Certes, I remember me not to have ever done aught that afforded me such pleasance and delight as putting the devil in hell; wherefore methinketh that whoso applieth himself unto aught other than God His service is a fool.'

Accordingly, she came ofttimes to Rustico and said to him,

I don't have the actual content to transcribe here.

with words and what with gestures, expounded it to them; whereat they set up so great a laughing that they laugh yet, and said, 'Give yourself no concern, my child; nay, for that is done here also, and Neerbale will serve our Lord full well with thee at this.' Thereafter, telling it from one to another throughout the city, they brought it to a common saying there that the most acceptable service one could render to God was to put the devil in hell, which byword, having passed the sea hither, is yet current here. Wherefore do all you young ladies, who have need of God's grace, learn to put the devil in hell, for that this is highly acceptable to Him and pleasing to both parties and much good may grow and ensue thereof.

VATSYAYANA
(c350 AD)

On Kissing

The *Kama Sutra* of Vatsyayana seems to have been written between the first and fourth centuries AD, by an author called Mallanaga, who belonged to the Vatsyayana *gotra*, and is known by its name. It originally took the form of a collection of aphorisms, later linked and explained by a commentator. Though writing for a society in which marriages were arranged, Vatsyayana lays great stress on courtship, the wooing of the wife, and her sexual satisfaction, and throughout the book – which includes passages on social behaviour, as well as an almost scientific examination of the art of sexual love – he is intent on reconciling *Kama*, or the life of the senses, with the other two activities central to man, *Dharma* (religious obligation) and *Artha* (social wellbeing) in complete harmony. The book first appeared in English in 1883, translated by Sir Richard Burton and F.F. Arbuthnot, and published by the Kama Shastra Society of Benares, which they had founded in order to publish erotic classics of India. The following section, in their translation, is entitled *On Kissing*.

It is said by some that there is no fixed time or order between the embrace, the kiss, and the pressing or scratching with the nails or fingers, but that all these things should be done generally before sexual union takes place, while striking and making the various sounds generally takes place at the time of the union. Vatsyayana, however, thinks that anything may take place at any time, for love does not care for time or order.

On the occasion of the first congress, kissing and the other things mentioned above should be done moderately, they should not be continued for a long time, and should be done alternately. On subsequent occasions, however, the reverse of all this may take place, and moderation will not be necessary, they may continue for a long time, and, for the purpose of kindling love, they may be all done at the same time.

The following are the places for kissing: the forehead, the eyes, the cheeks, the throat, the bosom, the breasts, the lips, and the interior of the mouth. Moreover the people of the Lat country kiss also on the following places: the joints of the thighs, the arms and the navel. But Vatsyayana thinks that though kissing is practised by these people in the above places on account of the intensity of their love, and the customs of their country, it is not fit to be practised by all.

Now in a case of a young girl there are three sorts of kisses:

The nominal kiss
The throbbing kiss
The touching kiss

When a girl only touches the mouth of her lover with her own, but does not herself do anything, it is called the 'nominal kiss'.

When a girl, setting aside her bashfulness a little, wishes to touch the lip that is pressed into her mouth, and with that object moves her lower lip, but not the upper one, it is called the 'throbbing kiss'.

When a girl touches her lover's lip with her tongue, and having shut her eyes, places her hands on those of her lover, it is called the 'touching kiss'.

Other authors describe four other kinds of kisses:

The straight kiss
The bent kiss
The turned kiss
The pressed kiss

When the lips of two lovers are brought into direct contact with each other, it is called a 'straight kiss'.

When the heads of two lovers are bent towards each other, and when so bent, kissing takes place, it is called a 'bent kiss'.

When one of them turns up the face of the other by holding the head and chin, and then kissing, it is called a 'turned kiss'.

Lastly when the lower lip is pressed with much force, it is called a 'pressed kiss'.

There is also a fifth kind of kiss called the 'greatly pressed kiss', which is effected by taking hold of the lower lip between two fingers, and then, after touching it with the tongue, pressing it with great force with the lip.

As regards kissing, a wager may be laid as to which will get hold of the lips of the other first. If the woman loses, she should pretend to cry, should keep her lover off by shaking her hands, and turn away from him and dispute with him saying, 'let another wager be laid'. If she loses this a second time, she should appear doubly distressed, and when her lover is off his guard or asleep, she should get hold of his lower lip, and hold it in her teeth, so that it should not slip away, and then she should laugh, make a loud noise, deride him, dance about, and say whatever she likes in a joking way, moving her eyebrows and rolling her eyes. Such are the wagers and quarrels as far as kissing is concerned, but the same may be applied with regard to the pressing or scratching with the nails and fingers, biting and striking. All these however are only peculiar to men and women of intense passion.

When a man kisses the upper lip of a woman, while she in return kisses his lower lip, it is called the 'kiss of the upper lip'.

When one of them takes both the lips of the other between his or her own, it is called 'a clasping kiss'. A woman, however, only takes this kind of kiss from a man who has no moustache. And on the occasion of this kiss, if one of them touches the teeth, the tongue and the palate of the other, with his or her tongue, it is called the 'fighting of the tongue.' In the same way, the pressing of the teeth of the one against the mouth of the other is to be practised.

Kissing is of four kinds: moderate, contracted, pressed, and soft, according to the different parts of the body which are kissed, for different kinds of kisses are appropriate for different parts of the body.

When a woman looks at the face of her lover while he is asleep and kisses it to show her intention or desire, it is called a 'kiss that kindles love'.

When a woman kisses her lover while he is engaged in business, or while he is quarrelling with her, or while he is looking at something else, so that his mind may be turned away, it is called a 'kiss that turns away'.

When a lover coming home late at night kisses his beloved, who is asleep on her bed, in order to show her his desire, it is called a 'kiss that awakens'. On such an occasion the woman may pretend to be asleep at the time of her lover's arrival, so that she may know his intention and obtain respect from him.

When a person kisses the reflection of the person he loves in a mirror, in water, or on a wall, it is called a 'kiss showing the intention'.

When a person kisses a child sitting on his lap, or a picture, or an image, or figure, in the presence of the person beloved by him, it is called a 'transferred kiss'.

When at night in a theatre, or in an assembly of caste men, a man coming up to a woman kisses a finger of her hand if she be standing, or a toe of her foot if she be sitting, or when a woman is shampooing her lover's body, places her face on his thigh (as if she was sleepy) so as to inflame his passion, and kisses his thigh or great toe, it is called a 'demonstrative kiss'.

There is also a verse on this subject as follows:

'Whatever things may be done by one of the lovers to the other, the same should be returned by the other, i.e. if the woman kisses him he should kiss her in return, if she strikes him he should also strike her in return.'

LONGUS
(c400–500)

A Wanton Information

Longus was a Greek writer whose life is shrouded in mystery. His only known work is a book entitled *Pastoral Matters concerning Daphnis and Chloe* – a delightfully simple country idyll, many times translated (among others by M.L.P. Courier and George Moore). The most charming translation remains, however, one of the earliest – that by George Thornley in 1657.

Thus Philetas: 'Love, sweet Chloe, is a god, a young Youth, and very fair, and wing'd to flye. And therefore he delights in youth, follows beauty, and gives our phantasie her wings. His power's so vaste that that of Jove is not so great. He governs in the Elements, rules in the Stars, and domineers even o're the gods that are his Peers. Nor have you only dominion o're your Sheep and Goats, for Love has there his range too. All flowers are the words of Love. Those Plants are his creations, and Poems. By him it is that the rivers flow, and by him the winds blow. I have known a Bull that has been in Love, and run bellowing through the Meadows as if he had been prickt with a Goad; a he-goat too so in Love with a Virgin-she that he has followed her up and down through the woods, through the Launs. And I myself, when I was young, was in love with Amaryllis, and forgot to eat my meat and drink my drink; and for many tedious nights never could compose to sleep: my panting heart was very sad and anxious, and my body shook with cold: I cryed out oft, as if I had bin thwackt and basted back and sides: and then again was still and mute, as if I had layen among the dead: I cast myself into the Rivers, as if I had been all on a fire: I call'd on Pan, that he would help me, as having sometimes bin himself catcht with the Love of peevish Pitys: I praised the Echo, that with kindnesse it restored and trebbled to me the dear name of Amaryllis: I broke my pipes, because they could delight and lead the sturdy herds which way I would, and could not draw the froward girle. For there is no med'cine for Love, neither meat, nor drink, nor any Charm, but only Kissing, and Embracing, and lying naked together.'

[32]

from *Daphnis and Chloe*

When it was day, and their flocks were driven to the field, [Daphnis and Chloe] ran to kisse and embrace one another with a bold, impatient fury, which before they never did. Yet of that third remedy which the old Philetas taught, they durst not make experiment: for that was not onely an enterprise too bold for Maids, but too high for young Goatherds. Therefore still, as before, they spent their nights without sleep and with remembrance of what was done, and with complaint of what was not. 'We have kist one another, and are never the better; we have clipt and embrac'd, and that's as good as nothing too. Therefore to lye together naked is the onely remaining remedy of Love. That must be tryed by all means; there's something in it without doubt more efficacious than in a kisse.'

While they indulg'd these kind of thoughts they had, as it was like, their sweet, erotic, amorous dreams; and what they did not in the day, that they acted in the night, and lay together stark naked, kissing, clipping[1], twining limbs. But the next day, as if they had bin inspired with some stronger Numen, they rose up and drove their flocks with a kind of violence into the fields, hasting to their kisses again; and when they saw one another, smiling sweetly ran together. Kisses past, Embraces past, but that third Remedy was wanting; for Daphnis durst not mention it, and Chloe too would not begin; till at last, even by chance, they made this essay of it: They sate both close together upon the trunck of an old Oak, and having tasted the sweetnesse of kisses, they were ingulf'd insatiably in pleasure, and there arose a mutual contention and striving with their clasping arms, which made a close compression of their lips; and when Daphnis hugg'd her to him with a more violent desire, it came about that Chloe inclin'd a little on her side, and Daphnis following his kisse, fell o' the top of her. And remembering that they had an image of this in their dreams the night before, they lay a long while clinging together. But being ignorant what was after that to be done, and thinking that this was the end of amorous fruition, most part of the day spent in vain, they parted, and drove their flocks home from the fields with a kind of hate to the oppression of the night.

[1] *clipping*   embracing

It was now the beginning of the Spring, the Snow was gone, the Earth uncovered, and all was green, when the other Shepherds drove out their flocks to pasture, and Chloe and Daphnis before the rest, as being servants to greater Shepherds. And forthwith they took their course up to the Nymphs, and that Cave, thence to Pan and his pipes; afterwards to their own Oak, where they sate down to look to their flocks, and kisse and clip insatiably. They sought about for flowers too to crown the Statues of the Nymphs. The soft breath of Zephyrus and the warm Sun had brought some forth; and there were then to be found the Violet, the Daffodil, the Primrose, with the other primes and dawnings of the Spring. And when they had crown'd the Statues of the gods with them, they made a Libation with new milk from the Sheep and from the Goats. They began too to play on the Pipe, and to provoke and challenge the Nightingale with their Musick and Song. The Nightingales answer'd softly from the Groves, and resuming their long intermitted Song began to jug and warble their Tereus and Ity's again. Here and there, not without pleasure, the bleating of the flocks was heard, and the Lambs came skipping and inclined themselves obliquely under the damms to riggle and nussle at their dugs. But those which had not yet teemed, the Rams pursued; and when with some pains they had made them stand, one rid another. There were seen too the Chases of the he-goats, and their lascivious ardent leaps. Sometimes they had battels for the she's, and every one had his own wives, and kept them sollicitously, that no skulking adulterer should set upon them.

The old men, seeing such incendiary fights as these, were prickt to Venus: but the Young, and such as of themselves did itch, and for some time had longed for the pleasure of Love, were wholly inflamed with what they heard, and melted away with what they saw, and lookt for something far more excelent than kisses and embraces were: and amongst them was Daphnis chief. Therefore he, as being now grown up and lusty by keeping at home, and following easie businesse all the Winter, was carried furiously to kissing, and stung with the desire to embrace and close; and in what he did was now more curious and more rampant than ever before. And therefore he began to ask of Chloe that she would give him free leave to do with her what he listed, and that she would lye naked with him naked, and longer too than they were wont: For there was nothing but that remaining of the Institutes of old Philetas, and that he would try as the onely Canon, the onely med'cine, to ease the pain of Love.

But Chloe asking him whether anything remain'd more than kissing, embracing and lying together upon the ground; or what he could do by lying naked upon a naked Girle?

'That' (quoth he) 'which the Rams use to do with the Ewes, and the he-Goats with the She's. Do you not see how after that work neither these run away nor those weary themselves in pursuit of them; but afterwards how enjoying a common pleasure, they feed together quietly. That as it seems is a sweet practice, and such as can master the bitternesse of Love.'

'How, Daphnis? And dost thou not see the she-Goats and the Ewes, the he-Goats and the Rams, how these do their work standing, and those suffer standing too? These leaping and those admitting them upon their backs? And yet thou askest me to lye down, and that naked. But how much rougher are they than I, although I have all my Clothes on?'

Daphnis is persuaded, and laying her down, lay down with her, and lay long; but knowing how to do nothing of that he was mad to do, lifted her up, and endeavour'd to imitate the Goats. But at the first finding a mere frustration there, he sate up, and lamented to himself that he was more unskillful than a very Tup in the practice of the mystery and the Art of Love.

But there was a certain neighbour of his, a landed man, Chromis by name, and was now by his age somewhat declining. He married out of the City a young, fair and buxome girle, one that was too fine and delicate for the Country and a Clown. Her name was Lycaenium; and she observing Daphnis as every day in the morning he drove out his goats to the fields, and home again at first twilight, had a great kind to purchase the youth by gifts to become her sweetheart. And therefore once when she had sculkt for her opportunity and catcht him alone, she gave him a curious fine pipe, some precious honey-combs and a new Scrip of Stag-skin: but durst not break her mind to him because she could easily conjecture at that dear love he bore to Chloe. For she saw him wholly addicted to the girle: which indeed she might well perceive before by the winking, nodding, laughing and tittering that was between them: but one morning she made Chromis believe that she was to go to a woman's labour, and followed softly behind them two at some

[35]

distance, and then slipt into a thicket and hid herself, and so could hear all that they said, and see too all that they did; and the lamenting untaught Daphnis was perfectly within her reach. Wherefore she began to condole the condition of the wretched Lovers, and finding that she had light upon a double Opportunity; this, to the preservation of them; that, to satisfie her own wanton desire, she projected to accomplish both by this device.

The next day, making as if she were to go a Gossiping again, she came up openly to the Oak where Daphnis and Chloe were sitting together; and when she had skilfully counterfeited that she was feared, 'Help, Daphnis, help me' (quoth she), 'An Eagle has carried away from me the goodliest Goose of twenty in a flock, which yet by reason of the great weight she was not able to carry to the top of that her wonted high crag, but is fallen down with her into yonder Cops. For the Nymph's sake, and this Pan's, do thou Daphnis go in to the Wood and rescue my Goose. For I dare not go in my selfe alone.'

Now Daphnis suspecting nothing of that that was intended, gets up quickly and taking his staff followed Lycaenium, who lead him a great way off from Chloe. But when they were come to the thickest part of the wood, and she had bid him sit down by a Fountain: 'Daphnis' (quoth she) 'Thou dost love Chloe, and that I learned last night of the Nymphs. Those tears which yesterday thou didst pour down were shown me in a dream by them, and they commanded me that I should save thee and teach thee the secret practices of Love. But those are not Kisses, nor embracing, nor yet such things as thou seest the Rams and the he-goats do. There are other leaps, there are other friskins than those, and far sweeter than them. For unto these there appertains a much longer duration of pleasure. If thou woulds't be rid of thy misery, and make an Experiment of that pleasure and sweetnesse which you have sought and mist so long, come on, deliver thy self to me a sweet Schollar, and I, to gratifie the Nymphs, will be thy Mistris.'

At this Daphnis as being a rustick Goat-herd, a Sanguin Youth, and burning in desire, could not contain himself for meer pleasure, and that Lubency[1] that he had to be taught; but throwes himself at the foot of Lycaenium and begs of her That she would teach him quickly that Art by which he should be able, as he would, to do Chloe;

[1] *Lubency*   pleasure

[36]

and he should not only accept it as a rare and brave thing sent from the gods, but for her kindnesse he would give her too a young Kid, some of the finest new-milk Cheeses; nay, besides, he promised her the dam her self. Wherefor Lycaenium now she had found the Goat-herd so willing and forward beyond her expectation, began to instruct the Lad thus – She bid him sit down as near to her as possibly he could, and that he should kisse her as close and as often as he used to kisse Chloe; and while he kist her to clip her in his arms and hugg her to him, and lye down with her upon the ground. As now he was sitting, and kissing, and lay down with her; She, when she saw him itching to be at her, lifted him up from the reclination on his side, and slipping under, not without art, directed him to her Fancie, the place so long desired and sought. Of that which happened after this, there was nothing done that was strange, nothing that was insolent: the Lady Nature and Lycaenium shewed him how to do the rest. This wanton Information being over, Daphnis, who had still a Childish Pastorall mind, would presently be gone, and run up to Chloe, to have an experiment with her, how much he had profited by that magistery, as if indeed he had bin afraid lest staying but a little longer he could forget to do his trick.

SHAYKH NEFZAWI
(c1530)

Everything for the Best!

The Perfumed Garden was the third of the ancient manuals of sexual technique privately published for members of the Kama Shashtra Society of London and Benares, and came out in 1886 in the translation of Sir Richard Burton, who had discovered a French version of the work made in the 1850s in Algeria. It discusses human sexual activity seriously, but not without wit, offering chapters on *Women who Deserve to be Praised*, *Men who are to be Held in Contempt*, *The Causes of Impotence in Men*, as well as long lists of Arabic names for the sexual organs – the penis was known as 'the tinkler', 'the pigeon', 'the striker', 'the impudent one', while the woman offered man 'the hedgehog', 'the duellist', 'the glutton' or 'the delicious one.' The following chapter is entitled *Relating to the Act of Generation*.

Know, O Vizar (and God protect you!), that if you wish for coition, in joining with the woman you should not have your stomach loaded with food and drink, only in that condition will your cohabitation be wholesome and good. If your stomach is full, only harm can come of it to both of you; you will have threatening symptoms of apoplexy and gout, and the least evil that may result from it will be the inability of passing your urine, or a weakness of sight.

Let your stomach then be free from excessive food and drink, and you need not apprehend any illness.

Before setting to work with your wife excite her with toying, so that the copulation will finish to your mutual satisfaction.

Thus it will be well to play with her before you introduce your verge and accomplish the cohabitation. You will excite her by kissing her cheeks, sucking her lips and nibbling at her breasts. You will lavish kisses on her navel and thighs, and titillate the lower parts. Bite at her arms, and neglect no part of her body; cling close to her bosom, and show her your love and submission. Interlace your legs with hers, and press her in your arms, for, as the poet has said:

from *The Perfumed Garden*

Under her neck my right hand has served her for a cushion,
And to draw her to me
I have sent out my left hand
Which bore her up as a bed.

When you are close to a woman, and you see her eyes getting dim, and hear her, yearning for coition, heave deep sighs, then let your and her yearning be joined into one, and let your lubricity rise to the highest point; for this will be the moment most favourable to the game of love. The pleasure which the woman then feels will be extreme; as for yourself, you will cherish her all the more, and she will continue her affection for you, for it has been said:

If you see a woman heaving deep sighs, with her lips getting red and her eyes languishing, when her mouth half opens and her movements grow heedless; when she appears to be disposed to go to sleep, vacillating in her steps and prone to yawn, know that this is the moment for coition; and if you there and then make your way into her you will procure for her an unquestionable treat. You yourself will find the mouth of her womb clasping your article, which is undoubtedly the crowning pleasure for both, for this before everything begets love and affection.

The following precepts, coming from a profound connoisseur in love affairs, are well known:

Woman is like a fruit, which will not yield its sweetness until you rub it between your hands. Look at the basil plant; if you do not rub it warm with your fingers, it will not emit any scent. Do you not know that the amber, unless it be handled and warmed, keeps hidden within its pores the aroma contained in it. It is the same with woman. If you do not animate her with your toying, intermixed with kissing, nibbling and touching, you will not obtain from her what you are wishing; you will feel no enjoyment when you share her couch, and you will waken in her heart neither inclination nor affection, nor love for you; all her qualities will remain hidden.

It is reported that a man, having asked a woman what means were the most likely to create affection in the female heart, with respect to the pleasures of coition, received the following answer:

O you who question me, those things which develop the taste for coition are the toyings and touches which precede it, and then the close embrace at the moment of ejaculation!

Believe me, the kisses, nibblings, suction of the lips, the close embrace, the visits of the mouth to the nipples of the bosom, and the sipping of the fresh saliva, these are the things to render affection lasting.

In acting thus, the two orgasms take place simultaneously, and enjoyment comes to the man and the woman at the same moment. Then the man feels the womb grasping his member, which gives to each of them the most exquisite pleasure.

This it is which gives birth to love, and if matters have not been managed this way the woman has not had her full share of pleasure, and the delights of the womb are wanting. Know that the woman will not feel her desires satisfied, and will not love her rider unless he is able to act up to her womb; but when the womb is made to enter into action she will feel the most valiant love for her cavalier, even if he be unsightly in appearance.

Then do all you can to provoke a simultaneous discharge of the two spermal fluids; herein lies the secret of love.

One of the servants who have occupied themselves with this subject has thus related the confidences which one of them made to him:

O you men, one and all, who are soliciting the love of woman and her affection, and who wish that sentiment in her heart to be of an enduring nature, toy with her previous to coition; prepare her for enjoyment, and neglect nothing to attain that end. Explore her with the greater assiduity, and, entirely occupied with her, let nothing else engage your thoughts. Do not let the moment propitious for pleasure pass away; that moment will be when you see her eyes humid, half open. Then go to work, but, remember, not till your kisses and toyings have taken effect.

After you have got the woman into a proper state of

excitement, O men! put your member into her, and, if you then observe the proper movements, she will experience a pleasure which will satisfy all her desires.

Lie on her breast, rain kisses on her cheeks, and let not your member quit her vagina. Push for the mouth of her womb. This will crown your labour.

If, by God's favour, you have found this delight, take good care not to withdraw your member, but let it remain there, and imbibe an endless pleasure! Listen to the sighs and heavy breathing of the woman. They witness the violence of the bliss you have given her.

And after the enjoyment is over, and your amorous struggle has come to an end, be careful not to get up at once, but withdraw your member cautiously. Remain close to the woman, and lie down on the right side of the bed that witnessed your enjoyment. You will find this pleasant, and you will not be like a fellow who mounts the woman after the fashion of a mule, without any regard to refinement, and who, after the emission, hastens to get his member out and to rise. Avoid such matters, for they rob the woman of all her lasting delight.

In short, the true lover of coition will not fail to observe all that I have recommended; for, from the observances of my recommendations will result the pleasure of the woman, and these rules comprise everything essential in that respect.

God has made everything for the best!

SIR THOMAS MALORY
(d1471)

Sir Launcelot and Elaine

Malory, a Warwickshire knight, spent some time in prison for attempted
murder and various other offences, and occupied himself by setting down
tales of Arthurian England – many of them from French sources, among
these the adventures of that 'best of earthly knights', Sir Launcelot. In
Book XI, Malory tells how, by a trick, Launcelot begot his son, Sir
Galahad, in the castle of King Pelles, 'king of the foreign country, and
cousin nigh unto Joseph of Arimathea.'

And fain would King Pelles have found the mean to have had Sir
Launcelot to have lain by his daughter, fair Elaine. And for this
intent: the king knew full well that Sir Launcelot should get a child
upon his daughter, the which should be named Sir Galahad, the
good knight, by whom all the foreign country should be brought out
of danger, and by him the Holy Grail should be achieved.

Then came forth a lady that hight[1] Dame Brisen, and she said
unto the king, 'Sir, wit ye well Sir Launcelot loveth no lady in the
world but all only Queen Guenever; and therefore work ye by
counsel, and I shall make him to lie with your daughter, and he shall
not wit but that he lieth with Queen Guenever.'

'O fair lady, Dame Brisen,' said the king, 'hope ye to bring this
about?'

'Sir,' said she, 'upon pain of my life let me deal;' for this Brisen
was one of the greatest enchantresses that was at that time in the
world living.

Then anon by Dame Brisen's wit she made one to come to Sir
Launcelot that he knew well. And this man brought him a ring from
Queen Guenever like as it had come from her, and such one as she
was wont for the most part to wear; and when Sir Launcelot saw
that token wit ye well he was never so fain[2].

'Where is my lady?' said Sir Launcelot.

'In the Castle of Case,' said the messenger, 'but five mile thence.'

[1] *hight*   was called.
[2] *fain*   glad

from *The Morte d'Arthur*

Then Sir Launcelot thought to be there the same night. And then this Brisen by the commandment of King Pelles let send Elaine to this castle with twenty-five knights unto the Castle of Case. Then Sir Launcelot against night rode unto that castle, and there anon he was received worshipfully with such people to his seeming as were about Queen Guenever secret. So when Sir Launcelot was alit, he asked where the queen was. So Dame Brisen said she was in her bed; and then the people were avoided, and Sir Launcelot was led unto his chamber.

And then Dame Brisen brought Sir Launcelot a cupful of wine; and anon as he had drunken that wine he was so assotted and mad that he might make no delay, but withouten any let he went to bed; and he weened that maiden Elaine had been Queen Guenever. Wit you well that Sir Launcelot was glad, and so was that lady Elaine that she had gotten Sir Launcelot in her arms. For well she knew that same night should be gotten upon her Galahad that should prove the best knight of the world; and so they let together until undern[1] on the morn; and all the windows and holes of that chamber were stopped that no manner of day might be seen.

And then Sir Launcelot remembered him, and he arose up and went to the window.

And anon as he had unshut the window the enchantment was gone; and then he knew himself that he had done amiss.

'Alas,' he said, 'that I have lived so long; now am I shamed.'

So then he gat his sword in his hand and said, 'Thou traitoress, what art thou that I have lain by all this night? Thou shalt die right here of my hands.'

Then this fair lady Elaine skipped out of her bed all naked, and kneeled down afore Sir Launcelot, and said, 'Fair courteous knight, comen[2] of kings' blood, I require you have mercy upon me, and as thou art renowned the most noble knight of the world, slay me not, for I have in my womb him by thee that shall be the most noblest knight of the world.'

'Ah, false traitoress,' said Sir Launcelot, 'why hast thou betrayed me? Anon tell me what thou art.'

'Sir,' she said, 'I am Elaine, the daughter of King Pelles.'

[1] *undern*   nine o'clock or later
[2] *comen*   descended

[43]

'Well,' said Sir Launcelot, 'I will forgive you this deed;' and therewith he took her up in his arms, and kissed her, for she was as fair a lady, and thereto lusty and young, and as wise, as any was that time living.

[Some time after the birth of Galahad, Elaine came to the court at Camelot; but though Launcelot 'thought she was the fairest woman that ever he saw in his life days', he would not speak to her or acknowledge her. So, like her father before her, Elaine had recourse to Dame Brisen.]

At night Queen Guenever commanded that Dame Elaine should sleep in a chamber nigh her chamber, and all under one roof; and so it was done as the queen commanded. Then the queen sent for Sir Launcelot and bad him come to her chamber that night: 'Or else I am sure,' said the queen, 'that ye will go to your lady's bed, Dame Elaine, by whom ye gat Galahad.'

'Ah, madam,' said Sir Launcelot, 'never say ye so, for that I did was against my will.'

'Then,' said the queen, 'look that ye come to me when I send for you.'

'Madam,' said Sir Launcelot, 'I shall not fail you, but I shall be ready at your commandment.'

This bargain was soon done and made between them, but Dame Brisen knew it by her crafts, and told it to her lady, Dame Elaine.

'Alas,' said she, 'how shall I do?'

'Let me deal,' said Dame Brisen, 'for I shall bring him by the hand even to your bed, and he shall ween[1] that I am Queen Guenever's messenger.'

'Now well is me,' said Dame Elaine, 'for all the world I love not so much as I do Sir Launcelot.'

So when time came that all folks were abed, Dame Brisen came to Sir Launcelot's bed's side and said, 'Sir Launcelot du Lake, sleep you? My lady, Queen Guenever, lieth and awaiteth upon you.'

'O my fair lady,' said Sir Launcelot, 'I am ready to go with you where ye will have me.'

---

[1] *ween*   think

from *The Morte d'Arthur*

Sir Launcelot threw upon him a long gown, and his sword in his hand; and then Dame Brisen took him by the finger and led him to her lady's bed, Dame Elaine; and then she departed, and left them in bed together. Wit you well the lady was glad, and so was Sir Launcelot, for he weened that he had another in his arms.

Now leave we them kissing and clipping, as was kindly[1] thing; and now speak we of Queen Guenever that sent one of her women unto Sir Launcelot's bed; and when she came there she found the bed cold, and he was away; so she came to the queen and told her all.

'Alas,' said the queen, 'where is that false knight become?'

Then the queen was nigh out of her wit, and then she writhed and weltered as a mad woman, and might not sleep a four or five hours. Then Sir Launcelot had a condition that he used of custom, he would clatter in his sleep, and speak oft of his lady, Queen Guenever. So as Sir Launcelot had waked as long as it had pleased him, then by course of kind he slept, and Dame Elaine both. And in his sleep he talked and clattered as a jay, of the love that had been betwixt Queen Guenever and him. And so as he talked so loud the queen heard him there as she lay in her chamber; and when she heard him so clatter she was nigh wood[2] and out of her mind, and for anger and pain wist not what to do. And then she coughed so loud that Sir Launcelot waked, and he knew her heming. And then he knew well that he lay not by the queen; and therewith he leapt out of his bed as he had been a wood man, in his shirt, and the queen met him in the floor; and thus she said:

'False traitor knight that thou art, look thou never abide in my court, and avoid my chamber, and not so hardy, thou false traitor knight that thou art, that ever thou come in my sight!'

'Alas,' said Sir Launcelot; and therewith he took such an heartly sorrow at her words that he fell down to the floor in a swoon. And therewithal Queen Guenever departed.

And when Sir Launcelot awoke of his swoon, he leapt out at a bay window into a garden, and there with thorns he was all to-cratched in his visage and his body; and so he ran forth he wist not whither, and was wild wood as ever was man; and so he ran two year, and never man might have grace to know him.

[1] *kindly* natural
[2] *wood* mad

LI YU
(1611–1680)

Looking and Enjoying

Li Yu, a Chinese essayist, dramatist and novelist, wrote the *Jou Pu Tuan* (sometimes translated as *The Prayer Mat of Flesh*, sometimes as *The Before Midnight Scholar*) during the first half of the seventeenth century. It has been unobtainable in China virtually ever since, and was relatively unknown in the West until published in Germany by Franz Kuhn in 1959. It is an erotic novel, but also reveals a great deal about the manners and morals of Li Yu's time. In the following scene, the hero, having made love to three young maidens, is seduced by their aunt Chen.

Although not too fat she was well favoured in the right places. When he lay on top of her she took him in her arms, and embracing him tightly, kissed him and called him 'my darling.' Immediately his whole body was seized, before even bestirring himself in any way, by a sense of blissful, almost ecstatic well-being such as he had never before experienced, though he was hardly a novice in love. My esteemed readers may wonder how so.

Let me explain. There are two varieties of beautiful women: one is beautiful to look upon, the other is beautiful to enjoy. When a woman is beautiful to look upon, it does not necessarily mean that she is beautiful to enjoy, or vice versa. Our history records only a single case, since ancient times, of a woman, among those wielding political influence at court, who combined both these advantages: that was the beautiful Yang Kuei-fei, celebrated favourite of the Emperor Ming Huang (713–756) of the T'ang dynasty.

To be beautiful to look upon, a woman must possess three qualities: she must be rather slender than stout, rather small and delicate than large and portly, rather frail and shy than robust and forward. Our painters, therefore, have always painted the frail shy beauty, and never represented in painting the buxom and vigorous-spirited lady, for all artistic conceptions of beauty are for the beholder, not for the possessor. As to women beautiful to possess they too have three qualities: they must be rather buxom than skinny, rather large and portly than small and frail, rather robust

[46]

and self-assured than delicate and shy. Why does true enjoyment require these three qualities?

Well, I will tell you. In cohabitation a man expects three things from his companion, and it is these three things that he prizes in her: first, feminine warmth and softness; second, compatibility between her proportions and his; third, that she be able to withstand the weight of his body. To lie on a flat, skinny creature is like lying on a stone bed. It is not very pleasant; on the contrary, it is quite uncomfortable. How different when the He has a soft, buxom She for a companion; then he basks in warmth and softness, he feels as though bedded in cushions and pillows; even before he has begun to bestir himself, a feeling of pleasure wells up in him. In addition, there is the highly estimable power of buxom, well-upholstered women to confer warmth in winter and coolness in summer. Accordingly, women of luxuriant build are preferable for purposes of cohabitation, to skinny, cadaverous women.

Furthermore, it is a very dubious pleasure to have a little, short-legged woman for a bed companion. The consequence will be a discrepancy in bodily proportions. If upstairs he holds her head to head and breast to breast, downstairs his legs will be dangling in mid-air; that is very unpleasant. To hold a delicate little doll of this sort in his arms may well arouse feelings of tenderness and affection in a man, but never voluptuous delight. Accordingly, big women are preferable to little ones for purposes of love.

Finally, a woman's body must withstand a considerable weight when it comes to love making. A man, after all, is likely to weigh his ninety-five to a hundred and sixty-five pounds. It takes a robust woman to endure such pressure without difficulty. It is just too much for one of your frail, willowy damsels. Her companion will be afraid of crushing her. That is bound to depress him and cramp his style. What pleasure can he have when he has to hold his passions in check and satisfy his desires in homoeopathic doses? A lusty fight to the finish is out of the question. Accordingly, a robust woman is decidedly preferable, for purposes of love, to a timid, fragile, delicate young thing.

Thus we see that beautiful to look upon and beautiful to enjoy are two entirely different things. A woman who combines both qualities in her person has no need to possess all the outward charms in the world. If she is eight tenths beautiful to look upon, that will do; she will give her companion twelve tenths worth of enjoyment and satisfaction. Lady Hua Chen was this rare type: beautiful to look upon and beautiful to enjoy.

As our young man lay in her full bosom, upstairs enlaced by her round firm arms, and downstairs held firmly by her silken smooth thighs which were gracefully modelled for all their luscious fullness, he felt as though bedded on soft cushions, and was seized with an infinite well-being. Her bodily proportions were just right for him and his weight did not seem to trouble her in the least. Beside this sumptuous, luxuriant, mature beauty, all the others in whose arms he had lain until that hour seemed in some way deficient, either too flat and thin or too short-legged or bashful. None had ever given him such bliss.

ANON
(c1655)

A Mighty Lewd Book

In January 1668 that great book-collector Samuel Pepys visited Martin, his bookseller, in the Strand, and 'saw the French book which I did think to have had for my wife to translate, called *L'escholle des filles*, but when I came to look in it, it is the most bawdy, lewd book that ever I saw . . .' Three weeks later, he bought it ('in plain binding') and next day began reading it, finishing it late at night after an evening of drinking and singing with his friends. 'A lewd book', he concluded, in the home-made code he used for the sexual passages in the Diary, 'but what doth me no wrong to read for information sake (but it did hazer my prick para stand all the while); and after I had done it, I burned it, that it might not be among my books to my shame.'

Pepys read *L'escholle des filles* in the French edition for which its co-publisher, Michel Millot, had been arrested, imprisoned and threatened with hanging. But by the time it was on sale in the Strand, there was probably already an English version available. Later, this too had its troubles and disappeared from circulation for a while. But it survived, and went into various editions.

The book consists of a dialogue between Susanna and Fanchon, who in *The School of Venus* became Katy and Fanny. One girl educates the other in the nature of sexual love, discussing many aspects of it; physiology, sexual techniques, the differing psychology of man and woman, various degrees of physical beauty. . . . Though obviously intended to titillate, the book is to a large degree educative, sensible and enthusiastic, and has its charms.

KATY I tell you what, since Mr Roger has fucked me, and I know what is what, I find all my mother's stories to be but bugbears and good for nothing but to fright children. For my part, I believe we were created for fucking, and when we begin to fuck we begin to live, and all people's actions and words ought to tend thereto. What strangely hypocritical ignorants are they who would hinder it in us young people because they cannot do it themselves? Heretofore, what was I good for but to hold down my head and sew? Now nothing comes amiss to me. I can hold an argument on any subject, and that which makes me laugh is this;

[49]

if my mother chide, I answer her smartly, so that she says I am very much mended, and she begins to have great hopes of me.

FANNY And all this while she is in darkness as to your concerns.

KATY Sure enough, and so she shall continue as I have ordered matters.

FANNY Well, and how goes the world with you now?

KATY Very well, only Mr Roger comes not so often to see me as I could wish.

FANNY Why, you are well acquainted with him then?

KATY Sure enough, for we understand each other perfectly.

FANNY But did not what he did unto you at first seem a little strange?

KATY I'll tell you the truth. You remember you told me much of the pleasure and tickling of fucking? I am now able to add a great deal more of my own experience, and can discourse as well of it as any one.

FANNY Tell me then. I believe you have had brave sport, I am confident Mr Roger must be a good fuckster.

KATY The first time he fucked me I was on the bed, in the same posture you left me, making as if I had been at work. When he came into the chamber, he saluted me and asked me how I did. I made him a civil answer and desired him to sit down, which he soon did close by me, staring me full in the face, and all quivering and shaking asked me if my mother was at home, and told me he met you at the bottom of the stairs and that you had spoken to him about me, desiring to know if it were with my consent. I returned no answer, but smiled; he grew bolder and immediately kissed me, which I permitted without struggling, tho' it made me blush as red as fire for the resolution I had taken to let him do what he would unto me. He took notice of it and said, 'What do you blush for, child? Come, kiss me again.' In doing of which he was longer than usual and thrusted his tongue into my mouth. Tis a folly to lie, that way of kissing pleased me, that if I had not before received your instructions I should have granted him whatever he demanded.

FANNY Very well.

KATY I received his tongue under mine, which he riggled about, then he stroked my neck, sliding his hand under my handkerchief he handled my breasts, thrusting his hands as low as he could.

from *L'Escholle des Filles*

FANNY A very fair beginning.

KATY The end will be as good. Seeing he could not reach low enough, he pulled out his hands again and whilst he was kissing and embracing me, by little and little he pulled up my coats 'till he felt my bare thighs.

FANNY We call this getting of ground.

KATY Look here, I believe very few wenches have handsomer thighs than I, for they are white, smooth and plump.

FANNY I know it, for I have often seen and handled them before now, when we lay together.

KATY Feeling them, he was overjoyed, protesting he never felt the like. In doing this his hat, which he had laid on his knees, fell off, and I casting my eyes downwards perceived something swelling in his breeches, as if it had a mind to get out.

FANNY Say you so, madam?

KATY That immediately put me in mind of that stiff thing, which you say men piss with and which pleaseth us women so much. I am sure when he first came into the chamber 'twas not so big.

FANNY No, his did not stand then.

KATY When I saw it I began to think there was something to be done in good earnest, so I got up and shut the door . . . Having made all sure, I returned and he, taking me about the neck and kissing me, would not let me sit as before on the bed but pulled me between his legs and, thrusting his hand into the slit of my coat behind, handled my buttocks, which he found plump, round and hard. With his other hand he takes my right hand and, looking me in the face, put it into his breeches.

FANNY You are very tedious in telling your story.

KATY I tell you every particular. He put his prick into my hand and desired me to hold it.

FANNY This relation makes me mad for fucking.

KATY This done, says he, 'I would have you see what you have in your hand,' and so made me take it out of his breeches. I wondered to see such a damned great tarse, for it is quite another thing when it stands. He perceiving me a little amazed said, 'Do not be frightened, girl, for you have about you a very convenient place to receive it,' and upon a sudden pulls up my smock.

FANNY This is what I expected all this while.

KATY Then he thrust me backwards, put down his breeches, put by

[51]

his shirt and draws me nearer to him.

FANNY Now begins the game.

KATY I soon perceived he had a mind to stick it in. I desired him to hold a little for it pained me. Having breathed, he made me open my legs wider and, with another hard thrust, went a little farther in. He told me that he would not hurt me much more and I should have nothing but pleasure for the pain I should endure, and that he endured a share of the pain for my sake, which made me patiently suffer two or three thrusts more. Endeavouring still to get more ground, he takes and throws me backwards on the bed, but being too heavy he took my two thighs and put them on his shoulders, he standing on his feet by the bedside. This way did give me some ease, yet I desired him to get off, which he did.

FANNY What a deal of pleasure did you enjoy! For my part, had I such a prick, I should not complain.

KATY Stay a little, I do not complain for all this. Presently he came and kissed me and handled my cunt afresh. Being still troubled with a standing prick and not knowing 'what to do with himself, he walked up and down the chamber 'till I was fit for another bout.

FANNY Poor fellow, I pity him; he suffered a great deal.

KATY Mournfully pulling out his prick before me, he takes down a little pot of pomatum which stood on the mantletree of the chimney. 'Oh,' says he, 'this is for our turn,' and taking some of it he rubbed his prick all over with it to make it go in the more glib.

FANNY He had better have spit upon his hand and rubbed his prick therewith.

KATY At last he thought of that and did nothing else. Then he placed me on a chair and by the help of the pomatum got in a little further, but seeing he could do no great good that way, he made me rise and laid me with all four on the bed, and having once more rubbed his tarse with pomatum he charged me briskly in the rear.

FANNY What a bustle here to get one poor maidenhead! My friend and I made not half this stir. We had soon done and never flinched for it.

KATY I tell you the truth verbatim. My coats being over my shoulders, holding out my arse I gave him a fair mark enough. This new posture so quickened his fancy that, no longer regarding my crying out, he kept thrusting on with might and main, 'till at last he perfected the break and took entire possession of all.

FANNY Very well, I am glad you escaped a thousand little accidents which attend young lovers, but let us come to the sequel.

KATY It now began not to be so painful. My cunt fitted his prick so well that no glove could come straighter on a man's hand. To conclude, he was sovereign at his victory, called me his love, his dear and his soul.

FANNY Very good.

KATY He asked me if I were pleased. I answered, 'yes'. 'So am I,' said he, hugging me close to him, his hands under my buttocks.

FANNY This was to encourage and excite him.

KATY The more he pushed, the more it tickled me, that at last my hands on which I leaned failed me and I fell flat on my face.

FANNY I suppose you caught no harm by the fall?

KATY None, but he and I dying with pleasure fell in a trance, he only having time to say, 'There have you lost your maidenhead, my fool.'

JEAN FRANÇOIS MARIE AROUET DE VOLTAIRE
(1694–1778)

The Young Circassian

François Marie Arouet, who assumed the name Voltaire, was born in Paris but spent most of his life in exile in England, Prussia and Switzerland. A sceptic who while believing in God rejected particular religions, he employed a piercing wit and the most elegant of styles to attack injustice and further the causes of tolerance and freedom. *Candide* (1759) is perhaps his most amusing and readable masterpiece: an adventure story, full of ironic comedy. In the following extract Candide, the innocent hero who has been carefully taught that 'all's for the best in this best of all possible worlds', has become a great and influential figure in Isfahan, but finds the people ungrateful for his wise laws and encouragement of the arts.

Candide, in the bitterness of his grief, wrote a very pathetic letter to the Rev. Ed-Ivan-Baal-Denk. He painted to him in such lively colours the present state of his soul, that Ed-Ivan, greatly affected with it, obtained the Sophi's consent that Candide should resign his employments. His Majesty, in recompense of his services, granted him a very considerable pension. Eased from the weight of grandeur, our philosopher immediately sought after Pangloss's Optimism in the pleasures of a private life. He till then had lived for the benefit of others, and seemed to have forgotten that he had a seraglio.

He now called it to remembrance, with that emotion which the very name inspires. Let every thing be got ready, says he to his first eunuch, for my visiting the women. My Lord, answered the shrill-piped Gentleman, it is now that your Excellence deserves the title of Wise. The men, for whom you have done so much, were not worthy of your attention; but the women – That may be, said Candide, modestly.

Embosomed in a garden, where art had assisted nature to unfold her beauties, stood a small house, of simple and elegant structure; and by that means alone very different from those which are to be seen in the suburbs of the finest city in Europe. Candide blushed as he drew near it. The air round this charming retreat diffused a delicious perfume; the flowers, amorously intermingled, seemed here to be guided by the instinct of pleasure, and preserved for a long time their various beauties. Here the rose never lost its brilliancy: the view of a rock from which the waters precipitated themselves, with a murmuring and confused noise, invited the soul to that soft melancholy which is ever the forerunner of pleasure. Candide enters, trembling, into a saloon, where taste and magnificence were united: his senses are drawn by a secret charm: he casts his eyes on young Telemachus, who breathes on the canvas, in the midst of the nymphs of Calypso's court. He next turns them to Diana, half naked, who flies into the arms of the tender Endymion; his agitation increases at the sight of a Venus, faithfully copied from that of Medicis: his ears on a sudden are struck with a divine harmony; a company of young Circassian females appear covered with their veils; they form round him a sort of dance, agreeably designed, and much more suitable to the scene than those trifling ballets that are performed on as trifling stages, after the representation of the death of Caesar and Pompey.

At a signal given they throw off their veils, and discover faces full of expression, that lend new life to the diversion. These beauties studied the most seducing attitudes, without appearing to have studied them: one expressed in her looks a passion without bounds; another a soft languor, which waits for pleasures without seeking them: this fair stoops and raises herself precipately, to give a cursory view of those enchanting charms which the fair sex display so freely at Paris; and that other throws aside a part of her cymar to show a leg which alone is capable of inflaming a mortal of any feeling. The dance ceases, and they remain fixed, as it were in the most seducing attitudes.

This pause recalls Candide to himself. The fire of love takes possession of his breast: he darts the most ardent looks on all around him; imprints warm kisses on lips as warm, and eyes that swim in liquid fire: he passes his hands over globes whiter than alabaster, whose elastic motion repels the touch; admires their proportion; perceives little vermilion protruberances, like those rose buds which only wait the genial rays of the sun to unfold them: he kisses them with rapture, and his lips for some time remained as if glued to the spot.

Our philosopher next admires, for a while, a majestic figure, of a fine and delicate shape. Burning with desire, he at length throws the handkerchief to a young person, whose eyes he had observed to be always fixed upon him, and which seemed to say, Teach me the meaning of a trouble I am ignorant of; and who, blushing at the secret avowal, became a thousand times more charming. The eunuch, in a moment, opens the door of a private chamber, consecrated to the mysteries of love. The lovers enter; and the eunuch whispers to his master, Here it is, my lord, you are going to be truly happy. I hope so, with all my heart, said Candide.

The ceiling and walls of this little retreat were covered with looking-glass: in the midst was placed a couch of black satin, on which Candide threw the young Circassian, and undressed her with incredible haste. The lovely creature let him do as he pleased, and gave him no other interruption but to imprint kisses, full of fire, on his lips. My lord, said she to him in the Turkish language, how fortunate is your slave to be thus honoured with your transports! An energy of sentiment can be expressed in every language by those who truly feel it. These few words enchanted our philosopher: he was no longer himself; all he saw, all he heard, was new to him. What difference between Mistress Cunégonde, grown ugly, and ravished by Bulgarian freebooters, and a Circassian girl of eighteen, till then an unspotted virgin. This was the first time of the wise Candide's enjoying her. The objects which he devoured were reflected in the glasses; on what side soever he cast his eyes, he saw upon the black satin the most beautiful and fairest form imaginable, and the contrast of colours lent it a new lustre, with round, firm and plump thighs, an admirable fall of loins, a— but I am obliged to have a regard to the false delicacy of our language. It is sufficient for me to say that our philosopher tasted, again and again, that portion of happiness he was capable of receiving; and that the young Circassian in a little time proved his sufficing reason.

JOHN CLELAND
(1709–89)

The Woman of Pleasure

John Cleland, having lost his job with the East India Company in Bombay, came back to London and wrote *The Memoirs of a Woman of Pleasure* for a bookseller called Ralph Griffiths, of St Paul's Church Yard, in 1748. He was paid twenty guineas for it, and Griffiths is said to have made ten thousand pounds on the deal. The book is probably the most elegant piece of English erotica to be written expressly to titillate the reader. It has been through innumerable editions, and its publishers in England and America have appeared many times before various courts, accused of publishing obscene matter. Some have been found guilty, some have been proved innocent; but Cleland's heroine, Fanny Hill, has triumphantly survived, no doubt at least in part because of her naïve charm. Happily, after many vicissitudes, at the end of the novel she marries her Charles, and settles into wedlock – a path 'strew'd with roses purely, and those eternally unfading ones.'

But here she is on the morning after her first seduction by the lover to whom she remains, in her fashion, true to the end.

Late in the morning I wak'd first; and observing my lover slept profoundly, softly disengag'd myself from his arms, scarcely daring to breathe for fear of shortening his repose; my cap, my hair, my shift, were all in disorder from the rufflings I had undergone; and I took this opportunity to adjust and set them as well as I could: whilst, every now and then, looking at the sleeping youth with inconceivable fondness and delight, and reflecting on all the pain he had put me to, tacitly own'd that the pleasure had overpaid me for my sufferings.

It was then broad day. I was sitting up in the bed, the cloaths of which were all tossed, or rolled off, by the unquietness of our motions, from the sultry heat of the weather; nor could I refuse myself a pleasure that solicited me so irresistably, as this fair occasion of feasting my sight with all those treasures of youthful beauty I had enjoy'd, and which lay now almost entirely naked, his shirt being truss'd up in a perfect whisp, which the warmth of the room and season made me easy about the consequence of. I hung over him enamour'd indeed! and devoured all his naked charms with only two eyes, when I could have wish'd them at least a hundred, for the fuller enjoyment of the gaze.

Oh! could I paint this figure, as I see it now, still present to my transported imagination, a whole length of an all-perfect, manly beauty in full view. Think of a face without a fault, glowing with all the opening bloom and vernal freshness of an age in which beauty is of either sex, and which the first down over his upper lip scarce began to distinguish.

The parting of the double ruby pout of his lips seem'd to exhale an air sweeter and purer than what it drew in: ah! what violence did it not cost me to refrain the so tempted kiss!

Then a neck exquisitely turn'd, grac'd behind and on the sides with his hair, playing freely in natural ringlets, connected his head to a body of the most perfect form, and of the most vigorous contexture, in which all the strength of manhood was conceal'd and soften'd to appearance by the delicacy of his complexion, the smoothness of his skin, and the plumpness of his flesh.

The platform of his snow-white bosom, that was laid out in a manly proportion, presented, on the vermilion summit of each pap, the idea of a rose about to blow.

Nor did his shirt hinder me from observing the symmetry of his limbs, that exactness of shape, in the fall of it towards the loins, where the waist ends and the rounding swell of the hips commences; where the skin, sleek, smooth and dazzling white, burnishes on the stretch over firm, plump, ripe flesh, that crimp'd and ran into dimples at the least pressure, or that the touch could not rest upon, but slid over as on the surface of the most polished ivory.

His thighs, finely fashioned, and with a florid glossy roundness, gradually tapering away to the knees, seem'd pillars worthy to support that beauteous frame; at the bottom of which I could not, without some remains of terror, some tender emotions too, fix my eyes on that terrible machine, which had, not long before, with such fury broke into, torn, and almost ruin'd those soft, tender parts of mine that had not yet done smarting with the effects of its rage; but behold it now! crest fall'n, reclining its half-capt vermilion head over one of his thighs, quiet, pliant, and to all appearance incapable of the mischiefs and cruelty it had committed. Then the beautiful growth of the hair, in short and soft curls round its root, its whiteness, branch'd veins, the supple softness of the shaft, as it lay foreshorten'd, roll'd and shrunk up into a squab thickness, languid, and borne up from between his thighs by its globular appendage, that wondrous treasure-bag of nature's sweets, which, rivall'd round, and purs'd up in the only wrinkles that are known to please, perfected the prospect, and all together formed the most interesting moving picture in all nature, and surely infinitely superior to those nudities furnish'd by the painters, statuaries, or any art, which are purchased at immense prices; whilst the sight of them in actual life is scarce sovereignly tasted by any but the few whom nature has endowed with a fire of imagination, warmly painted by a truth of judgement to the spring-head, the originals of beauty, of nature's unequall'd composition, above all the imitation of art, or the reach of wealth to pay their price.

But every thing must have an end. A motion made by this angelic youth, in the listlessness of going off sleep, replac'd his shirt and the bedclothes in a posture that shut up that treasure from longer view.

I lay down then, and carrying my hands to that part of me in which the objects just seen had begun to raise a mutiny that prevail'd over the smart of them, my fingers now open'd themselves in easy passage; but long I had not time to consider the whole difference, *there*, between the maid and the now finish'd woman, before Charles wak'd, and turning towards me, kindly enquir'd how I had rested and scarce giving me time to answer, imprinted on my lips one of his burning rapture-kisses, which darted a flame to my heart that from thence radiated to every part of me; and presently, as if it had proudly meant revenge for the survey I had smuggled of all his naked beauties, he spurns off the bed-clothes, and trussing up my shift as high as it would go, took his turn to feast his eyes on all the gifts nature had bestowed on my person; his busy hands, too, rang'd intemperately over every part of it. The delicious austerity and hardness of my yet unripe budding breasts, the whiteness and firmness of my flesh, the freshness and regularity of my features, the harmony of my limbs, all seem'd to confirm him in his satisfaction with his bargain; but when curious to explore the havoc he had made in the centre of his over-fierce attack, he not only directed his hands there, but with a pillow put under, placed me favourably for his wanton purpose of inspection. Then, who can express the fire his eyes glisten'd, his hands glow'd with! whilst sighs of pleasure, and tender broken exclamations, were all the praises he could utter. By this time his machine, stiffly risen at me, gave me to see it in its highest state and bravery. He feels it himself, seems pleas'd at its condition, and, smiling loves and graces, seizes one of my hands, and carries it with a gentle compulsion to his pride of nature, and its richest masterpiece.

I, struggling faintly, could not help feeling what I could not grasp, a column of the whitest ivory, beautifully streak'd with blue veins, and carrying, fully uncapt, a head of the liveliest vermilion: no horn could be harder or stiffer; yet no velvet more smooth or delicious to the touch. Presently he guided my hand lower, to that part in which nature and pleasure keep their stores in concert, so aptly fasten'd and hung on to the root of their first instrument and minister, that not improperly he might be styl'd their purse-bearer too: there he made me feel distinctly, through their soft cover, the contents, a pair of roundish balls, that seem'd to play within, and elude all pressure but the tenderest, from without.

But now the visit of my soft warm hand in those so sensible parts had put everything into such ungovernable fury that, disdaining all further preluding, and taking advantage of my commodious posture, he made the storm fall where I scarce patiently expected, and where he was sure to pay it: presently, then, I felt the stiff insertion between the yielding, divided lips of the wound, now open for life; where the narrowness no longer put me to intolerable pain, and afforded my lover no more difficulty than what heighten'd his pleasure, in the strict embrace of that tender, warm sheath, round the instrument it was so delicately adjusted to, and which, now cased home, so gorged me with pleasure that it perfectly suffocated me and took away my breath; then the killing thrusts! the unnumber'd kisses! every one of which was a joy inexpressible; and that joy lost in a crowd of yet greater blisses! But this was a disorder too violent in nature to last long: the vessels, so stirr'd and intensely heated, soon boil'd over, and for that time put out the fire; meanwhile all this dalliance and disport had so far consum'd the morning, that it became a kind of necessity to lay breakfast and dinner into one.

JACOPO CASANOVA
(1725–1798)

Trio – and Quartet

Born in Venice, Casanova had an adventurous life in Eastern Europe before returning to Venice in 1755, when he was imprisoned as a spy. Escaping after eighteen months he fled to Paris, where he became director of state lotteries. Later, he again took up a life of (chiefly amorous) adventure, before settling down as librarian to Count Waldstein in Bohemia, where he died not long after completing his memoirs – the revelations of a real-life Don Juan. In the following extract he has manoeuvred himself into a bedroom with two young women, M.M. and C.C., determined to enjoy them both.

C.C. got up and sat on M.M.'s lap, and the two girls began to caress each other, amusing as well as arousing me. Far from stopping them, I encouraged them, for I was inclined to look on at a sport which had often pleased me.

M.M. picked up a book of erotic engravings by Meursius, showing women making love to each other, and looking me straight in the face asked if I would like a fire lit in the alcove. I said that would be an excellent idea, for the bed was quite large enough for the three of us. (I knew precisely what she had in mind: she thought that her friend the Ambassador might be watching us from some concealed spy-hole, and knew that in the alcove we could not be seen.)

A table was laid in front of the alcove, and supper was served. We all fell to with a sound appetite. While M.M. was teaching C.C. to make punch, I fell to admiring the progress of the latter's beauty.

'In the past nine months,' I said, 'your breasts must have reached perfection.'

'Oh, they are just like mine!' said M.M. 'Do you want to see?' And she unlaced her friend's dress, the latter making no objection, and then undid her own, so that I could compare the four beautiful globes – which merely fired me with the desire to compare their whole bodies.

I placed Meursius' *Academie des Dames* on the table, and showed them a picture which I would like to see them counterfeit.

M.M. asked C.C. if she would agree; C.C. pointed out that to do so perfectly, they would have to undress completely, and get into bed. The idea appealed, and within a few minutes we were all naked and ready for the pleasures of love. The two girls attacked each other without delay, like lithe tigresses fighting to devour each other.

The sight of their loving contest soon had its effect upon me: but which should I first attempt to love? C.C. attracted me most strongly – but then M.M. would accuse me of lying, for had I not assured her that I loved her alone? C.C. was slimmer than M.M., although her hips were broader and her thighs stronger. The down which shaded C.C.'s body was blond; that of M.M. was brown. Both seemed equally ardent and skilful in a game of love which showed no signs of tiring, let alone ending.

Aflame with lust, I fell upon them, with the pretence of separating them – and in so doing finding myself between the legs of M.M., who threw me off, when C.C. welcomed me to her arms with enthusiasm, and within a minute had brought me to my death, dying with me in an access of pleasure, neither of us giving a thought to the natural dangers of our actions.

When we had recovered, we both fell upon M.M. – C.C. wishing to show her gratitude for the gift of my first love, and myself eager to revenge myself for having been forced to be unfaithful to her! I caressed her for a full hour, while C.C. looked on with pleasure at the sight of her friend's enjoyment of a lover proving his metal.

Exhausted with pleasure, I persuaded the girls to sleep at last, having set the clock to wake us at four, when we would have two more hours for delight before we had to leave. And once awake, indeed, the sight of our nakedness once more invigorated us: I strove first with C.C., then with M.M. – all three of us, afire with the lust of Furies, tearing and thrusting at every part of each other's bodies, each of us seeming to be of both sexes at once in the trio which we performed. Half an hour before dawn, we parted, our strength utterly exhausted, ashamed to admit the fact, but at the same time proud of it – and even yet not wholly satisfied.

Some years later, travelling with a widow, Madame Dubois, who he had not yet succeeded in seducing, he arrived at Berne, and took a walk in the early evening.

from the *Memoirs*

At the top of a hill which hung over a plateau crossed by a small river, I found a flight of steps – about a hundred of them – leading to what seemed to be a row of about forty bathing machines. As I stood looking at them, a pleasant-faced fellow approached me, and asked if I wanted to bathe. When I said I would, he opened the door of one of the cabins – and immediately I was surrounded by a crowd of women attendants. The man said that I could choose whichever I wanted to look after me, and that one *écu* would pay for the bath, the girl, and breakfast! Like the Grand Turk, I inspected the harem, and threw my handkerchief to the most attractive of the girls.

We went into the cabin, and she fastened the door and in a matter-of-fact way undressed me completely, placing a cotton cap on my head to protect my hair. I got into the water, and no sooner was I in than she undressed and climbed in with me. Then she massaged the whole of my body – that is, except for one part, which I guarded with my hands. When I felt thoroughly relaxed, I ordered coffee. She climbed out of the bath, opened the cabin door, called my order to someone outside, and climbed back in – all completely unconscious of her nakedness. An old woman delivered the coffee, which my companion again climbed from the bath to receive and bring to me, holding the tray while I drank.

Without taking any special notice of her, it was quite clear to me that she was as attractive as man could wish, with fine features and eyes, rounded breasts, a springy curve to her back, and everything else to match. Her hands were certainly rough, as indeed are those of young women who work for their living; and it might be that the skin of her body was no softer. Nor did she have the distinction, the subtlety, or the nobility of carriage, and certainly not the modest reserve, of a young woman of quality. But clearly she had every other virtue a girl of eighteen needs to tempt a man of quick passion. And yet she did not move me.

Why not? I fear that man needs artificiality, coquetry, to tempt him. Why should it be that, since we do not commonly go about stark naked, and sensually the face we show to the world really cannot matter, it is still the face which sparks our lusts? Why should we decide after one glance at her face that the whole woman is beautiful or plain? Why should we even be content with a pretty face, though her secret parts fall far short of its enticing beauty? Would it not be sensible to cover our faces, and leave our bodies

[63]

nude, so that the revelation of a face which matches the loveliness of the body becomes a kind of happy bonus? Then we would fall in love with true beauty, and if the face, revealed at last, proved to be plain – *tant pis*! A plain woman, indeed, would be content to seduce us with her body, and refuse to reveal her face; a pretty woman need not wait to be asked. The plain woman would only consent to our making love to her on condition that she remained masked – and if in the end she revealed her face, it would only be after convincing us by other means that a plain face is no bar to the enjoyment of love. And is it not true that only the variety of women's faces tempts us to infidelity? If every face were the same, a man would remain forever faithful to the first woman to whom he made love. If this reasoning sounds stupid, then I am stupid; but it is nevertheless my opinion.

When I left the bath, the attendant dried me with towels, put on my shirt, and dressed my hair – still completely naked. I pulled on the rest of my clothes, and when she had buckled my shoes, she also dressed, herself having dried off naturally in the warm air. As I left I gave her a *petit écu*, and six francs for herself – which she scornfully returned. Her pride not only irritated but upset me, and I went back to the hôtel in a bad temper.

After supper, I could not help telling Dubois about my experience. The girl could not have been pretty, she suggested, or I would certainly have fallen upon her! She would quite like to see her, to find out for herself. I said I would be happy to take her to the bath-houses, but thought she should dress as a man. She silently left the room, and in fifteen minutes there appeared a handsome young fellow in a coat borrowed from Le Duc – though below the waist his appearance was something equivocal, as the full curve of Dubois' buttocks declined to fit into Le Duc's breeches! I gave her the choice of mine, and we decided to take our excursion next morning.

At six o'clock she came for me, dressed in a blue overcoat which perfectly disguised her sex. I quickly dressed, and we walked to La Matthe (as the place was called). Excited at the prospect before her, my companion was so pleased with herself that anyone looking closely at her would have discovered her sex; she wrapped her coat closely about her.

At the bottom of the steps, the bath-keeper greeted us, and asked if we wanted a cabin for four. I acquiesced, and we were shown into one. The group of girls again appeared, and I pointed out to Dubois the girl who had failed to seduce me; she chose her. I chose another – tall and handsomely built. Then we locked the door.

Naked except for the cotton cap, I was soon in the water, followed by my assistant. My friend was not so quick: the unusual situation dismayed her, and she seemed to be wishing she had not come, though she laughed to see my muscular girl massaging me. Ashamed to remove her shift before her assistant, she also hesitated to undress before me; one shame eventually cancelled out the other, and she allowed me to get out of my bath, help her undress, and place her in hers.

The two Swiss girls showed no surprise at the revelation of Dubois' sex; no doubt they had seen it all before. Indeed, they immediately began some activities which were nothing new to me, though Dubois had never seen such a display. Like images in a mirror, they imitated the caresses I offered her; she was amazed at the enthusiasm with which my girl, playing the man, made love to the other. I was more than a little surprised myself, in spite of my memories of the enthusiasm shown by M.M. and C.C. six years earlier – and nothing could be more inspiriting than that!

I would really never have thought that anything could have distracted me from the pleasure of holding naked in my arms the body of a woman I loved, and whose beauties seemed to me to be most perfect; but the immoderate ecstacies of the two Maenads took her eyes as well. Despite her breasts, Dubois asserted, the girl I had chosen must really be a boy! Seeing us looking closely at her, she turned, displaying a large clitoris, longer than my little finger, and completely rigid. I pointed this out to Dubois, who could not believe it was what it was! Indeed, to convince her, I had to persuade her to examine it. It looked exactly like a finger, though of course without a fingernail, and more flexible. Mistaking her interest, the Swiss girl, who obviously had an eye for Dubois, offered to show her its practical use; but she did not wish it, and I would not have enjoyed the process, either. So she returned to her companion, with such enthusiasm and lust that while in one way we were disgusted, in another we could not help being aroused by the sight of their raptures. Dubois, indeed, was so affected that she surrendered to me everything I asked, even running before me in her invention. We made love for two hours before returning to the inn entirely happy. I gave the girls a *louis* each, but we were determined never to return to the baths. We did not need the lovemaking of the two girls to prompt us to new pleasures of our own, and for the rest of the time we were at Berne we made each other entirely happy.

RESTIF DE LA BRETONNE
(1734–1806)

Monsieur Nicolas

Restif was born on the borders of Burgundy and Champagne, the son of a
farmer. At first a printer, he published his first novel when he was 32, and
became a prolific author – so prolific that he composed his work at the
printer's, thus saving time and money. His best-known novel, *Le Paysan
perverti*, achieved a certain notoriety, but he is now remembered chiefly
for his sixteen-volume autobiography, at first regarded by critics as the
work of 'the Rousseau of the gutter.' Restif claimed however that he was
not writing his confessions, but 'laying bare the springs of the human
heart.' As the following extracts show, his book is not without humour.

I have already said that all Bonne Sellier's lodgers [in Paris] were
her husbands. Simple-minded travellers, who have seen only one
household in each savage tribe, come and give us what they have
seen as the general rule. It is as if I went and told foreigners, and
even my compatriots: 'In Paris, it is the rule for men who lodge in a
house, even if there are thirty of them, all to be entitled to their
landlady's favours.' Yet I should be even better justified than
certain travellers, for among women who conformed to this rule I
have known not only Bonne Sellier, but Madame Lallemand, and a
Madame Debus, another printers' landlady, in whose house the
mother and two quite pretty daughters passed through the hands of
all the lodgers. And since then, in 1768, I have seen the same thing
in the Cour d'Albret, at the top of the Rue des Carmes, in a lodging-
house for law students and medical students. There were four
women there; the grandmother, the mother, and two daughters.
The grandmother was still appetising because she had good blood
in her; the mother, who had been a widow for a long time, was a
fine-looking woman; the elder daughter was a charming girl of
about nineteen, and Madelon, the younger daughter, a child of
fourteen or fifteen. The grandmother would come to make your bed
while you were in it and would tease you so well that her remaining
charms would tempt you. Next, when the landladies saw that you
were beginning to grow accustomed to the ways of the house, the
mother would come to do your room. You had her for some time,

and it was the way you behaved with her which determined whether you would have the daughters: a scoundrel had only the grandmother, who saved the mother from him, while the mother saved the elder daughter from a shady character. But after a decent young man had enjoyed the mother for some time and treated her well, the elder daughter, in a provocative *déshabillé* revealing the naked body beneath, would come to make the chosen lodger's bed. She would get him to court her for a little while; finally, if she was satisfied with his sentiments and his behaviour, she would make him happy. You had to be the epitome of virtue and decency to get as far as the child of fifteen. The young girl would be fitted out in battle dress; the happy man would give a small collation, at the end of which he would be told: 'You are a friend of the house: you have shown that you deserve to possess its houri, and we are leaving her to you for an hour.' And the mother would withdraw. All these pleasures took place day by day, never at night; you could never obtain anything except when somebody came to make your bed. I spent ten months in that house, in 1768. But let us return to Madame Lallemand, who was the principle heroine of the adventure I am about to relate.

Madame Lallemand had gone back to live in the Rue Jacinthe, at the corner of the Rue Galande. The lower part of this house was occupied by a coffee-house keeper whose wife, a handsome brunette, had an unnatural temperament, which I had not yet encountered in women. I had not seen this former landlady of mine since leaving her house. One day she met me and gently reproached me with my indifference. As it was Monday, I went the same evening to see that whore of a woman, with the intention of inviting her to supper and of taking advantage at the same time of her extreme facility. I arrived too late: it was half-past six. We chatted: I knelt before her as soon as she had dismissed her little maid. I was very bold: I told her that I loved her. She answered me with a remark which I have often quoted since to my friends: 'Heavens! Why didn't you tell me before?' We made an assignation for five o'clock the next day, and I left her before the arrival of her lodgers.

On the Tuesday, I arrived long before the appointed hour. Instead of five o'clock, I came at three. The kitchen door was open: I saw nobody there; the little maidservant, knowing that her mistress was busy, had gone off to gossip somewhere. The key was not in the door of the front apartment, but when I pushed it with one finger it opened. I went in quietly. I made out somebody through the movement of the shadows in the bedroom at the back, although the curtain was carefully drawn. I guessed that it was some lover, and I was surprised that Madame Lallemand should not have been satisfied with a rendezvous as important as ours; but I was not annoyed to have a story I could tell Boudard. I went up to the door, and I heard the sound of kisses. One of the two people, who was moving about a good deal, gave a kick which moved the curtain. I then saw two women, Madame Lallemand, and her neighbour Madame Beugnet. The latter's firm white bosom, which was completely naked, was being covered with kisses by my former landlady, while two lecherous hands, mutually occupied . . . Never was anybody so surprised as I was then. I innocently assumed that pretty Maximine Mâri was a sensual woman who, having a jealous husband, did not dare risk herself with a man. In this belief I turned the handle of the glazed door and went in. The two women gave a shriek. I offered my ardent services to the beautiful wife of the coffee-house keeper, using expressions in keeping with my erroneous opinion. Her answers struck me as unintelligible. Madame Lallemand explained them to me. 'Dammit,' I cried, 'you are cheating Nature. By Venus, you shall be ridden by a man!' And I laid down the conditions for my future discretion. Madame Beugnet went first, because she did not want me to have Madame Lallemand. But those two women caressed each other while I was enjoying them, and they agreed that it was an additional spice which they had never known before. Reader, I depict what I have seen, what I have done. A new Petronius, I conceal nothing from you. Know your century, or rather, know all centuries! The passions and their perversions were always the same, and always had the same effects.

I have said I was faithful to Zéphire with her companions. That truth might lead you into error. I must tell all, if I am not to deceive you. Here is another of my turpitudes, all the more surprising in that it took place in a time of virtue, and that nothing seemed to foreshadow it. I was respecting my intended and abstaining from other women: I was living more virtuously than I had ever done before, and I was beginning to imagine that one could become accustomed to it. But what is going to show the danger of books such as the *Le Portier des Chartreux*, *Thérèse Philosophe*, *La Religieuse en chemise*, and others like them, is the sudden and terrible eroticism which they aroused in me after long abstinence. A great libertine, that Molet whom I have already mentioned and who was a fellow-lodger of mine at Bonne Sellier's, had come to see me one Sunday morning when I was still in bed, and had brought me the first of these books, which I had only glimpsed at La Macé's. Filled with a lively curiosity, I took it eagerly and started reading in bed; I forgot everything, even Zéphire. After a score of pages, I was on fire. Manon Lavergne, a relative of Bonne Sellier, came on behalf of my former landlady to bring my linen and Loiseau's, which Bonne continued to wash for us. I knew what Manon's morals were like. I threw myself upon her. The young girl did not put up very much resistance.

I resumed my reading after she had gone. Half an hour later there appeared Cécile Decoussy, my sister Margot's companion, who came on her behalf to ask why she no longer saw anything of me. Without any regard for this young blonde's position (she was about to be married), or for the atrocious way in which I was bringing shame on my sister in the person of her friend, I put so much fury into my attack that, alarmed as much as surprised, she thought that I had gone mad. I returned to my baneful reading.

About three quarters of an hour later Thérèse Courbisson arrived, laughing and bantering. 'Where is he, that lazy scamp? Still in bed!' And she came over to tickle me. I was waiting for her. I seized her almost in the air, like a feather, and with only one hand I pulled her under me. 'Oh! After what you've just done to Manon? A fine man you are!' She was caught before she could finish; and, as she was very partial to physical pleasure, she did nothing more but help me. At last she tore herself from my arms because she heard my landlord coming upstairs. She went out, leaving the door open. I finished my book.

The bed had warmed me up; the three pleasures I had enjoyed were just a spur to my senses: I got up with the intention of going to fetch Zéphire, of bringing her to my room, and of abandoning myself with her to my erotic frenzy. At that moment someone scratched at my door, which I had only pushed to. I started, thinking it was Zéphire. 'Who is it?' I cried. 'Come in.' 'Séraphine,' said a voice which I thought I recognised. I trembled, thinking it was Séraphine Destroches who had come to scold me for my behaviour with her companion Decoussy. 'Who is it?' I repeated. 'Séraphine Jolon.' The only person I had ever known by that name was the housekeeper of a painter who was our neighbour in the Rue de Poulies, and I had whispered sweet nothings to her once or twice; but then Largeville had turned up, and Jeannette Demailly, and I had left the house. Reassured, I opened the door. It was she. 'I have come,' the pretty girl said to me, 'on behalf of Madamoiselle Fagard, now Madame Jolon, my sister-in-law, who begs you to introduce me and recommend me to Mademoiselle Delaporte, who thinks highly of you and can render me a great service.' 'Immediately,' I said; 'sit down, pretty neighbour.' She was charming. As she turned round, she showed me a perfect figure. I seized her, and pushed her back on to the bed. She tried to defend herself. That was adding fuel to the fire. I did not even take time to shut the door. I finished, I began again. 'I . . . did . . . not . . . tell . . . you,' gasped Séraphine, 'that . . . my sister Jolon . . . was waiting for me.' This thought spurred me on towards a treble. I was like a madman, when the door opened. It was Agathe Fagard. 'Help! Help!' cried Séraphine. I left her uncovered; I jumped up, kicked the door to, threw the lovely brunette on to my bed, and submitted her to a sixth triumph no less vigorous than the first, carried away as I was by the force of my imagination. Agathe Fagard had not yet recovered from her surprise when, appeased by an almost simultaneous triple effort, I blushed at my frenzy and apologised to the two sisters-in-law. 'He has to be seen to be believed!' said Séraphine. I used all the arguments I could to calm them and only just succeeded. Such is the effect of erotic literature.

THE MARQUIS DE SADE
(1740–1814)

Adventure at a Monastery

Donatien Alphonse, Count Sade, was born in pre-Revolutionary France to a manner of life in which the feelings of servants, and women in particular, were of no account – a fact which enabled him to indulge his sadistic tastes to such an extent that at the request of his mother-in-law the King signed a *lettre de cachet* which resulted in his spending a quarter of a century in prison. The most famous of his books, *Justine*, is by no means as horrific as, say, the *120 Journées de Sodome*; in fact there is some evidence to suggest that it began as a satire in the manner of Voltaire's *Candide*. It seems to owe much to Laclos' *Les Liaisons Dangereuses*, that novel of cold sexual intrigue, which had been published six years before Sade completed the *ms* of the first version of *Justine* – in only a fortnight. In the following episode, Justine, having undergone various adventures, takes refuge in a monastery, where she finds four monks, including the Superior, amusing themselves with four girls.

'Come,' said Raphael, whose prodigiously inflamed desires seemed to have reached the point at which it was no longer possible to restrain them, 'it is time to immolate the victim. Let each of us prepare to submit her to his favourite pleasure.'

And this coarsest of men, having placed me on a sofa in the attitude most propitious to his execrable pleasures, had me held down by Antonin and Clément. . . .*

Clément was the next to approach me. Already inflamed by his Superior's behaviour, he was even more excited by the things he had done while observing this. He declared that he would represent no more danger for me than his confrère had done, and that the place where his homage was to be paid would leave me without peril to my virtue. He made me get down on my knees, and fastening himself to me while in this position exercised his perfidious passions on me in a place which prevented me, during the sacrifice, from expressing any complaint as to its irregularity.

*the dots are Sade's, and not an indication of any omission from the original text.

from *Justine*

Jérôme followed. His temple was the same as that of Raphael, but he did not approach the sanctuary. Content to remain in the courtyard, and moved by primitive episodes, the obscenity of which it is impossible to describe, he was unable to accomplish his desires except by barbarous means. . . .

'What favourable preparations,' exclaimed Antonin, as he seized hold of me. 'Come along, my little chicken, come along and let me avenge you for the irregularity of my confrères. Let me gather, at last, the delightful fruits abandoned to me by their intemperance!'

But the details? . . . Great God! . . . I cannot possibly describe them to you. One might have said that this flagitious villain – who was the most lecherous of the four, even though he appeared the least removed from nature's ways – only consented to approach me with a little less unconformity, providing he could compensate himself for this lesser depravity by outraging me more thoroughly, and for a longer period. . . . Alas, if at times I had previously allowed my imagination to wander over the pleasures of sex, I believed them chaste as the God who inspires them, given by nature as a compensation to human beings, and born of love and tenderness. I had been far from believing that man, following the behaviour of certain ferocious beasts, was able to enjoy himself only by making his partners shriek with pain. My experience was so violent that the sufferings natural to the breaking of my virginity were the least I had to support in this dangerous attack. But it was at the moment of his crisis, which Antonin terminated with such furious cries, with such murderous excursions over every part of my body, and bitings so like the bloody caresses of a tiger, that I felt for the moment I was the prey of some savage animal who could only be appeased by devouring me. Once these horrors had ceased, I fell back on the altar of my immolation, motionless, and almost unconscious.

Raphael ordered the women to look after me and give me something to eat. But in that cruel moment a raging torrent of grief and desolation was sweeping through my heart. I finally lost the treasure of my virginity – for which I would have sacrificed my life a hundred times. Nor could I accept the fact that I had been dishonoured by those from whom I had expected the greatest assistance and moral support. My tears flowed abundantly, my cries echoed around the room. I rolled on the floor, tore my hair, and begged my butchers to put me to death. But although these profligate wretches had become completely hardened to such scenes, and were far more interested in tasting of new pleasures with my companions, than in calming my pain or comforting me, they were nevertheless sufficiently troubled by my cries to send me off to rest in a place where lamentations could not be heard. . . . Omphale was ready to take me there when the perfidious Raphael, still looking at me with lubricity, despite the cruel state I was in, said that he did not want me sent away before I had once more become his victim. . . . Hardly had he conceived this project than it was executed. . . . His desires, however, needed an additional degree of stimulation, and it was not until he had employed the cruel methods of Jérôme that he found the necessary strength for the accomplishment of this new crime. . . . What excesses of debauchery! Great God! – was it possible that these lubricious beasts could be so ferocious as to choose the moment of crisis of a moral pain so violent as mine, to make me suffer an equally barbarous physical one?

'By all that's merry!' exclaimed Antonin, as he also took me again, 'it's good to follow the example of one's Superior; and nothing is so appetising as a second offence. They tell me that pain inclines one to pleasure. I'm sure this beautiful child is going to make me the happiest of men!'

And despite my repugnance, despite all my cries and pleas, I became for a second time the wretched target of this contemptible satyr. . . . At length they allowed me to go.

CHODERLOS DE LACLOS
(1741–1803)

The Sweet Distraction

Choderlos de Laclos wrote his famous novel *Les Liaisons Dangereuses* in 1781 and '82, while serving in the French Army. The book, published in 1782, was an immediate sensation – not because it is a masterpiece of construction, elegance and style, but for other reasons. Everyone read it – Marie Antoinette had a richly-bound edition in her library, though without a title on its spine, for it was considered extremely indelicate and immoral.

The book deals with cold-blooded seduction. Here, Valmont, the anti-hero, tells Madame de Merteuil, his friend, in one of the letters which make up the narrative, of his attempt on Cécile, a precocious child whose sensual appetite is yet unawakened. Valmont persuades her fiancé, Danceny, to instruct her to allow the seducer to copy the key to her bedroom, on the pretence of delivering Danceny's love-letters to her the more easily.

The little Volanges girl is indeed very pretty; and though it is very stupid of Danceny to be in love with her, perhaps it would be no less stupid of me not to seek to find with her some distraction from my loneliness. . . . Her pretty glance, her fresh young lips, her naïve air, even her gaucheness underlined the thought; so I decided to act, and success has crowned my attempt.

And are you wondering how I managed to supplant the absent beloved? What kind of seduction proved proper to her age and inexperience? Don't bother: the answer is, none. No doubt you are used to using the weapons of your sex, and triumphing by finesse; I simply took for granted the rights of a man, and subjugated her by my authority. Sure of being able to get at her, I was sure of success, and to gain my ends I used no lies, no pretences at all – or at least, none worthy of the name.

I profited by the very first letter that Danceny sent me for his beloved, and after I had given her the clandestine signal that we had prearranged to let her know that I had such a message, I found every excuse for not actually letting her have it: the impatience she showed was as nothing to mine – and having contrived the delay, I offered a solution.

[75]

The young lady slept in a room which had a door giving directly onto the corridor; but with reason, her mother kept the key! It was just a matter of my getting hold of it. Nothing could then be easier. I only had to have it for two hours in order to have a perfect copy made. Then arrangements, interviews, nocturnal meetings, all became easy and certain: except that – would you believe it? – the timid child took fright and refused me the key! Anyone else might have been dismayed; I only saw in her refusal the change of a piquant pleasure. I wrote to Danceny and complained of this refusal, and was so convincing that the dullard did not rest until he had got from his tremulous mistress her agreement to my demand and her confidence in my discretion.

I was very pleased, I must say, to have changed rôles in this way, and to have persuaded the young man to do for me what he counted on my doing for him! The thought doubled, in my eyes, the effect of the adventure; so as soon as I had the precious key, I hastened to make use of it; and that was last night.

After making sure that all was quiet in the château, I armed myself with a dark lantern, and having made what preparations were demanded by time and circumstance, made my first visit to your pupil. Everything was prepared (she had seen to that herself) to enable me to come to her without any noise. She was in her first sleep, and the sound sleep of that age; I came to her bedside without wakening her, so quietly that I might have passed for a dream; but thinking of the effect of surprise, and the noise which it often causes, I preferred to rouse the pretty sleeper carefully, and indeed prevented the cry which I had feared.

After having calmed her immediate fears, I risked a few liberties – after all, I had not come there without a reason. No one had told her, in her convent, how many perils endanger the timid innocent, and what one has to do to avoid being taken by surprise; for giving all her attention, all her strength, to avoiding being kissed, she left the rest of her body undefended; of which I took advantage! I altered my approach, and soon commanded the field. At that moment we were both almost lost: the little girl, terrified, tried to cry out in real earnest; happily, her voice was strangled by her tears. She threw herself towards the bell-rope, but I quickly held her arm.

'What are you doing?' I asked; 'you will be lost for ever! If someone comes, what can that matter to me? Who could you from *Les Liaisons Dangereuses*

persuade that I am not here at your invitation? Who other than you could have enabled me to come to you? And this key which I had from you, which I could have got from no one else – for what other reason would you have given it me?' This brief lecture allayed neither her anger nor her grief; but in the end she submitted. I do not know whether it was my eloquence; it was certainly not my gestures! One hand was occupied in force, the other in love; what orator could pretend to grace in that situation? If you imagine the scene vividly, *you* will understand that everything was now favourable for an attack; but for myself, I understand nothing – as you say, the simplest woman, a schoolgirl, can lead me like a child.

She, desolate as she was, knew that she must now take some course, come to some arrangement. Prayers did not sway me, so she had to make me an offer. You think I sold the situation dearly? Not at all – I promised everything in exchange for a kiss. It is true that after that first kiss, I forgot my promise; but I had good reason. Was the kiss taken, or given? Forced to resolve that problem, we agreed on a second kiss; and that it should be received. Then I guided her timid arms around my body, and pressed hers with one of my arms – rather more lovingly; and the soft kiss was well received – indeed, perfectly received: Love himself could not have done better.

Such good faith deserved a reward, and I responded to the demand. My hand was drawn back, and I found – I cannot think how – that my person was in its place. You suppose that I pressed on actively? Not at all. I began to enjoy the leisuredly approach, I assure you. Once sure of arriving, why hurry the journey?

Seriously, I was very happy to observe for once the strength of *the moment*, and found I needed no other help. I had to fight against love – and love sustained by modesty or shame, and strengthened above all by the offence which I had given, which was great. *The moment* was all; and that being ripe, everything was offered, everything available. Love – absented itself.

To make sure of my theories, I was cunning enough not to offer more force than she could have overcome. It was only if my charming enemy abused my skill by trying to escape, that I delayed her by mention of that same fear which had already had such a happy effect on her. Without any other persuasion, the tender mistress, forgetting her oaths, at first gave way and then consented; not that after the first embrace reproaches and tears did not return

[77]

in full flood; but I simply ignored them, whether they were true or feigned. As is always the case, they ceased as soon as I began to give her reason for more. Indeed, what with weakness and reproach, reproach and weakness, we did not separate until we had satisfied each other, and mutually agreed upon another meeting tonight.

I did not go back to my room until dawn, worn out and tired through lack of sleep; depend upon it, however, that I made the sacrifice of coming down for breakfast this morning. I love, the morning after an affair, to observe the effects! And you have no idea of them – what embarrassment in her face! What difficulty in walking! Eyes cast down, and so large, so weary! The round face so long! Nothing could be more amusing.

ANON
(c1750)

The Rose and the Thorns

In 1760 there appeared in English a translation of a book of semi-erotic fairy-stories which had appeared a little previously in France as *Tant Mieux pour Elle; Tant Mieux pour Lui*, attributed to a certain Abbé de Voisenon. The English version was entitled *Did you Ever See such Damned Stuff?, or, So Much the Better*. The stories are parodies of some of the anticlerical fairy-stories which had appeared in France at the turn of the century. One concerns the rivalry, for the hand of the Princess Tricolora, of Prince Toadstool (under the protection of the Fairy Burning-Spite) and Prince Discreet (protected by the Fairy Sly). Gaining a temporary victory, Prince Toadstool marries the Princess, and the couple are escorted to the marriage bed.

Scarce had the company cleared the room before a voice was heard to pronounce these words: 'He is not *there* yet!'

'Madam,' said Toadstool, 'allow me to give this voice the lie.'

Tricolora observed a modest silence, which authorised a husband's rights: he was proceeding to avail himself of it, when the Princess made a face, a complaint, and a motion. Toadstool, full of respect, reined in his rapture, and asked what ailed her.

'My lord,' said she, 'something very extraordinary is the matter with me.'

'Do you feel pain in any part?' pursued Toadstool.

'My lord, it is more embarrassing than painful.'

'Permit me, madam, to see.'

'I dare not,' replied the Princess; 'if you knew but where it is you would not ask me.'

'Your saying so,' answered Toadstool, 'points out to me where it is.'

At these words, he examined; but how great must be his astonishment at seeing a rose surrounded with thorns.

'Ah,' said he, 'madam, what a beautiful rose is there! Pray, is it a mark you was born with?'

'My lord,' said the Princess, 'I believe it is but now come there.'

'That is very odd,' said Toadstool; 'this must either be a trick played me, or meant me for a piece of gallantry. But I perceive some letters: they are perhaps a motto. Allow me to use a light to read them: the character is very small: I fancy it is Elzevir.'

Toadstool went and brought a candle; but he found a change of decoration. There were now neither rose nor thorns; in their place he saw two monstrous fingers that were making cuckold's horns at him. Toadstool put himself into a violent passion; can you blame him?

'Madam,' cried he, 'you have got a gallant, and these are his fingers.'

'My lord, what do you mean? You use me ill.'

'Madam, be so good as to stand up, that I may see whether that will make no alteration.'

The Princess stood up, but the fingers were still there. Toadstool tried to think, but as he had always been an enemy to thinking, thinking was at this juncture an enemy to him, as indeed it generally is to those who have not got a habit of it.

'This will now appear, Princess,' said he with an air of satisfaction, 'all this is nothing but a joke, and a cursed stupidity of the Fairy Sly, who wants to obstruct my joys by giving me umbrage about you. I remark however that those two fingers cannot hinder me from giving you proof of my esteem. They will doubtless disappear the instant I shall show I despise them.'

He had then, as things appeared, a misplaced desire, and indeed his wrong head never suggested to him any other: and that desire he was proceeding to satisfy. But the two fingers just then became a pair of claws, and squeezed him unmercifully. He screamed out, and what redoubled his torments was that the Princess, by an involuntary impulsion, at the same time he was thus held fast, walked or rather ran in a retrograde motion round the room with as much speed as the fleetest greyhound could do in its course forward.

'S'death, madam!' he cried out, 'you are mad: what do you mean? Stop, stop!'

'Indeed, my lord, I cannot,' answered she, continuing to draw him in that manner several times around the room without ceasing.

'Madam,' said Toadstool, 'this is not to be borne. You ruin me. I shall never be good for anything as long as I live.'

At length, after a full quarter of an hour or more, Tricolora fell from *Did you Ever See such Damned Stuff?, or, So Much the Better*

backward into an armchair, and Toadstool, released with a jerk, rolled down upon the floor, quite senseless.

ANON
(c1785)

A Word or two to the Engraver

To the editor of the second edition of *The Exhibition of Female Flagellants*, published by George Peacock from 66, Drury Lane, London, in 1785, an anonymous correspondent calling himself Philobodex wrote a letter giving a little advice on the illustrations proper in a work on flagellation.

In the first place it will consist of a display of Female Backsides, for though I think a Lady's Bum uncovered an agreeable and diverting object, I would not give a farthing to see a man's Arse – this I believe is only agreeable to persons of a certain description, too bad to be countenanced. But to see the representation of an agreeable young lady having her petticoats pulled up, and her pretty pouting Backside laid bare, and seeming to feel the tingling stripes of a Rod, is amusing enough.

Now a word or two to the Engraver. Let him portray the Lady's Backside, which no doubt will be the principal figure in the piece, round, plump and large; rather over than under the size which the usual proportion of painters and statuaries would allow; let him in general present it full and completely bared to the eye; though in some plates for variety he may give it us sidelong, or a little bit of the Lady's under-petticoat or shift shading some part of it, and let it be remembered that if he has that complete knowledge of his subject I imagine he has, and is a man of genius, a large field is open before him to display it in. He may show us several different sorts of Backsides, all of them natural and proper; all of them elegant and handsome (for there is almost as much difference in tails as in heads) but not all alike; he certainly will not give the little round firm backside of fifteen to five and thirty, nor the full mellow bum of the middle-aged lady to the boarding-school Miss. . . .

It is probable that in some of these prints there will be other figures besides the principal, the bare-arsed lady; now though we cannot have the satisfaction of seeing the pretty bums of them all, an ingenious delineator might so contrive it to heighten the lusciousness of the whole piece so that one by some careless posture might show her legs, another her breasts, and the dress of others might be so managed as to give us the idea of a very large and full backside concealed under the swelling drapery. Thus would each plate present us with a very beautiful and entertaining *tout ensemble*, and these little circumstances and adjuncts prove a seasonable relief to the eye fatigued and overpowered by the blaze of beauty from the naked arse of the Lady enjoying the sweets of the Birch, darting full upon us without the least bit of petticoat or smock interposing, by way of cloud to ease our parched senses.

P.S. I thought it unnecessary to advise you that all the figures should be dressed; every lady should have her shift on at least; nakedness must always in these matters be partial, to give the highest degree of satisfaction.

CAPT. FRANCES GROSE
(c1785)

From Abbess to Windward

Frances Grose, an antiquarian whose gambling debts forced him into authorship, published his *Classical Dictionary of the Vulgar Tongue* in 1785. Little is known of his life (how or why, for instance, he came to call himself 'Captain'). He died in Dublin in 1791, leaving his dictionary to be plundered by other dictionary-makers for at least a century.

ABBESS, or Lady Abbess. A bawd, the mistress of a brothel.

APPLE DUMPLIN SHOP. A woman's bosom.

ARMOUR. In his armour, to fight in armour; to make use of Mrs Philips's ware (a condom).

ARTICLE. A wench. A prime article: a handsome girl. 'She's a prime article', she's a devilish good piece, a hell of a *goer*.

BACKGAMMON PLAYER. A sodomite.

BALUM RANCUM. A hop or dance, where the women are all prostitutes. N.B. The company dance in their birthday suits.

BEARD SPLITTER. A man much given to wenching.

BITER. A wench whose cunt is ready to bite her arse: a lascivious, rampant wench.

BLOW THE GROUNDSELS. To lie with a woman on the floor.

BOB TAIL. A lewd woman, or one that plays with her tail; also an impotent man, or an eunuch.

BRIM. (Abbreviation of brimstone). An abandoned woman; perhaps originally a passionate or irascible woman, compared to brimstone for its inflammability.

BROTHER STARLING. One who lies with the same woman, that is, builds in the same nest.

BUNTER. A low, dirty prostitute, half whore and half beggar.

BURNER. A clap. 'The blowen tipped the swell a burner', the girl gave the gentleman a clap.

BURNT. Poxed or clapped. 'He was sent out a sacrifice, and came home a burnt offering', a saying of seamen who have caught the venereal disease abroad.

BUSHEL BUBBY. A full-breasted woman.

BUTTERED BUN. One lying with a woman that has just laid with another man is said to have a buttered bun.

BUTTOCK BALL. The amorous congress.

BUTTOCKING SHOP. A brothel.

CAB. A brothel. 'Mother, how many tails have you in your cab', how many girls have you in your bawdy house?

CARVEL'S RING. The private parts of a woman. Ham Carvel, a jealous old doctor, being in bed with his wife, dreamed that the Devil gave him a ring, which, so long as he had it on his finger, would prevent his being made a cuckold; waking, he found he had got his finger the Lord knows where.

CHICKEN-BREASTED. Said of a woman with scarce any breasts.

CLICKET. Copulation of foxes, and thence used, in a canting sense, for that of men and women, as 'The cull and the mort are at clicket in the dyke', the man and woman are copulating in the ditch.

CLOVEN, CLEAVE, OR CLEFT. A term used for a woman who passes for a maid, but is not.

COCK ALLEY or COCK LANE. The private parts of a woman.

COCK BAWD. A male keeper of a bawdy-house.

COCKISH. Wanton, forward. 'A cockish wench', a forward, coming girl.

CODS. The scrotum. Also a nickname for a curate: a rude fellow meeting a curate, mistook him for the rector, and accosted him with the vulgar appellation of Bollocks the Rector. 'No, sir,' answered he, 'only Cods the curate, at your service.'

COFFEE HOUSE. A necessary house. 'To make a coffee-house of a woman's cunt,' to go in and out and spend nothing.

COMMODITY. A woman's commodity, the private parts of a modest woman, and the public parts of a prostitute.

CONVENIENT. A mistress.

COVENT GARDEN ABBESS. A bawd.

COVENT GARDEN AGUE. The venereal disease. 'He broke his shins against Covent Garden railings,' he caught the venereal disease.

COVENT GARDEN NUN. A prostitute.

CRINKUM CRANKUM. A woman's commodity.

CONDOM. The dried gut of a sheep, worn by men in the act of coition, to prevent venereal infection. Said to have been invented by one Colonel Condom. These machines were long prepared and sold by a matron of the name of Philips, at the Green Canister in Half-Moon Street, in the Strand. That good lady having acquired a fortune, retired from business; but learning that the town was not well served by her successors, she, out of a patriotic zeal for the public welfare, returned to her occupation, of which she gave notice by divers hand-bills, in circulation in the year 1776.

DAIRY. A woman's breasts. 'She sported her dairy', she pulled out her breast.

DELLS. Young, buxom wenches, ripe and prone to venery, but who have not lost their virginity, which the *upright man* claims by virtue of his prerogative; after which they become free for any of the fraternity. Also a common strumpet.

DIDDEYS. A woman's breasts or bubbies.

DILDO. Penis-succedanaeus, called in Lombardy *Passo Tempo*.

TO DOCK. To lie with a woman. 'The cull docked the dell all the darkmans,' the fellow laid with the wench all night. 'Docked smack smooth,' one who has suffered an amputation of his penis from a venereal complaint.

DOG'S RIG. To copulate till you are tired, and then turn tail to it.

DOUBLE JUGG. A man's back side.

DRY BOB. Copulation without emission.

DUCHESS. A woman enjoyed with her pattens on, or by a man in boots, is said to be made a duchess.

TO EDGE. To excite, stimulate, provoke; or as it is vulgarly called, to egg a man on.

EVE'S CUSTOM-HOUSE. Where Adam made his first entry.

FANCY MAN. A man kept by a lady for secret services.

FEN. A bawd, or common prostitute.

FLASH MAN. A bully to a bawdy house. A whore's bully.

FLAT COCK. A female.

FLESH BROKER. A match-maker, a bawd.

FLOGGING CULLY. A debilitated lecher, commonly an old one.

FRENCH DISEASE. The venereal disease, said to have been imported from France. French gout: the same. 'He suffered by a blow over the snout with a French faggot-stick', he lost his nose by the pox.

FRENCHIFIED. Infected with the venereal disease. 'The mort is Frenchified,' the wench is infected.

FROE, or VROE. A woman, wife or mistress. 'Brush to your froe, or bloss and wheedle for crop,' run to your mistress, and sooth and coax her out of some money.

FRUITFUL VINE. A woman's private parts, i.e. that flowers every month, and bears fruit in nine months.

FUMBLER. An old or impotent man.

GAME. At bawdy-houses, lewd women: 'Mother have you any game,' mother, have you any girls? 'Game pullet,' a young whore, or forward girl in the way of becoming one.

GAP STOPPER. A whoremaster.

GAYING INSTRUMENT. The penis.

GINGAMBOBS. A man's privities.

GOAT. A lascivious person. Goat's jig, making the beast with two backs, copulation.

GREEN GOWN. To 'give a girl a green gown,' to tumble her on the grass.

TO GRIND. To have carnal knowledge of a woman.

HAT. 'Old hat,' a woman's privities, because frequently felt.

HOITY-TOITY. 'A hoity-toity wench,' a giddy, thoughtless, romping girl.

HORN MAN. A person extremely jealous of his wife is said to be horn mad. Also a cuckold, who does not cut or breed his horns easily.

HORSE BUSS. A kiss with a loud smack, also a bite.

HUMMUMS. A bagnio, or bathing house.

JACK WHORE. A large masculine overgrown wench.

TO JOCK, or JOCKUM CLOY. To enjoy a woman.

TO KEEP IT UP. To prolong a debauch. 'We kept it up finely last night;' 'mother, your tit won't keep,' your daughter will not preserve her virginity.

LACED MUTTON. A prostitute.

LADYBIRDS. Light or lewd women.

LEFT-HANDED WIFE. A concubine; an allusion to an ancient German custom according to which when a man married his concubine, or a woman greatly his inferior, he gave her his left hand.

LETCH. A whim of the amorous kind, out of the common way.

TO LIB. To lie together.

LIBKEN. A house to lie in.

LOBCOCK. A large relaxed penis.

MACKEREL. A bawd.

MADGE. The private parts of a woman.

MADGE CULLS. Sodomites.

MAN TRAP. A woman's commodity.

MELTING MOMENTS. A fat man and woman in the amorous congress.

MISS. A miss or kept woman; a harlot.

MISS LAYCOCK. The monosyllable.

MOLL PEATLY'S GIG. A rogering bout.

MOLLY. A Miss Molly, an effeminate fellow, a sodomite.

MUFF. The private parts of a woman. 'To the well wearing your muff, mort,' to the happy consummation of your marriage, girl: a health.

MUTTON MONGER. A man addicted to wenching.

MUTTON. 'In her mutton,' having carnal knowledge of a woman.

NOTCH. The private parts of a woman.

NUB. Coition.

NUGGING HOUSE. A brothel.

NUNNERY. A bawdy house.

ONE OF US, ONE OF MY COUSINS. A woman of the town, a harlot.

PETTICOAT PENSIONER. One kept by a woman for secret services.

PETTISH. Passionate.

PIECE. A wench. 'A damned good or bad piece,' a girl who is more or less active and skilful in the amorous congress. Hence the (Cambridge) toast, 'May we never have a *piece* (peace) that will injure the constitution.'

PISS-PROUD. Having a false erection. 'That old fellow thought he had an erection, but his cock was only piss-proud,' said of any old fellow who marries a young wife.

PLUG TAIL. A man's penis.

PRAY. 'She prays with her knees upward,' said of a woman much given to gallantry and intrigue.

PROUD. Desirous of copulation. 'A proud bitch,' a bitch at heat, or desirous of a dog.

PUBLIC LEDGER. A prostitute, because, like that paper, she is open to all parties.

PUNK. A whore.

PUSHING SCHOOL. A fencing school, also a brothel.

RANTALLION. One whose scrotum is so relaxed as to be longer than his penis, i.e. whose shot pouch is longer than the barrel of his piece.

RANTUM SCANTUM. 'Playing at rantum skantum,' making the beast with two backs.

RASCAL. A rogue or villain, a rascal originally meaning a lean, shabby deer at the time of changing his horns, penis, &c, whence, in the vulgar acceptation, rascal is conceived to signify a man without genitals; the regular vulgar answer to this reproach, if uttered by a woman, is the offer of an ocular demonstration of the virility of the party so defamed. Some derive it from *rascaglione*, an Italian word signifying a man without testicles, an eunuch.

RELISH. Carnal connection with a woman.

TO ROGER. To bull, or lie with a woman; from the name of Roger being frequently being given to a bull.

ROOM. 'She lets out her fore room and lies backwards,' saying of a woman suspected of prostitution.

RUN GOODS. A maidenhead, being a commodity never entered.

SALT. Lecherous; 'a salt bitch,' a bitch at heat, or proud bitch.

TO SCREW. To copulate. 'A female screw,' a common prostitute.

TO SHAG. To copulate. 'He is but bad shag,' he is no able woman's man.

SHORT-HEELED WENCH. A girl apt to fall on her back.

SNOOZING KEN. A brothel. 'The swell was spiced of his screens in a snoozing ken,' the gentleman was robbed of his banknotes in a brothel.

SOCKET MONEY. A whore's fee or hire.

SPANISH GOUT. The pox.

STALLION. A man kept by an old lady for secret services.

STRAPPING. Lying with a woman.

TO STRUM. To have carnal knowledge of a woman.

STRUMPET. A harlot.

SUGAR STICK. The virile member.

TO SWIVE. To copulate.

TACKLE. A man's tackle, the genitals.

TAIL. A prostitute.

TO TAP. 'To tap a girl,' to be the first seducer, in allusion to a beer barrel.

THOMAS. 'Man Thomas,' a penis.

THOROUGH-GOOD-NATURED-WENCH. One who being asked to sit down, will lie down.

TOOLS. The private parts of a man.

TRUMPERY. An old whore, or goods of no value.

TO TUP. To have carnal knowledge of a woman.

TWIDDLE-DIDDLES. Testicles.

TWIDDLEPOOP. An effeminate looking fellow.

TWO HANDED PUT. The amorous congress.

VELVET. To tip the velvet, to put the tongue into a woman's mouth.

UNRIGGED. Undressed, or stripped. 'Unrig the drab,' strip the wench.

WAGTAIL. A lewd woman.

TO WAP. To copulate. 'If she won't wap for a winne, let her trine for a make,' if she won't lie with a man for a penny, let her hang for a halfpenny. 'Mort wap-a-pace,' a woman of experience, or very expert at the sport.

WASP. An infected prostitute, who like a wasp carries a sting in her tail.

WELL-HUNG. 'The blowen was nutts upon the kiddey because he is well-hung,' the girl is pleased with the youth because his genitals are large.

WHIFFLES. A relaxation of the scrotum.

WHIRLYGIGS. Testicles.

WHOREMONGER. A man that keeps more than one mistress. A country gentleman who kept a female friend, being reproved by the parson of the parish, and styled a whoremonger, asked the parson whether he had a cheese in his house, and being answered in the affirmative, 'Pray,' says he, 'and does that one cheese make you a cheesemonger?'

WHOREPIPE. The penis.

WIFE IN WATER COLOURS. A mistress or concubine; watercolours being, like their engagements, easily effaced or dissolved.

WILLING TIT. A free horse or a coming girl.

WINDWARD PASSAGE. One who uses or navigates the windward passage, a sodomite.

ANON
(1788–93)

The Good Whores' Guide

Harris' List of Covent Garden Ladies, or Man of Pleasure's Kalendar was an annual publication which listed the women of pleasure of eighteenth century London. Twentieth century British law makes such a publication impossible (indeed, there was a prosecution a decade ago, when one was attempted); Harris provided a kind of *Good Whores' Guide* which was often as honest and uncompromising as could be.

1788

MISS B————RN, No. 18, Old Compton Street, Soho.
This accomplished nymph has just attained her eighteenth year, and fraught with every perfection, enters a volunteer in the field of Venus. She plays on the piano forte, sings, dances, and is mistress of every *Manoeuvre* in the amorous contest that can enhance the coming pleasure; is of the middle stature, fine auburn hair, dark eyes, and very inviting countenance, which ever seems to beam delight and love. In bed she is all the heart could wish, or eye admire, every limb is symmetry, every action under cover truly amorous; her price is two pounds ten.

MISS W————D, at a Hairdressers', Windmill Street.
This young charmer is of the middle size, and the resplendent black of her lively eyes is finely controlled by the fairness of her complexion and lightness of her hair: her teeth are good, and her temper complying. She is really a delicious piece, and her *terra incognita* is so very agreeable to every traveller therein, that it hath ceased to deserve that name, and is become a well known and much frequented country; freely taking in the stranger, raising up them that *fall*, making the *crooked straight*, and although she does not pretend to restore sight to the blind, she'll place him in such a direction that he cannot mistake the way; and for one guinea will engage he returns the same way back without any direction at all.

[91]

1789

MISS T——M—S, No. 28, Frith Street, Soho.
'Days of ease and nights of pleasure' is a motto this lewd girl never means to depart from; nor does she wish to be *closely* connected with any lover that does not possess an equal share of lewdness and amorous fire with herself. Mr G——n, a gentleman of her own cast, altho' not long lived in the capacity of keeper, was with her for some months, during which time she *drained* him of all his amorous warmth, and being disabled in respect to duty, she no longer thought him worth her bed. Her temper is haughty and imperious, her complexion of darker tint, being of the mule breed, and she stands upon the tempting precipice of eighteen; those that love a true copper-bottomed frigate, and can spare a few guineas, will think himself [*sic*] happy on board. If report says true, this swarthy female was the companion of a certain princely commander, during his voyage home from America. She dresses very genteel, and is accomplished in musick, etc.

1790

MISS B—NF——LD, No. 9, Poland Street
Miss B is about nineteen years old, tall, genteel, and very handsome, being quite fair, with blue eyes, light red hair, and fine regular teeth. She is a very agreeable companion upon all occasions, and approves herself in bed a *devotee* to Venus, who has well studied the mysteries of that Goddess. She is frequently mounted *à la militaire*, and as frequently performs the rites of the love-inspiring queen according to the *equestrian* order, in which style she is said to afford uncommon delight, being perfect in her paces, having studied under a professed riding-master who has taught her the *ménage* in the highest perfection. For these lessons, which she daily and nightly gives, she expects two or three guineas at least.

1793

MISS GODF——Y, No. 22, Upper Newman Street
This lady is a kind of boatswain in her way, and when she speaks, every word is uttered with a thundering and vociferous tone. She is

a fine, lively little girl, about twenty-two, very fond of dancing, has dark eyes and hair, well shaped, and an exceedingly good bedfellow, will take brandy with any one, or drink and swear, and though but little, will fight a good battle. We apprehend this lady would be an extraordinary good companion for an officer in the army, as she might save him the trouble of giving the word of command. She resides in the first floor.

MISS SH——RD, No. 46, Googe Street
A very desirable companion, though in the *knowing* style, she is *up to a thing or two*, and is not to be had by a *queer cull*. She is of middle size, inclined to be fat, and may be said, if we draw a *kind view* of things, or argue *a posteriori*, inclined to be luscious. Her face is one of those where love seems to have chosen his seat for casting his darts from, especially from her eyes, which, for a certain peculiar cast, is all life, spirit and fire; indeed, it seems rather to flame than burn. Her hand and arm are uncommonly neat; and her leg, thigh, and the *demesnes* adjacent remarkably tempting. She drinks but little, swears less, and has that great attractive recommendation to every woman – an apparent modesty, which, if a woman wants the reality is certainly the best substitute for it. She is without doubt a most pleasing *pupil* of *pleasure*, and perfectly competent to the instruction of those who desire to be announced *Students* in the *mysteries of Venus*. She is about twenty, and a single guinea will content her. This lady's apartments are on the first floor; has several city friends, and lawyers from Gray's Inn and the Temple.

MISS J——NSON, No. 17, Willow Walk, near the Dog and Duck
This pretty filly is of a middling size, near twenty. Norfolk gave her her birth. Her countenance is rather pleasant, with fine black eyes that are very attractive, good teeth, and a fine skin, and of so amorous constitution that in the arms of an equally lewd partner she never wishes to fall into the arms of sleep; the *dairy hills* of delight are beautifully prominent, firm and elastic, the *sable coloured grot* below with its coral-lipped *janitor* is just adapted to the sons of Venus. It is a pity that this girl did not receive some sort of education; however, as there are people who admire a vulgarity of expression and a coarseness of manner which they account a kind of rustic *naïveté*, and which they prefer to the polish, education or

attractions of *bieuseance* [*sic*], it is no wonder if she has a few customers, though her clothes are always at the pawnbrokers. She seems always low spirited, except when the liquor exhilarates her spirits; extremely illiterate, ungrateful to her benefactors, peevish, and addicted to swearing and to low company, this girl in a short time will be in the lowest class of prostitutes; however as she is young, she is still worthy the attention of an *amateur* who would rescue her from prostitution, as we think she still possesses a little sensibility. She is the only girl that frequents the Dog and Duck worth mentioning; her price from five shillings to half a guinea.

HONORÉ DE BALZAC
(1799–1850)

The Danger of being an Innocent

Balzac told his mistress, Countess Hanska, that he thought of his *Contes Drolatiques* as his 'principal title to fame in days to come.' He may have been joking; but he took enormous trouble over these erotic tales, writing them for instance in accurate archaic French, and modelling them on the stories of Rabelais and Marguerite of Navarre. In the story part of which is reprinted below, a young man brought up in a monastery is married to an innocent young girl, whose mother, the Lady d'Amboise, is the mistress of Lord de Braguelogne, Civil Lieutenant of the Châtelet Ambit of Paris. After great feasting and joking, the two innocents are conducted to their bridal chamber.

Now that our gentle innocent beheld the delightful maid vouchsafed him, she was tucked well down between the sheets, and, though devilish curious, was sternly turned away from him. Her glance, however, was as sharp as the point of a halberd, and inwardly she kept telling herself that what she had to do was obey. She was, you see, also utterly ignorant, so merely waited on the desires of the gentleman of rather ecclesiastical appearance to whom, after all, she now belonged.

Seeing the situation, young Moncontour went to the bedside, scratched behind his ear, then knelt down, at which exercise he was expert.

'Have you said your prayers?' he whispered, as if butter would not melt in his mouth.

'No,' she replied, 'I forgot. Do you think I should?'

So the young couple began their conjugal life by calling on God for aid, which was in itself not unseemly, except that it was not God, only Old Nick who heard them and replied, God at the moment being completely preoccupied by that abominable new Protestant faith.

'What did they tell you to do?' inquired the husband.

'Love you,' said she, in all simplicity.

'They didn't tell me that,' he said. 'But I do, all the same.

[95]

Moreover, I am ashamed to say, I love you more than I used to love God.'

These words did not seem to worry the bride too much.

'If it won't disturb you too much, I should awfully like to get into bed with you,' resumed the husband.

'I will be pleased to make room. I am anyway supposed to be under you,' she said.

'All right then,' he said, 'only please don't look. I am going to undress and get in.'

At this virtuous announcement, the maid most expectantly turned the other way, for this was the first time she had found only the thin partition of a girl's shift between herself and a young man.

In due course the booby comes and slips cautiously into the bed. In this way husband and wife found themselves indeed united, though not at all in the way you are thinking of.

Have you ever seen a monkey freshly brought from overseas first given a walnut? Knowing by monkey imagination how tasty the food hidden inside the shell is, he sniffs and turns it about a thousand monkeyish ways, muttering I know not what between his teeth. Oh, how lovingly he examines it, how studiously, how he holds it and pulls it about and turns it over and angrily shakes it, and often, if it is a monkey of no great breed or sense, in the end he leaves it alone.

Just so our poor innocent who, as day was breaking, was compelled to confess to his darling wife that as he had not a notion how to accomplish his duty, nor even exactly what the duty was, nor even where to find the office, so to speak, he would have to make some inquiries about it, seeking assistance and, as he put it, a supporting hand.

'You must,' she said, 'since, unfortunately, I shall not be able to teach you.'

Indeed, despite all their devices, all manner of attempts and the countless extraordinary things which boobs will try, things which would never even occur to anybody who knows what love is, the young couple fell asleep, quite despondent at not having succeeded in cracking their conjugal nut. However, at least they had sufficient gumption to agree both to profess to having been very satisfied with their first night.

When the young wife rose, still a virgin, totally unqueened, she boasted valiantly about it all and said she had the king of husbands. But, when it came to being ragged and teased about it, she was like anyone else who knows nothing, she piled it on a bit too much. Everybody indeed found that she was a bit too free with her tongue, for when a certain Lady de la Roche-Carnon prompted a young girl named de la Bourdaisière, who was also ignorant of such matters, to ask the bride 'how many loaves her husband put in the oven,' she overdid it again and cried: 'Twenty-four.'

Now, as the young husband went droopily about, which hurt his wife very much (for she was following him out of the corner of her eye all the time, hoping to see his innocence come to an end), the ladies of the company got the idea into their heads that the pleasures of the first night had cost him a little too dearly. They also thought that the bride must already be feeling rather rueful at having exhausted him already.

Now came the wedding breakfast, with all the prickly wisecracks which in those days were so much in taste. Somebody, for instance, made the remark that the bride looked very open, another that somewhere in the castle during the night he had heard a lot of knocking, a third that somebody's loaf had come out of the oven very soft, and yet another that after such a night there were two families that had lost something they would never get back again, and there were countless other salty observations and sly references which, unfortunately, were all Greek to the young groom. However, on account of the wealth of the families and their neighbours and other guests, nobody had really been to bed at all, there had been dancing and rollicking and roistering all night, as is usual at weddings with the nobility.

All this satisfied the Lord de Braguelogne, while Lady d'Amboise, well primed by the thought of the nice things happening to her daughter, was with a view to a gallant encounter eyeing the Civil Lieutenant with eyes as sharp as a kestrel's. But the poor Civil Lieutenant, so knowledgeable about court bailiffs and sergeants, and quick to seize all the rogues and pickpockets of Paris, made out he did not perceive the opportunity offered him, especially as it came from a mistress of so long-standing. For the love of this grand lady was getting rather burdensome to him. Indeed, it was only from a lively sense of what was proper that he stuck to her at all. It was, he thought, not seemly for a Lieutenant of the police to change his mistresses like a gentleman-in-waiting. After all, he was in charge of public decency, police and religion.

Nevertheless, there would have to be an end to his rebellion. The day after the wedding, most of the guests left, and this meant that Lady d'Amboise, Lord de Braguelogne and the grandparents could go to bed at last. Hence, as supper drew nigh, the good Lieutenant was the recipient of summonses so explicit that it was no more seemly than it would have been had they come from the magistrates' court, to oppose any procrastinatory arguments.

Before supper, therefore, Lady d'Amboise made signs (more than a hundred), aimed at extracting good old Braguelogne from the room where he had settled down to entertain the bride. But in place of the Lieutenant it was that innocent of a bridegroom who emerged. He thought he would like to take a stroll in the air with his dear young wife's mamma. The reason was that the innocent had suddenly conceived an idea which had grown like a mushroom, namely, he would make inquiry of this good lady (since he thought her of most circumspect behaviour), about the task before him. Yes, recalling the saintly precepts of his spiritual pastor, who had always told him to seek information on any matter from 'elderly folk with experience of life', he proposed to entrust his situation to Lady d'Amboise.

Being all timidity and shyness, however, before he could find how to put the matter, he took a few turns up and down the garden. Lady d'Amboise for her part was extremely glum, being shockingly put out by the blindness, deafness and apparently deliberate paralysis of the senses of Lord de Braguelogne. . . .

[At last] the young innocent of a bridegroom brought himself to pipe up his *introit* to this most pepperishly worked-up female. The result was that the very first circumlocution caught fire in her mind like a hot spark on tinderwood in the soldier's musket, and it at once occurred to her that she might do far worse than try her own son-in-law as a stop-gap, and so now she murmured to herself: 'Oh darling young beard, how sweet you do smell. . . . Oh, pert pretty nose, all dewy and fresh. . . . Oh untried beard, oh silly beard, oh virgin beard, oh nose full of delight, oh springtime beard, oh master key of love!'

She had to keep this up the whole length of the garden (and it was a large garden too) before she had connived with the booby that when night fell he should leave his room and slip into hers, where she promised to teach him more than his father knew. The novitiate husband was very pleased with this, and thanked Lady d'Amboise, only begging her to keep it secret. . . .

[Meanwhile] the young bride, full of thought of the worry it must be to her young husband not to know the way to accomplish this matter essential to marriage, but completely at a loss to guess what it might be, conceived the notion of saving him perhaps considerable worry, shame and trouble by finding out for herself. In this it was her intention to make him a pleasant surprise and please him and when night came, teach him his duty, and be in a position to say: '*This is what it is all about, dear love!*'

So, having been brought up by the old dowager with great respect for elderly folk, she thought she might discourse gracefully with the good Lieutenant of Paris and in so doing extract from him the sweet mystery of coition. At this moment, full of shame at thus being entangled in agonising reflections on the night's task before him without saying a word to his sportive companion, Lord Braguelogne remarked bluntly to the pretty young bride how lucky she was to have such a nice young husband.

'Yes,' she said, 'he is very nice indeed.'

'Too nice, perhaps?' murmured the Lieutenant, with a smile.

To cut a long story short, things went so smoothly between these two that Lord de Braguelogne suddenly struck up a very different canticle, one trilling with delight and also with promises, regarding the matter under discussion, to spare nothing to disobfuscate the understanding of Lady d'Amboise's daughter, that young person engaging to call on him for her first lesson.

Take account too that the said Lady d'Amboise after supper dinned a shrill music into Braguelogne's ears about his scant recognition of the benefits she had brought him, her estate, her money, her loyalty and all that, and even after half an hour of it she had not spilled one quarter of her wrath. They brandished a hundred blades against each other, yet kept the sheaths on them all.

Meanwhile the young couple, nicely gone to bed, each cogitated inwardly how to slip away, in order to delight the other. At last our dim one declared that he felt all of a flutter, he did not know why, he would have to go out for a breath of fresh air. Immediately, his unqueened spouse suggested that perhaps a little moonlight might do him good. Then the good innocent said how sorry he was for his little one, being left all alone for a moment.

In short, both of them, one after the other, quit the bridal bed, in great haste to acquire wisdom. They visited their authorities, who also, as you may imagine, were most impatient. Thus they acquired excellent instruction. What sort, exactly?

I cannot say, because in this matter everybody has his own education system and his own practices. Of all the sciences, this is the one in which the basic principles are most fluid. You may however count on it that there never were pupils who more eagerly acquired the teaching in any tongue, in any form of conjugation or any other discipline. And when at last the two spouses returned to their nest, they were delighted to communicate to each other what they had discovered during their scholarly peregrinations.

'Why, darling,' suddenly cried the bride in astonishment, 'you already know better than my teacher.'

From such fascinating experiment, delight entered the young couple's home and with it went perfect fidelity, for at the very outset of their marriage they each found by experience how much better equipment their partner had than any of their mentors, even including their special subject masters. Hence for the remainder of their days they stuck to the legitimate substance of each other's bodies. Hence too it was that in his old age Lord Moncontour used to say to his friends: 'Take my advice, be cuckolded green, not ripe.'

Which is the true morality for married codpieces.

MARY WILSON
(fl 1800–30)

The Essential Point

'Mary Wilson, Spinster', was associated with a number of erotic books during the first three decades of the nineteenth century. In 1824, in *The Voluptuarian Cabinet*, she published her plans for 'promoting Adultery on the part of Married Women and Fornication on the part of Old Maids and Widows.' There is no evidence that a sufficient number of ladies subscribed to her scheme to enable it to be carried out.

I have purchased very extensive premises, which are situated between two great thoroughfares, and are entered from each by means of shops devoted entirely to such trades as are exclusively resorted to by ladies. In the area between the two rows of houses I have erected a most elegant temple, in the centre of which are large saloons entirely surrounded with boudoirs most elegantly and commodiously fitted up. In these saloons, according to their classes, are to be seen the finest men of their species I can procure, occupied in whatever amusements are adapted to their taste, and all kept in a high state of excitement by good living and idleness. The ladies will never enter the saloons even in their masks, but view their inmates from a darkened window in each boudoir. In one they will see fine, elegantly dressed young men playing at cards, music, &c. – in others athletic men wrestling or bathing, in a state of perfect nudity. In short, they will see such a variety of the animal that they cannot fail of suiting their inclinations. Having fixed upon one she should like to enjoy, the lady has only to ring for the chambermaid, call her to the window, point out the object, and he is immediately brought to the boudoir. She can enjoy him in the dark, or have a light and keep on her mask. She can stay for an hour or a night, and have one or a dozen men as she pleases, without being known to any of them. A lady of seventy or eighty years of age can at pleasure enjoy a fine, robust youth of twenty, and to elevate the mind to the sublimest raptures of love, every boudoir is surrounded with the most superb paintings of Aretino's Postures after Julio Romano and Ludovico Carracci, interspersed with large mirrors; also a sideboard covered with the most delicious viands and richest wines. The whole expense of the Institution is defrayed by a subscription from each lady of one hundred guineas per annum, with the exception of the refreshments which are to be paid for at the time.

The greatest possible pains have been taken to preserve order and regularity, and it is impossible that any discovery can take place by the intrusion of police or enraged cuckolds, as will be demonstrated to every lady before she pays her subscription, and as is more fully detailed in the private prospectus to be had of Madame de Gomez, the subdirectress, at the Institution, who will also furnish them with a catalogue of the most extensive collection of bawdy books in French, Italian and English, which has ever been collected, and which I have purchased at the expense of £2,000 for the use of my patronesses. The different saloons have been decorated by one of the first painters of the age, with designs from Mr Knight's work on the ancient worship of Priapus, which renders them one of the most singular exhibitions of Europe. No male creature is to be admitted into any part of the temple but the saloons, and those only the trusty, tried and approved functionaries who are well paid for their services, and not let in to gratify curiosity. Having thus made it my study to serve my own sex in a most essential point, I trust to their liberality for encouragement in my arduous undertaking, and am, Ladies, your most obedient servant, Mary Wilson.

THE WHORE'S CATECHISM

The Whore's Catechism, said to be translated by Mary Wilson from the French, was published and printed by another woman – but were either of them really women? – Sarah Brown, at Princes Place, Pimlico, in 1830. (Ms Wilson, incidentally, had a rather more respectable address: she dated her Foreword from Hall Place, St Johns Wood.)

Q What is a whore?

A A girl who, having laid modesty completely aside, no longer blushes at yielding herself to the promiscuous gratification of sensual pleasures with the opposite sex.

Q What are the most requisite qualities for a whore to possess?

A Impudence, complaisance and metamorphosis.

Q What do you mean by impudence?

A I mean that a girl who gives herself up to lascivious commerce should be ashamed of nothing. All parts of her body are to be exposed to the men with as little ceremony as she would expose them to herself, viz. her breasts, her cunt, and her backside are to be thought no more of when with a strange man whom she has to amuse, than a modest woman of the palm of her hand, which she does not blush to expose.

Q What do you mean by complaisance in a whore?

A It is an allurement by which she artfully retains the most casual customers. Assuming the air of a thorough good nature, she yields herself cheerfully to the various whims, leches and caprices of men, by which means she retains them as in a net, and obliges them, in spite of themselves, to return another time to the object who has so well gratified a momentary passion.

Q What do you mean by metamorphosis?

A I mean that a perfect whore should, like the fabled Proteus of old, be able to assume every form, and to vary the attitudes of pleasure according to the times, circumstances, and temperaments. A thoroughbred whore has made her particular study for the various methods of giving pleasure to men, for there is a difference between amusing a man of a cold constitution and a man of a warm one – between exciting a vigorous youth and a wornout débauché. Nature, more impressed with the one, requires only to be relieved in the regular way; and, more moderate with the other, requires different degrees of titillation, situations more voluptuous, coaxings and frictions more piquant and more lewd. The whore who only exposes her bottom to a young Ganymede, will make him discharge almost to blood, while the same action shall produce but an ordinary sensation in another. The jerks and heaves of a strong, lustful woman will plunge the man of vivid temperament into a torrent of delight, while they would be death to the effeminate strokes of the decrepid old lecher.

Q Ought a whore to administer as much pleasure to the man who only gives her a crown as to him who pays her liberally?

A The great art of a courtesan who would acquire a reputation, is to avoid appearing mercenary. She must study her men, and with some refuse the proffered fee. She will meet with those who will be susceptible of this delicacy, and be touched by the apparent disinterestedness shown them, imagining that she is more taken with their person than their money. The pleasure that does not appear to them to be bought is more piquant and more thought of, and a whore is often a great gainer by this kind of artifice.

Q May a girl avail herself of all the finesse of her sex, and whatever acts of fascination she possesses, in order to obtain as much money as possible from those who visit her?

A Yes. As long as no fraud is made use of, and good faith directs the temptations, she may employ the art of a siren. In doing this she is only following her vocation, and the man has nothing to complain of but his own weakness in yielding to her fascination.

MARK TWAIN
(1835–1910)

The Conversation of the Tudors

Mark Twain, the author of *The Adventures of Tom Sawyer* and *Huckleberry Finn*, wrote his short mock-Elizabeth sketch *1601* for his friend the Rev. Joseph Twichell, pastor of the Asylum Hill Congregational Church at Hartford, Connecticut, in 1876. It was first printed on faked paper and old print, in a limited edition of fifty copies. Much reprinted in America, it is still relatively little-known in England. Though described by a Professor Edward Wagenknecht as 'the most famous piece of pornography in American literature,' *1601*, which takes the form of a conversation between the old Queen Elizabeth, Francis Bacon, Sir Walter Raleigh, Ben Jonson, Shakespeare and young Francis Beaumont, with the Duchess of Bilgewater (22), the Countess of Granby (26), Lady Helen Granby, her daughter (15) and two maids-of-honour, Lady Margery Boothy (65) and Lady Slice Dilberry (over 70), is largely scatological, and only perhaps just sufficiently erotic for inclusion here, mainly on the grounds of its fame.

Then fell they to talk about ye manners and customs of many peoples, and Master Shaxpur spake of ye boke of ye sieur Michael de Montaine, wherein was mention of ye custom of widows of Perigord to wear uppon ye headdress, in sign of widowhood, a jewel in ye similitude of a man's member wilted and limber, whereas ye queene did laugh and say widows in England doe wear prickes too, but betwixt the thighs, and not wilted neither, till coition hath done that office for them. Master Shaxpur did likewise observe how yt the sieur de Montaine hath also spoken of a certain emperor of such mighty prowess that he did take ten maidenheddes in ye compass of a single night, ye while his empress did entertain two and twenty lusty knights between her sheetes, yet was not satisfied; whereas ye merrie Countess Granby saith a ram is yet ye emperor's superior, sith he wil tup above a hundred yewes 'twixt sun and sun; and after, if he can have none more to shag, will masturbate until he hath enrich'd whole acres with his seed.

Then spake ye damned windmill, Sr Walter, of a people in ye uttermost parts of America, yt copulate not until they be five and thirty yeres of age, ye women being eight and twenty, and do it then but once in seven yeres.

Ye Queene – How doth that like my little Lady Helen? Shall we send thee thither and preserve thy belly?

Lady Helen – Please your highnesses grace, mine old nurse hath told me there are more ways of serving God than by locking the thighs together; yet am I willing to serve him yt way too, sith your highnesses grace hath set ye ensample.

Ye Queene – God' wowndes a good answer, childe.

Lady Alice – Mayhap 'twill weaken when ye hair sprouts below ye navel.

Lady Helen – Nay, it sprouted two yeres syne; I can scarce more than cover it with my hand now.

Ye Queene – Hear ye that, my little Beaumonte? Have ye not a little birde about ye that stirs at hearing tell of so sweete a neste?

Beaumonte – 'Tis not insensible, illustrious madam; but mousing owls and bats of low degree may not aspire to bliss so whelming and ecstatic as is found in ye downy nests of birdes of Paradise.

Ye Queene – By ye gullet of God, 'tis a neat-turned compliment. With such a tongue as thine, lad, thou'lt spread the ivory thighs of many a willing maide in thy good time, an' thy cod-piece be as handy as thy speeche.

Then spake ye Queene of how she met old Rabelais when she was turned of fifteen, and he did tell her of a man his father knew that had a double pair of bollocks, whereon a controversy followed as concerning the most just way to spell the word, ye contention running high between ye learned Bacon and ye ingenious Jonson, until at last ye old Lady Margery, wearying of it all, saith, *Gentles, what mattereth it how ye shall spell the word? I warrant ye when ye use your bollocks ye shall not think of it; and my Lady Granby, be ye content; let the spelling be, ye shall enjoy the beating of them on your buttocks, just the same, I trow. Before I had gained my fourteenth year I had learnt that them that would explore a cunt stop'd not to consider the spelling o't.*

Sir W – In sooth, when a shift's turned up, delay is meet for naught but dalliance. Boccaccio hath a story of a priest that did beguile a maid into his cell, then knelt him in a corner to pray for grace to be rightly thankful for this tender maidenhead ye Lord had sent him; but ye Abbot, spying through ye key-hole, did see a tuft of brownish hair with fair white flesh about it, wherefore when ye priest's prayer was done, his chance was gone, forasmuch as ye little maid had but ye one cunt, and that was already occupied to her content.

Then conversed they of religion, and ye mightie work ye old dead Luther did doe by ye grace of God. Then next about poetry, and Master Shaxpur did rede a part of his King Henry IV., ye which, it seemeth unto me, is not of ye value of an arsefull of ashes, yet they praised it bravely, one and all.

Ye same did rede a portion of his 'Venus and Adonis', to their prodigious admiration, whereas I, being sleepy and fatigued withal, did deme it but paltry stuff, and was the more discomforted in that ye blody bucanier had got his wind again, and did turn his mind to farting with such villain zeal that presently I was like to choke once more. God damn this windy ruffian and all his breed. I wolde that hell mighte get him.

They talked about ye wonderful defense which old Sr Nicholas Throgmorton did make for himself before ye judges in ye time of Mary; which was unlucky matter of broach, sith it fetched out ye quene with a *Pity yt he, having so much wit, had not enough to save his dotor's maidenhedde sound for her marriage-bed*. And ye quene did give ye damn'd Sr Walter a look yt made hym wince – for she hath not forgot he was her own lover in yt olde day. There was silent uncomfortableness now; 'twas not a good turn for talk to take, sith if ye quene must find offence in a little harmless debauching, when pricks were stiff and cunts not loathe to take ye stiffness out of them, who of this company was sinless; behold, was not ye wife of Master Shaxpur four months gone with child when she stood uppe before ye altar? Was not her Grace of Bilgewater roger'd by four lords before she had a husband? Was not ye little Lady Helen born on her mother's wedding-day? And, beholde, were not ye Lady Alice and ye Lady Margery there, mouthing religion, whores from ye cradle?

In time came they to discourse of Cervantes, and of the new painter, Rubens, that is beginning to be heard of. Fine words and dainty-wrought phrases from the ladies now, one or two of them being, in other days, pupils of that poor ass, Lille, himself; and I marked how that Jonson and Shaxpur did fidget to discharge some venom of sarcasm, yet dared they not in the presence, the queene's grace being ye very flower of ye Euphuists herself. But behold, these be they yt, having a specialty, and admiring it in themselves, be jealous when a neighbor doth essay it, nor can abide it in them long. Wherefore it was observable yt ye quene waxed uncontent; and in time labor'd grandiose speeche out of ye mouth of Lady Alice, who manifestly did mightily pride herself thereon, did quite exhauste ye quene's endurance, who listened tell ye gaudy speeche was done, then lifted up her brows, and with vaste irony, mincing saith *O shit*! Whereat they alle did laffe, but not ye Lady Alice, yt olde foolish bitche.

Now was Sr Walter minded of a tale he once did hear ye ingenious Margrette of Navarre relate, about a maid, which being like to suffer rape by an olde archbishoppe, did smartly contrive a device to save her maidenhedde, and said to him, *First, my lord, I prithee, take out thy holy tool and piss before me*; which doing, lo his member felle, and would not raise again.

LEOPOLD VON SACHER-MASOCH
(1835–1895)

The Slave

Sacher-Masoch was an Austrian novelist, a lawyer who writing in his spare time gained a reputation for his studies of life in small-town Poland, and in particular the relationship between Jews and Gentiles. He was a masochist – he gave his name to the psychological condition in which sexual pleasure is gained by suffering pain – and in his *Venus in Furs*, published in 1886, he wrote of a young aristocrat, Severin, who falls in love with the beautiful widow Wanda von Dunajew. He persuades her to whip him; at first she dislikes this, but later comes to enjoy it, and is content that he should sign a paper promising to be her abject slave.

She gently took hold of my hand, and my name appeared at the bottom of the paper. Wanda looked once more at the two documents, and then locked them in the desk which stood at the head of the ottoman.

'Now then, give me your passport and money.'

I took out my wallet and handed it to her. She inspected it, nodded, and put it with other things while in a sweet drunkenness I kneeled before her leaning my head against her breast.

Suddenly she thrusts me away with her foot, leaps up, and pulls the bell-rope. In answer to its sound three young, slender negresses enter; they are as if carved in ebony, and are dressed from head to foot in red satin; each one has a rope in her hand.

Suddenly I realise my position, and am about to rise. Wanda stands proudly erect, her cold beautiful face with its sombre brows and contemptuous eyes is turned towards me. She stands before me as mistress, commanding, gives a sign with her hand, and before I really know what has happened to me the negresses have dragged me to the ground, and have tied me hand and foot. As in the case of one about to be executed my arms are bound behind my back, so that I can scarcely move.

'Give me the whip, Haydée,' commands Wanda with unearthly calm.

The negress hands it to her mistress, kneeling.

[109]

'And now take off my heavy furs,' she continues, 'they get in my way.'

The negress obeyed.

'The jacket, there!' Wanda commanded.

Haydée quickly brought her the *kazabaika*, set with ermine, which lay on the bed, and Wanda slipped into it with two inimitably graceful movements.

'Now tie him to the pillar here!'

The negresses lifted me up, and twisting a heavy rope around my body, tied me standing against one of the massive pillars which supported the top of the wide Italian bed.

Then they suddenly disappeared, as if the earth had swallowed them.

Wanda swiftly approached me. Her white satin dress flowed behind her in a long train, like silver, like moonlight; her hair flared like flames against the white fur of her jacket. Now she stood in front of me with her left hand firmly planted on her hips, in her right hand she held the whip. She uttered an abrupt laugh.

'Now play has come to an end between us,' she said with heartless coldness. 'Now we will begin in dead earnest. You fool, I laugh at you and despise you; you who in your insane infatuation have given yourself as a plaything to *me*, the frivolous and capricious woman. You are no longer the man I love, but *my slave*, at my mercy even unto life and death.

'You shall know me.

'First of all you shall have a taste of the whip in all seriousness, without having done anything to deserve it, so that you may understand what to expect, if you are awkward, disobedient, or refractory.'

With a wild grace she rolled back her fur-lined sleeve, and struck me across the back.

I winced, for the whip cut like a knife into my flesh.

'Well, how do you like that?' she exclaimed.

I was silent.

'Just wait, you will yet whine like a dog beneath my whip!' she threatened, and simultaneously began to strike me again.

The blows fell quickly, in rapid succession, with terrific force upon my back, arms and neck; I had to grit my teeth not to scream aloud. Now she struck me in the face, warm blood ran down, but she laughed, and continued her blows.

'It is only now I understand you,' she exclaimed. 'It really is a joy to have someone so completely in one's power, and a man at that, who loves you – you do love me? – No? – Oh! I'll tear you to shreds yet, and with each blow my pleasure will grow. Now, twist like a worm, scream, whine! You will find no mercy in me.'

Finally she seemed tired.

She tossed the whip aside, stretched out on the ottoman, and rang.

The negresses entered.

'Untie him!'

As they loosened the rope, I fell to the floor like a block of wood. The black women grinned, showing their white teeth.

'Untie the rope around his feet.'

They did it, but I was unable to rise.

'Come over here, Gregor.'

I approached the beautiful woman. Never did she seem more seductive to me than today in spite of all her cruelty and contempt.

'One step further,' commanded Wanda. 'Now kneel down, and kiss my foot.'

She extended her foot beyond the hem of white satin, and I, the supersensual fool, pressed my lips on it.

ALGERNON CHARLES SWINBURNE
(1837–1909)

The Lash of the Sea

When Lord Tennyson died in 1892, and the Poet Laureateship became vacant, Queen Victoria said to her Prime Minister: 'I am told that Mr Swinburne is the best poet in the country.' But the general feeling was that Swinburne was 'unsuitable', and the nonentity Alfred Austin was appointed. Swinburne had published some extremely explicit sexual poems, and the manuscript of his novel *Lesbia Brandon* was much talked about, as was his private life. *Lesbia Brandon*, an incomplete novel unpublished in his lifetime, is by no means a bad novel, containing some magnificent description of topography, and thinly-disguised memoirs of the poet's childhood on the Isle of Wight – including his love of his cousin Mary, who in the book becomes the hero's (Herbert's) sister. The book also records Swinburne's twin passions – for the birch and the sea; the tutor, Denham, engaged to prepare Bertie for Eton, plays a notable part in the story.

Two days after his arrival, Denham saw good to open fire upon his pupil, and it was time indeed to apply whip and spur, bit and bridle, to the flanks and mouth of such a colt; the household authorities supported and approved the method of the breaker, under whose rigorous hand and eye he began to learn his paces bit by bit; a breaker who was hardly over-strict, and out of school hours amiable enough; and idle as the boy often was, he soon began to move on except in the mournful matter of sums. As Friday was consecrated to the worship of that numerical Moloch at whose altar more boys have bled than ever at that of Artemis, Herbert was horsed afresh every Friday for some time. He was soon taught not to appeal to his sister; once assured that he was in good training and not overworked, she gave him all condolence but no intercession. Nothing excessive was in effect expected of the boy; Denham had always a fair pretext for punishment and was not unjust or unkind; and in time Herbert learnt to be quiet and perverse; it had grown into a point of honour with him to take what fate sent him at his tutor's hands with a rebellious reticence, and bear anything in reason rather than expose himself to an intercession which he could

from *Lesbia Brandon*

not but imagine contemptuous; and thus every flogging became a
duel without seconds between the man and the boy. These
encounters did both of them some good; Herbert, fearless enough
of risk, had a natural fear of pain, which lessened as he grew familiar
with it, and a natural weight of indolence which it helped to quicken
and lighten; Denham eased himself of much superfluous discomfort
and fretful energy by the simple exercise of power upon the mind
and body of his pupil: and if the boy suffered from this, he gained
by it often; the talk and teaching of his tutor, the constant contact
of a clear trained intellect, served to excite and expand his own,
he grew readier and sharper, capable of new enjoyment and
advance. And Denham, a practised athlete whose strength of arm
Herbert knew to his cost, encouraged him to swim and ride and won
his esteem by feats which his slighter limbs were never to emulate. In
summer they went daily into the sea together, and the rougher it was
the readier they were for it; Herbert wanted no teaching to
make him face a heavy sea; he panted and shouted with pleasure
among breakers where he could not stand two minutes; the blow of
a roller that beat him off his feet made him laugh and cry out in
ecstacy: he rioted in the roaring water like a young sea-beast, sprang
at the throat of waves that threw him flat, pressed up against their
soft fierce bosoms and fought for their sharp embraces; grappled
with them as lover with lover, flung himself upon them with limbs
that laboured and yielded deliciously, till the scourging of the surf
made him red from the shoulders to the knees, and sent him on
shore whipped by the sea into a single blush of the whole skin,
breathless and untried. Denham had to drive him out of the water
once or twice; he was insatiable and would have revelled by the hour
among waves that lashed and caressed him with all their might and
all their foam. Standing where it was so shallow in the interval from
wave to wave that the seething water in its recoil only touched the
boy's knees, they waited for a breaker that rose to the whole height
of the man. Herbert would creep out to it quivering with delight,
get under the curve of it and spring right into the blind high wall of
water, then turn and dive straight with it as it broke and get his feet
again upon dry ground, sand or shingle as it pleased the water to
throw him; and return, a little cut or beaten as it might be, with
fresh laughter and appetite, into the sweet white trouble of the
waters. Denham, though not such a seagull, had a taste for all work

of this kind, and perhaps gave the boy something more than his fair credit; for the magnetism of the sea drew all fear out of him, and even had there been any discomfort or peril to face, it was rather desire than courage that attracted and attached him to the rough water. Once in among green and white seas, Herbert forgot that affliction was possible on land, and in his rapture of perfect satisfaction was glad to make friends with the man he feared and hated in school hours. The bright and vigorous delight that broke out at such times nothing could repress or resist; he appealed to his companion as to a schoolfellow, and was answered accordingly. 'He was a brick in the water,' Herbert told young Lunsford; 'like another fellow you know, and chaffs one about getting swished, and I tell him its a beastly chouse and he only grins.' This intimacy was broken by one tragic incident; bathing had been forbidden on all hands one stormy day before the sea had gone down, and Herbert, drawn by the delicious intolerable sound of the waves, had stolen down to them and slipped in; having had about enough in three or four minutes, he came out well buffeted and salted, with sea-water in his throat and nostrils and eyes; and saw his tutor waiting just above the watermark between him and his clothes. Finding him gone, Denham had quietly taken a tough and sufficient rod and followed without a superfluous word of alarm. He took well hold of Bertie, still dripping and blinded; grasped him round the waist and shoulders, wet and naked, with the left arm and laid on with the right as long and as hard as he could. Herbert said afterwards that a wet swishing hurt most awfully; a dry swishing was a comparative luxury. The sting of every cut was doubled or trebled, and he was not released till blood had been drawn from his wet skin, soaked as it was in salt at every pore: and came home at once red and white, drenched and dry. Nothing in his life had ever hurt him as much as these. He did not care to face again the sharp superfluous torture of these stripes on the still moist flesh; and from that day he was shy of facetious talk in the water or out: thus the second stage of his apprenticeship began.

CORA PEARL
(1838–1886)

An Evening in the Rue de Chaillot

Emma Elizabeth Crouch was born in Stonehouse, now a part of Plymouth, and by force of circumstance, beauty, and a will of iron, became by the 1860s one of the most notorious of all the courtesans of the Second Empire. Calling herself Cora Pearl, she set up house in the Rue de Chaillot, charging, it is said, the equivalent of £6000 for one night's entertainment. Towards the end of her life she was reduced to writing her memoirs and attempting to extort money from gentlemen by promising to omit their names. Perhaps because too many of them paid up, the memoirs proved appallingly dull when they finally appeared, written in indifferent French. The present extract is from the alleged early version, which appeared in German and in English, much later. It may be a forgery, but it is lively enough and uninhibited enough to suggest that it may indeed be the work of the girl who, while mistress of Prince Jerome Napoleon, swore like a trooper in French (with a thick Devonshire accent) and clapped a dish of trifle upon the head of a nobleman unfortunate enough to bore her.

It was in the autumn of 1864 that I gave my rival Anne de Chassaigne, known as Liane, her *congé*. At that time she had reached the height of her meagre attractions (having wasted herself upon stage-door Johnnies while a dancer at the *Folies*, she was now engaged in dances of a less public but more profitable nature). M. de Goubouges had delighted in bringing me an account of how Liane had invited a *coterie* of her most influential admirers to her apartment, and received them seated in a bath of milk (asses' milk, M. Goubouges opined; cows' milk would have been more fitting). Rising from this bath in a manner most calculated to expose her charms, she had summoned a pair of *filles de ferme* who had dried her with the most lascivious gestures and displays, whereupon she had withdrawn leaving – or so M. Goubouges reported – her audience in a fever of unassuaged lust. My informant was unnecessarily emphatic about the nature of Liane's charms and the manner in which she exhibited them, and had spread the story all over Paris.

A week later I invited six gentlemen to dinner. The irritating but indispensable M. de Goubouges was one, for his tattle I was in need of; then came the Duc de Tréage, the Prince C————, Colonel Marc Aubry, M. Paul of the Banque National, M. Perriport (the brother of the owner of the Restaurant Tric), and the actor Georges Capillon, a friend of Henri Meilhac, Offenbach's librettist, on whom I was eager to make an impression. I let it be known that the chief purpose of the occasion was to display the talents of my pastry chef, Salé, formerly with the Prince d'Orléans, but I hinted to Goubouges that the final dish was likely to be one of an unusual nature.

I received the gentlemen in my finest style, and entertained them to a dinner of excellent quality; the conversation was agreeable, the wines accomplished. When we had finished all but the final course, I excused myself in order to supervise its presentation. Slipping to the kitchen, I stepped out of my gown (when entertaining gentlemen it is never my habit to wear quantities of under clothing, and especially was this the case on this occasion) and mounting a chair lay upon a vast silver dish which Salé had borrowed for me from the Prince d'Orléans' kitchens. I lay upon my side, my head upon my hand.

Frémont stepped forward, accompanied by Yves [the newly employed footman] carrying as it were his palate – a large tray upon which was a set of dishes filled with marzipans, sauces and pastes, all of different colours. With that deftness and artistry for which he was so famed, Salé began to decorate my naked body with rosettes and swathes of creams and sauces, each carefully composed so that the heat of my body would not melt them before I came to table.

As Salé was laying trails of cream across my haunches and applying wreaths of tiny button flowers to the upper sides of my breasts, I could not help noticing that Yves, chosen like all my servants for a combination of personal charm and accomplishment, and a young man of obvious and increasingly virile promise, was taking a peculiar interest in the chef's work. The knuckles of his hands were whiter than would have been the case had the tray been ten times as heavy, and the state of his breeches proclaimed the fact that his attitude to his employer was one of greater warmth than respect.

Having finished the decoration by placing a single unpeeled

grape in the dint of my navel, Salé piled innumerable *meringues* about the dish, completing the effect with a dusting of icing sugar. The vast cover which belonged to the dish was then placed over me, and I heard Salé call the two other footmen into the room. Shortly I felt myself raised, and carried down the passage to the dining room. I heard the door opened, and the chatter of voices cease as the dish was carried in and settled upon the table.

When the lid was lifted, I was rewarded by finding myself the centre of a ring of round eyes and half-open mouths. M. Paul, as I had expected, was the first to recover, and with an affectation of coolness reached out, removed the grape, and slipped it slowly between his lips. Not to be outdone, M. Perriport leant forward and applied his tongue to removing the small white flower that Frémont had placed upon my right tit; and then all, except for M. Goubouges, who as I expected was as usual content simply to observe and record, were at me, kneeling upon their chairs or upon the table, their fingers and tongues busy at every part of me as they lifted and licked the sweetness from my body. The Prince was so inflamed by the circumstance that nothing would content him other than to have me there and then upon the table, to the ruination of the remaining decoration upon my body and the irritation of the other gentlemen, in whom only reverence for rank restricted violence.

So speedily did the Prince fetch off that they had not to wait long – *le laurier est tôt coupé*, as my friend Théo used to say. Since the centre of a dining table and a mess of *meringues* together with wine-glasses and forks is not the most convenient nor comfortable of pleasure-beds, the price of my comforting the other members of the party was that they should give me time at least to dispose myself on one of the nearby couches, where the Duc continued where the Prince had left off, M. Capillon as was his wont contenting himself with an energetic frigging (often the taste of members of his profession, I have frequently been disappointed to observe), while M. Paul offered his shaft to my lips and Colonel Aubry his to my sufficiently practised manipulation. Finally, M. Perriport, in a desperate state of agitation, was attempting to displace the Duc when his ecstacy overflowed, together with an access of language which seemed to me to betray a youth spent in less than polite circles.

The way in which (to offer an observation often made by me) gentlemen, whether they are intimates or no, are perfectly agreeable to make love to the same woman at the same time, is strange. It may be a circumstance of nature that one woman may in a trice satisfy six men or even more, while it is impossible for the most virile of fellows to satisfy more than three women in twenty minutes or so, but that men should positively seek such a *commission* of fellow lovers when they would hesitate to bathe themselves in the same water or put on each other's pantaloons, is surprising to me. However, such is very often the case, as it seems that the butting of one pair of buttocks may quicken the butting of another's. And often, as in this case, the result is a remarkably speedy accomplishment of all desires. My friends took their leave kindly, leaving me entirely satisfied that M. Goubouges' account of the occasion would entirely eclipse the memory of Liane's little bathing party; as indeed by noon of the next day proved to be the case. Shortly afterwards she became a postulant nun, under the name of Soeur Madeleine de la Pénitence.

I was not tired but elated by my triumph; and the rapid accomplishment of both the Prince's and the Duc's desires left me at a pitch of desire. So upon retiring to my bedroom to bath, I ordered that Yves should bring me my hot water, and when he did so ordered him to assist me. Up to that time I had always embraced the admirable French motto, *jamais avec les domestiques*; but my observation of the boy's passion for me had roused me to try him. As he gave me his hand to help me step into the bath, I told him to remove his uniform, for, said I, it had cost several hundred francs, and I was not eager it should be soiled.

To my surprise he not only threw it off with remarkable celerity, but his under clothes with it. (It has been my general observation that members of the lower orders, while as lusty as any gentleman, tend to satisfy themselves while removing as little outer clothing as is convenient for the purpose of the Act.) He then washed me all over with hands which were both clean and gentle, his manhood meanwhile paying me the compliment of raising and nodding at my beauties.

The sight of his marvellously promising person moved me to allow him to draw me from my bath and to the rugs beside the bed, where he dried me with his own body, proving that as I had suspected a footman was capable of much more stamina than any man of society. At least, that is what I believed him to prove; though even in the ecstacy to which his ministerings of hand, tongue and manhood thrice roused me, I retained the power to wonder at the extent of his understanding of the requirements of my sex. Unlike most men of whatever rank, he did not batter my gate until his ram broke, but as in a mirror seemed to attack me with my own weapons; how good a whore he would have made was what occurred to me, had it been the custom for men to enter our profession. The graceful, almost womanly but yet wholly masculine manner in which he seemed to subdue his own pleasure to my own (a quality rarely found) amazed me. It was some time before we were spent; and when at last it was so, I taxed him with being no servant. Nor was he; but the revelation of what he was, which was to bring me to a new pinnacle of fame, must be reserved to my next chapter.

ÉMILE ZOLA
(1840–1902)

Thérèse Raquin

In his earliest successful novel, *Thérèse Raquin*, published first as a serial in 1867, Zola shocked his readers with the immediacy and accuracy of his portrayal of intense sexual passion. He was to do so again in many novels, notably *La Terre* and *Nana*; but he was as successful in his first novel as in any other in accomplishing his aim, which was, as he said, 'given a highly-sexed man and an unsatisfied woman, to uncover the animal side of them and see that alone, then throw them together in a violent drama and note down with scrupulous care the sensations and actions of these creatures.'

Thérèse and her ineffectual, physically repulsive cousin and husband Camille, live with his mother in a flat above a small shop in Paris. Their childhood friend Laurent visits them after many years, and immediately seduces her. Unawakened until then, she becomes passionately involved with him; leaving his place of work during the afternoons, he comes to her.

As soon as he entered the passage, he began to feel intensely excited. The costume-jewellery seller sat just opposite the side entrance to the house. He waited until she was occupied with a girl who wanted to buy a ring or a pair of brass ear-rings. Then, quickly, he slipped into the doorway; he climbed the narrow, dark stairs, one hand on the slippery, damp walls. His feet nudged the stones of the steps; each time a foot jolted, he felt a hot quiver at his heart. A door opened. In it, in a sort of white haze, he saw Thérèse, in her slip, her petticoat, her hair tied tightly back in a bun behind her head. She closed the door, and hung round his neck. There was a strange smell about her, a smell of white linen and newly washed flesh.

Laurent, astonished, saw that his mistress was beautiful. He had never seen this woman before! Thérèse, strong and supple, held him, her head thrown back, and, across her face, flashes of emotion like lightning, passionate smiles. This loving face was transfigured with a madly feverish look; her wet lips, her shining eyes, made her radiant. The young girl, twisting and wriggling against him, had a strange beauty, as though lit by some inner light, flames running through her flesh. Her blood seemed to boil, her very nerves to radiate heat, intense and penetrating.

from *Thérèse Raquin*

Her first kiss betrayed the natural whore. Her unsatisfied body leapt ungovernably into love. She woke from a dream, born into passion. She passed from the sickly arms of Camille into the vigorous arms of Laurent, and it was the coming of a truly virile man which gave her the shock that woke her sleeping flesh. Every instinct of this tense woman broke into life with unthought-of violence; the blood of her mother, the African blood that boiled in her veins, began to course, to beat furiously in her slender, almost virgin body. She flaunted herself, offering herself to him with outright impudence. And, from head to foot, long shivers of passion shook her.

Now Laurent had never known a woman like this. He was surprised, and worried. Ordinarily, his mistresses failed to receive him with such abandon; he was accustomed to cool, indifferent kisses, to weary and bored embraces. The moans and shudders of Thérèse troubled him, if at the same time they awoke his sexual curiosity. When he left the girl, he staggered like a drunken man. Next day, regaining his calm and prudent senses, he wondered whether he would return to this lover whose kisses filled him with a fever. He decided at first to stay at home. Then he weakened. He wanted to forget, never again to see Thérèse in her nakedness, with her soft and strong caresses; but she was always there, implacable, holding out her arms. The physical suffering which the vision inflicted was unbearable.

He gave in, made another rendezvous, and returned to the Passage du Pont-Neuf. . . .

In that bare, cold room passed hours of passionate love, sinister brutality. Each new meeting brought a fiercer passion.

The girl seemed in love with daring and shamelessness. She never hesitated, never felt any fear. She threw herself into adultery with a sort of intense honesty, braving all danger, and even vain of her bravery. When her lover was coming, her only precaution was to tell her aunt that she was going to rest; and when she was upstairs, she walked and talked quite naturally, without bothering about the noise. Sometimes, in the beginning, Laurent was terrified.

'For God's sake!' he would whisper to Thérèse, 'keep a bit quieter. Madame Raquin'll come up!'

'Bah!' replied Thérèse, mockingly, 'you're always trembling. . . . She's glued behind the counter; why d'you think she'll come up? She's too afraid someone'll rob her. . . . Anyway, let her come up, if she wants. You can hide. . . . I thumb my nose at her. I love you.'

Laurent was not very reassured by these words. Passion had not yet put his peasant's caution to sleep. But soon habit led him to accept without fear the risks of these rendezvous in broad daylight, in Camille's room, a couple of yards from the old shopkeeper. His mistress kept repeating that danger always avoids those who stare boldly at it, and it seemed true. There could never have been a safer place for the lovers to meet than this, where no one would think of looking for them. They satisfied their lust in unbelievable tranquillity.

One day, however, Madame Raquin did come up, thinking her niece must be unwell. It had been nearly three hours since the girl had gone upstairs. Thérèse had had the audacity not to bolt the door which led into the dining-room.

When Laurent heard the footsteps of the old shopkeeper, climbing the wooden stairs, he began feverishly to search for his waistcoat, his hat. Thérèse began to laugh at his comic capers. She took him fiercely by the arm, thrust him to the foot of the bed, in one corner, and said in a quiet, firm voice:

'Stay there . . . don't stir.'

She threw all the men's clothes which lay about on top of him, and spread over everything a white petticoat that she had thrown off. She did all this with precise, calm movements, and without losing a jot of her calm. Then she lay down, dishevelled, half-naked, flushed and panting.

Madame Raquin quietly opened the door and came up to the bed without making a noise. The girl feigned sleep. Laurent sweated under the white petticoat.

'Thérèse', said the shopkeeper kindly, 'are you ill, my dear?'

Thérèse opened her eyes, yawned, turned over and said in a weary voice that she had a terrible migraine. Wouldn't her aunt let her sleep on? The old woman went as quietly as she had come.

The two lovers, laughing quietly, made love again with passionate violence.

'You see?' said Thérèse in triumph; 'we needn't worry. All the people here are blind. They're not in love.'

Nana

Nana, the most famous courtesan in Paris (perhaps based by Zola on Cora Pearl), entertains her elderly lover, Muffat.

When she eventually entered the room, she saw Muffat, sitting resignedly on a narrow divan, his face pale, his hands nervously twitching. She was upset, between pity and contempt for him. Poor man, so deceived by a treacherous wife! She felt like throwing herself at him, as a consolation. Yet there was a certain justice about the state he was in; he was an idiot over women; he would have to learn. All the same, she did pity him. They were scarcely a quarter of an hour at the Café Anglais, and went back together to the Boulevard Haussmann. It was eleven o'clock; before midnight she would, tenderly, get rid of him.

In the ante-chamber, she prudently gave Zoë her orders.

'Watch out, tell *him* not to make a noise if this one is still with me.'

'But where shall I put him, Madame?'

'Keep him in the kitchen; that's safest.'

Muffat, in the bedroom, was already taking off his coat. A big fire burned there. It was still the same – rosewood furniture, embroidered damask hangings and chair-covers, with big flowers on a grey background. Nana had twice thought of refurbishing it, at first in black velvet, then in white satin with pink bows; then when Steiner agreed, she insisted on his giving her cash, just to defraud him. She had only indulged the caprice of putting a tigerskin in front of the fire, and hanging a crystal chandelier from the ceiling.

'I'm not at all sleepy; I shan't go to bed,' she announced when she had closed the door.

The count accepted her statement with the submission of a man who no longer feared exposure. His sole preoccupation was not to annoy her.

'As you like,' he murmured. Still, he took off his boots before sitting in front of the fire.

One of Nana's pleasures was to undress before her wardrobe mirror, where she could see herself from head to foot. She let everything, even her chemise, fall to the floor; then, completely naked, she was lost in thought as she looked long at herself. A passion for her body, a ravishment with the satin of her skin and the

[123]

supple line of her torso, held her serious, attentive, absorbed in a love affair with herself. Often, her hairdresser found her like this; she did not even turn her head as he came in. But it often annoyed Muffat, to her surprise. What worried him? It wasn't for anyone else, it was for her.

This evening, in order to see herself more clearly, she lit six candles on their brackets. But as she slid out of her chemise, she stopped, preoccupied for a moment, a question on her lips.

'You've not read the article in *Figaro*? . . . It's on the table.'

She remembered Daguenet's laugh, and was troubled by a doubt. If Fauchery had written slightingly of her, she would have her revenge.

'They say it's all about me,' she said, affecting indifference. 'What do you think, darling?'

And, dropping her chemise, she waited naked while Muffat finished the article. He read slowly. Fauchery's piece, called *The Golden Fly*, was the story of a tart, born of four or five generations of drunkards, her blood adulterated by a long heredity of misery and drink, which became in her a feverous sexuality. She had grown up in the suburbs, on the pavements of Paris; adult and beautiful, beautiful like a flower on a stinking dunghill, she avenged the beggars and rejected ones from whom she had sprung. In her, the rottenness fermenting among the lowest of men rose to attack the aristocracy. She became a force of nature, a ferment of destruction, despite herself, corrupting the whole of Paris between her snowy thighs, causing the male city to turn sour just as women churn milk to curdle it. And at the end of the article she was compared to a fly, gilded by the sun, soaring out of the filth – a fly which lived on the rotting corpses of the roadside, and which, buzzing and dancing, glittering like precious stones, poisoned men just by settling on them, in the palace through whose windows she flew.

Muffat lifted his head, eyes fixed, looking into the fire.

'Well?' asked Nana.

He said nothing. He seemed to want to re-read the article. A chill ran down the back of his neck. The piece was badly written, a jumble of phrases, too many odd words and elaborate embroideries. Still, it had held him, and had suddenly brought home to him everything which he had been ignoring for the last months.

At last, he looked up. Nana was absorbed by the seductive sight of herself. She was bending her neck, looking closely in the glass at a little brown mole just above her right buttock; she touched it with the tip of her finger, turning so that she could see it better, no doubt finding it strange and pretty just where it was. Then she examined other parts of her body, amused and caught up once more in the vicious curiosity of childhood. She was always surprised to see herself like this; she had the astonished, glamorous air of a young girl discovering her puberty. Slowly, she opened her arms to display her full, Venus torso, bent at the waist, looked at herself from the front and from the back, held by the outline of her breasts, the curving round of her hips. And finally she pleased herself by making a game of swaying to the right, to the left, her knees parted, her belly and loins quivering like those of a belly-dancer.

Muffat looked at her. She frightened him. *Figaro* had fallen from his hands. In that minute of clear vision, he hated himself. That was it: in three months, she had corrupted his life; he felt disgusted by filth which he had not dreamed of. He saw in a moment, in his conscience, the accidental consequences of evil – himself poisoned, his family destroyed, a corner of society cracking and breaking down. And, unable to turn away his eyes, he looked fixedly at her, trying to be disgusted by her nudity.

She did not budge. One arm now behind her neck, one hand grasping the other, she threw back her head, her elbows thrust wide. He saw her half-closed eyes, her half-open mouth, her face lit by an amorous smile; and behind this, her chignon of yellow hair covering her back like the fleece of a lion. Bent over, with her side flexed, she displayed her broad loins, her breast which seemed as strong as that of a soldier, the muscles showing under the satin skin. A fine line, rounded at shoulder and buttock, ran from elbow to foot. Muffat saw that tender line, the sweep of white flesh bathed in gleams of gold, the fullness to which the candle-light lent the shine of silk. He thought of his former horror of women as of the monsters of the Scriptures, lubricious, like wild animals. Nana's body was covered with a fine velvet down of hair, and her hindquarters and sturdy thighs, the handfuls of flesh, deep hollows mysteriously shading her sex, reminded him of an animal. A golden animal, unselfconscious as a force of nature, and with a scent which devastated the world. Muffat stared, obsessed, possessed to the point at which, closing his eyes so as to see no more, he found the animal appeared in the darkness behind them, bigger and more terrible, more exaggerated in its pose. Now it would remain there, behind his eyes, a part of his flesh for ever.

GUY DE MAUPASSANT
(1850–1893)

The Window

Maupassant, whose relatively brief life was cut short by venereal disease, which attacked him physically and mentally, is best known as a writer of short stories. One extremely pornographic novel, *The Colonel's Nieces*, is attributed to him; but his *contes* – notably *Boule de Suif* – reveal a deep understanding of the nature of sensuality.

I met Madame de Jadelle in Paris this winter, and liked her enormously, at once. But then, you know her as well as I do – or almost as well. You know her humours, her romantic nature: forthright, impressionable, wilful, unconventional, fearless, always ready for adventure, disliking all prejudice – and yet sentimental, fastidious, easy to offend, sensitive and modest.

She was a widow. I adore widows, because I have a lazy nature. Thinking of marrying, I courted her. The more I knew her, the more I liked her; and at last I decided the time had come to make my proposal. I loved her, by then, indeed was almost too much in love with her. A man should not be too much in love when he marries, at least not with his prospective wife, for then he becomes a fool, losing all sense of himself, becoming stupid and crude. He must hold on to himself. If he loses his head on his wedding night, he may well find horns on his forehead a year later.

One day, then, I presented myself at her house, white-gloved, and said:

'Madame, I am fortunate enough to love you, and I come to ask whether I may hope to please you; I shall certainly endeavour to do so, and also to persuade you to take my name.'

She coolly answered: 'That is a matter for you. I have no idea whether I may, in the end, care for you; but nothing would interest me more than to discover whether that may be true. As a man, I quite like you. But what are you like in character, in disposition? What are your personal habits? Most marriages become stormy or immoral because the couple did not know each other well enough when they married. Slight things, an ethical conviction, a matter of religion, the tiniest irritating gesture, some bad habit or other, the merest fault is enough to make a man and wife deathless enemies, bitterly chained together, however passionate they may have been as lovers.

'I am determined not to marry a man whose nature I do not know intimately, every nook and corner of it. I must study him at leisure, and at close quarters, and for months.

'So I suggest that you spend the summer with me in the country, at my house at Lauville, where in quiet seclusion we can discover whether we can happily live together.

'Oh, I see your smile, and I know what you are thinking. No, no – I know enough about myself to know that I can safely issue that invitation. I scorn, I loathe the kind of love of which you are thinking. I assure you I shall keep my head. But you – do you accept?'

I kissed her hand.

'When shall I come to you, Madame?'

'On May the tenth. Then it's a bargain?'

'It's a bargain.'

And a month later, I was installed at Lauville. What an astonishing woman! She certainly studied me closely, morn till night. She loves horses, and we spent hours riding through the woods talking about every conceivable subject, for she was determined to discover my most secret thoughts, and equally to watch my every action.

And as for me, I began to love her madly, though without worrying about our mutual characters! I soon realised that I was studied even in sleep. Someone slept in the little room next to mine, entering it late at night, with the utmost care. At last I wearied of the incessant spying. I wanted to bring things to a head, and one evening became impatient. She put me down so firmly that I ceased to importune her; but became determined to pay her out, somehow or other, for the continual watchfulness with which she pestered me.

You know her maid, Césarine? The pretty little thing from Granville, where all the girls are beautiful? You remember – she's as fair as her mistress is dark?

One afternoon I persuaded her into my room, gave her five francs, and said:

'My dear, this is not to encourage you to do anything wrong, but I want to treat your mistress just as she treats me.'

She smiled with a mocking air. I went on:

'I know I'm being watched, day and night – whether I'm eating, drinking, dressing, shaving, putting on my socks . . .'

'Well, Sir,' she said, 'you see . . .' Then she stopped. I went on:

'You sleep in the room next to mine, and you listen to hear if I snore or talk in my sleep. Right?'

She began to laugh. 'Well, sir, you see . . .' And she stopped again.

'Well, it's hardly fair that your mistress should know everything about me, but that I should know nothing about her, whom I'm proposing to marry. And I do love her completely. I love her appearance, her mind, her heart; as far as that goes, I'm the happiest of men. But there are some things I would give a great deal to know.'

Césarine put my five francs in her pocket. I understood what that meant.

'You know, my dear, that we men think a great deal of certain . . . certain . . . well, physical factors, which certainly may not make a woman any more or less charming, but can alter her value where we are concerned. Now I wouldn't want you to speak ill of Madame de Jadelle, or even to reveal any secret faults which she might have. Just answer four or five frank questions for me. After all, you dress and undress her every day, and know her as well as you know yourself. So tell me: is she as plump as she seems to be?'

There was no answer.

'Come now, you know as well as I do that certain women pad themselves in a place where . . . well, where babies are fed, and also where they sit. Does she pad?'

Césarine hung her head. She said timidly:

'Ask all you want, sir; I'll answer all at once.'

'Well, then, some women have knock-knees, sometimes so bad that they rub together when they walk. Others have legs set so far apart that they are like the arch of a bridge, through which you can see a whole landscape. Both, mind you, are very pretty. What are your mistress' legs like?'

No answer.

I continued:

'Some women have a fine, full breast, with a deep line beneath; some have plump arms and a slim body; some are beautiful from in front, ill-shaped behind; some are beautiful from the back, and ill-shaped in front. They may all be very pretty, but I would very much like to know how your mistress is shaped. I'll be happy to give you more money for a full description.'

Césarine looked at me intently, and then, laughing, said:

'Except that she's a brunette, sir, Madame's shape is precisely like my own.' And she ran off.

Sold again!

Feeling such a fool, I was determined to get my revenge.

An hour later, I went into her little room, and unscrewed the bolts on the door.

I heard her go in at midnight, and followed her. She started to cry out, but I put my hand over her mouth, and very soon convinced myself (not with a great deal of difficulty) that unless Césarine was lying, Madame de Jadelle was very well-made indeed.

I may say that I very much enjoyed the process of verification, nor did Césarine seem to dislike it too much. At once sturdy and slim, she was a magnificent example of the Bas-Normande people, though innocent of certain little niceties that indeed Henry IV would also have scorned. I soon taught her about cleanliness, and loving perfumes gave her that very evening a little bottle of amber lavender.

We soon became close friends, and she was a delightful mistress, with a natural intelligence that made her a consummate lover. In Paris she could certainly have become a great courtesan. The delights she afforded me made it easy for me to wait patiently for Madame de Jadelle's decision. With her, I was impeccably behaved, agreeable, quiet. And as for her, she must have found me delightful, and gave certain signs that it would not be long before she would accept me. I must have been one of the happiest men in the world, quietly lying in the arms of a young girl of whom I was exceedingly fond, and waiting for the lawful embraces of the woman I adored.

This, Madame, is where you should stop listening, for I come to a somewhat delicate incident.

One evening when we were coming back from our daily ride, Madame de Jadelle was complaining of her grooms' inattention to her orders: 'They'd better take care, they'd better watch out. I know how to catch them out!' she repeated.

After a quiet night in my own bed, I woke early, full of energy, dressed, and went up to the turret in which I smoked my early morning cigarette. A spiral staircase led to a first floor room, lit by a large window.

I went up quietly in my felt-soled Moroccan slippers, and there was Césarine, leaning out of the window.

I could not see all of her, but only the lower half, the half that was towards me. The half I liked best! I might have preferred Madame de Jadelle's top half, of course, but the half which was before me was entirely delightful, scarcely covered by a short white petticoat.

I crept towards her quietly; she heard nothing. I knelt down, and carefully took hold of the two edges of the petticoat, lifting it quickly: there before me was the tight, round, plump, smooth shape of my mistress' secret face, and I put my lips to it – I do beg your pardon, Madame – and gave it the tender kiss of a lover to whom no action is forbidden.

I was somewhat surprised to smell not the scent of amber lavender, but of verbena. I had no time to consider the implications, for I received a tremendous blow in the face that almost broke my nose, and heard a violent cry which made my hair stand on end. The woman turned round. It was Madame de Jadelle.

Her hands beat the air as though she was about to faint; she stood there gasping, made as though to strike me – but then fled.

Ten minutes later, a very puzzled Césarine brought me a note.

'Madame de Jadelle hopes that M. de Brives will at once relieve her of his company.'

I left.

I'm still desolate. I have tried by every means to gain her forgiveness for my mistake. All in vain.

And do you know, since that moment I cherish in . . . in my heart . . . a faint smell of verbena which fills me with the longing desire to sense it once more in my nostrils?

EDWARD SELLON
(1818–1866)

Fair but Frail

Captain Edward Sellon, a determined pornographer, lived (if one is to trust his lively autobiography, *The Ups and Downs of Life*) a determinedly energetic sensual life, and many of his adventures were not so far removed in tone from those of the characters of Boccaccio, whose *Decameron* he translated robustly. His intrigues continued until the year of his death, and in a letter to a friend he related a typical adventure.

London, 4th March 1866

My dear Sir,

You will be very much surprised no doubt to find that I am again in England. But there are so many romances in real life that you will perhaps not be so much astonished at what I am going to relate after all.

You must know then that in our trip to the continent (Egypt it appears was a hoax of which I was to be the victim) we were to be accompanied by a lady! I did not name this to you at the time, because I was confident of my friend.

On Monday evening I sat for a mortal hour in his brougham near the Wandsworth Road Railway Station waiting for the 'fair but frail', who had done me the honour to send me a beautiful little pink note charmingly scented with violets, in which the dear creature begged me to be punctual! – and most punctual I was, I assure you, but alas! she kept me waiting a whole hour, during which I smoked no end of cigars.

At length she appeared, imagine my surprise! I! who had expected some swell or other, soon found myself seated beside the most beautiful young lady I ever beheld, so young that I could not help exclaiming, 'Why, my dear, you are a mere baby! How old, may I be permitted to ask?' She gave me a box on the ear, exclaiming 'Baby indeed! Do you know, sir, I am fifteen!' 'And you love Mr Scarsdale very much, I suppose?' said I as a feeler. 'Oh! *comme ça*!' she rejoined. 'Is he going to marry you at Vienna, or

Egypt?' I asked. 'Who's talking of Egypt?' said she. 'Why, I hope, my dear, our dear friend invited me to accompany him up to the third Cataract, and this part of the affair – you, I mean, my dear – never transpired until half-an-hour before I got that pretty little note of yours.' 'Stuff!' she said, 'he was laughing at you; we go no further than Vienna.' 'Good!' said I, 'all's fair in love and war,' and I gave her a kiss! She made no resistance, so I thrust my hand up her clothes without more ado. 'Who are you, my dear?' I enquired. 'Does your mother know you're out?' I ejaculated. 'I am coming out next summer,' said she. 'That is to say you *were* coming out next summer,' said I. 'Well, I shall be married then, you know,' said the innocent. 'Stuff,' said I in my turn. 'How, stuff?' she asked angrily, 'do you know he has seduced me?' 'No, my angel, I did not know it, but I thought as much. But don't be deceived, a man of Mr Scarsdale's birth won't marry a little cit like you.' She burst into tears. I was silent. 'Have you known him long?' she asked. 'Some years,' said I. 'And you really think he won't marry me?' 'Sure of it, my dear child.' 'Very well, I'll be revenged; look here, I like you.' 'Do you though, by Jove!' 'Yes, and—' I give you my word I was into her in a moment! What bliss it was! None who have not entered that heaven can fathom it! But alas, we drew near the station, and I only got one poke complete. She pressed my hand as I helped her out of the brougham at Chatham and Dover Station, as much as to say, 'You shall have me again.' Scarsdale was there to receive her. Not to be tedious, off we started by the Mail, and duly reached Dover, went on board the boat, reached Calais, off again by train. Damned a chance did I get till we were within ten or twelve versts of Vienna. Then my dear friend fell asleep, God bless him! The two devils of passengers who had travelled with us all the way from Calais had alighted at the last station – here was a chance!! We lost not an instant. She sat in my lap, her stern towards me! God! what a fuck it was. 'See Rome and die!' said I in a rapture. This over we were having what I call a straddle fuck when lo! Scarsdale woke up! I made a desperate effort to throw her on the opposite seat, but it was no go, he had seen us. A row of course ensued, and we pitched into each other with hearty good will. He called me a rascal for tampering with his fiancée, I called him a scoundrel for seducing so young a girl! And we arrived at Vienna! 'Damn it!' I said as I got out of the train with my cut lip and nose bleeding, 'here's a cursed piece of business.'

OSCAR WILDE (attr.)
(1854–1900)

The Reverse of the Medal

Oscar Wilde, the author of one of the finest comedies in the language, *The Importance of Being Earnest*, was at the height of his fame sentenced to two years' hard labour for homosexual practices. *Teleny*, or *The Reverse of the Medal*, issued in a private edition of two hundred copies in 1893, has often been attributed to him. It tells the story of a young man, Camille des Grieux, and his hopeless adoration for René Teleny, a pianist. The first volume of the book is almost entirely heterosexual in tone; the second volume almost entirely homosexual. The style certainly occasionally recalls Wilde, as does the melodramatic conclusion of the book. In the following scene des Grieux, driven to desperation by a love he thinks cannot be returned, finds himself on one of the London bridges, and is about to throw himself into the Thames when Teleny appears out of the darkness to stop him.

'Leave me alone! Why did you not let me die? This world is hateful to me, why should I drag on a life I loathe?'

'Why? For my sake.' Thereupon he whispered softly, in that unknown tongue of his, some magic words which seemed to sink into my soul. Then he added, 'Nature has formed us for each other; why withstand her? I can only find happiness in your love, and yours alone; it is not only my heart but my soul that panteth for yours.'

With an effort of my whole being I pushed him away from me, and staggered back.

'No, no!' I cried, 'do not tempt me beyond my strength; let me rather die.'

'Thy will be done, but we shall die together, so that at least in death we may not be parted. There is an afterlife; we may then, at least, cleave to one another like Dante's Francesca and her lover Paulo. Here,' said he, unwinding a silken scarf that he wore round his waist, 'let us bind ourselves closely together, and leap into the flood.'

I looked at him, and shuddered. So young, so beautiful, and I was thus to murder him! The vision of Antinöus as I had seen it the first time he played appeared before me.

He had tied the scarf tightly round his waist, and he was about to pass it round me.

'Come.'

The die was cast. I had not the right to accept such a sacrifice from him.

'No,' quoth I, 'let us live.'

'Live,' added he, 'and then?'

He did not speak for some moments, as if waiting for a reply to that question which had not been framed in words. In answer to his mute appeal I stretched out my hands towards him. He – as if frightened that I should escape him – hugged me tightly with all the strength of irrepressible desire.

'I love you!' he whispered, 'I love you madly! I cannot live without you any longer.'

'Nor can I,' said I faintly; 'I have struggled against my passion in vain, and now I yield to it, not tamely, but eagerly, gladly. I am yours, Teleny! Happy to be yours, yours for ever and yours alone!'

For all answer there was a stifled hoarse cry from his innermost breast; his eyes were lighted up with a flash of fire; his craving amounted to rage; it was that of a wild beast seizing his prey; that of the lonely male finding at last a mate. Still his intense eagerness was more than that; it was also a soul issuing forth to meet another soul. It was a longing of the senses, and a mad intoxication of the brain.

Could this burning, unquenchable fire that consumed our bodies be called lust? We clung as hungrily to one another as the famished animal does when it fastens on the food it devours; and as we kissed each other with ever-increasing greed, my fingers were feeling his curly hair, or paddling the soft skin of his neck. Our legs being clasped together, his phallus, in strong erection, was rubbing against mine no less stiff and stark. We were, however, always shifting our position, so as to get every part of our bodies in as close contact as possible; and thus feeling, clasping, hugging, kissing, and biting each other, we must have looked, on that bridge amid the thickening fog, like two damned souls suffering eternal torment.

The hand of Time had stopped; and I think we should have continued goading each other in our mad desire until we had quite lost our senses – for we were both on the verge of madness – had we not been stopped by a trifling incident.

[135]

A belated cab –wearied by the day's toil – was slowly trudging its way homeward. The driver was sleeping on his box; the poor, broken-down jade, with its head drooping almost between its knees, was likewise slumbering – dreaming, perhaps, of unbroken rest, of new-mown hay, of the fresh and flowery pastures of its youth; even the slow rumbling of the wheels had a sleepy, purring, snoring sound in its irksome sameness.

'Come home with me,' said Teleny, in a low, nervous and trembling voice; 'come and sleep with me,' added he, in the soft, hushed and pleading tone of the lover who would fain be understood without words.

I pressed his hands for all answer.

'Will you come?'

'Yes,' I whispered, almost inaudibly.

This low, hardly-articulate sound was the hot breath of vehement desire; this lisped monosyllable was the willing consent to his eagerest wish.

Then he hailed the passing cab, but it was some moments before the driver could be awakened and made to understand what was wanted of him.

As I stepped in the vehicle, my first thought was that in a few minutes Teleny would belong to me. This thought acted upon my nerves as an electric current, making me shiver from head to foot.

My lips had to articulate the words 'Teleny will be mine,' for me to believe it. He seemed to hear the noiseless murmur of my lips, for he clasped my head between his hands, and kissed me again and again.

Then, as if feeling a pang of remorse – 'You do not repent, do you?' he asked.

'How can I?'

'And you will be mine – mine alone?'

'I never was any other man's, nor ever shall be.'

'You will love me for ever?'

'And ever.'

'This will be our oath and our act of possession,' added he.

Thereupon he put his arms around me and clasped me to his breast. I entwined my arms round him. By the glimmering, dim light of the cab-lamps I saw his eyes kindle with the fire of madness. His lips – parched with the thirst of long-suppressed desire, of the pent-up craving of possession – pouted towards mine with a painful expression of dull suffering. We were again sucking up each other's being in a kiss – a kiss more intense, if possible, than the former one. What a kiss that was!

The flesh, the blood, the brain, and that undefined subtler part of our being seemed all to melt together in an ineffable embrace.

A kiss is something more than the first sensual contact of two bodies; it is the breathing forth of two enamoured souls.

But a criminal kiss long withstood and fought against, and therefore long yearned after, is beyond this; it is as luscious as forbidden fruit; it is a glowing coal set upon the lips; a fiery brand that burns deep, and changes the blood into molten lead or scalding quicksilver.

Teleny's kiss was really galvanic, for I could taste its sapidity upon my palate. Was an oath needed, when we had given ourselves to one another with such a kiss? An oath is a lip-promise which can be, and is, often forgotten. Such a kiss follows you to the grave.

Whilst our lips clung together, his hand slowly, imperceptibly, unbuttoned my trousers, and stealthily slipped within the aperture, turning every obstacle in its way instinctively aside, then it lay hold of my hard, stiff, and aching phallus which was glowing like a burning coal.

This grasp was as soft as a child's, as expert as a whore's, as strong as a fencer's. . . .

Some people, as we all know, are more magnetic than others. Moreover, while some attract, others repel us. Teleny had – for me, at least – a supple, mesmeric, pleasure-giving fluid in his fingers. Nay, the simple contact of his skin thrilled me with delight.

My own hand hesitatingly followed the lead his hand had given, and I must confess the pleasure I felt in paddling him was really delightful.

Our fingers hardly moved the skin of the penis; but our nerves were so strained, our excitement had reached such a pitch, and the seminal ducts were so full, that we felt them overflowing. There was, for a moment, an intense pain, somewhere about the root of the penis – or rather, within the very core and centre of the reins, after which the sap of life began to move slowly, slowly, from within the seminal glands; it mounted up the bulb of the urethra, and up the narrow column, somewhat like mercury within the tube of a thermometer – or rather, like the scalding and scathing lava within the crater of a volcano.

It finally reached the apex; then the slit gaped, the tiny lips parted, and the pearly, creamy fluid oozed out – not all at once in a gushing jet, but at intervals, and in huge, burning tears.

At every drop that escaped out of the body, a creepy almost unbearable feeling started from the tips of the fingers, from the ends of the toes, especially from the innermost cells of the brain; the marrow in the spine and within all the bones seemed to melt; and when the different currents – either coursing with the blood or running rapidly up the nervous fibres – met within the phallus (that small instrument made out of muscles and blood-vessels) a tremendous shock took place, a convulsion which annihilated both mind and matter, a quivering delight which everyone has felt, to a greater or lesser degree – often a thrill almost too intense to be pleasurable.

Pressed against each other, all we could do was try and smother our groans as the fiery drops slowly followed one another.

The prostration which followed the excessive strain of the nerves had set in, when the carriage stopped before the door of Teleny's house – that door at which I had madly struck with my fist a short time before.

CHARLES DEVEREAUX
(c1889)

Precocious Child

Venus in India, published first in Brussels in 1889, purports to be the autobiography of a British army officer who served on the North West Frontier of India. Inspired by a reading of Gautier's *Mademoiselle de Maupin*, he set down at length his amorous adventures with various ladies, among them the daughters of his Colonel. The two volumes Captain Devereaux produced (volume three was never published) are full of vigour and by no means without humour.

I might have kept up my acquaintance more vigorously with the Selwyns but for Mabel. That little girl, ever since I had tickled her mound at Nowshera, evidently looked forward to being had by me very soon, and she was more than daring whenever I visited her family. She plagued beyond bearing. Her delight was by word, look or gesture, to make my yard stand, no matter whether her mother was beside her, and my embarrassment was simply enormous. Pretending to consider herself as a mere child, she would, in spite of her mother's too feeble chidings, seat herself on my lap, and, hiding her hand under her, feel for and clutch my infernal fool of an organ, which would stand furiously for her though I wished it cut off at such moments. If I happened to be spending an evening at her father's house, and to be engaged in a game of chess with one of the two girls, Mabel would find her opportunity, slip unnoticed under the table, crawl to my knees, and with her nimble fingers, unbutton my trousers, and putting in her little exciting hand take possession of all she found there. I should have laughed at it only that I was terrified lest this very forward play be discovered, I had to sit tight up against the table, and do my best to seem unconcerned, whilst Mabel's moving hand was precious nearly making me spend! A catastrophe, I am thankful to say, she never quite succeeded in bringing about. I took my opportunities to beg and implore her to be more careful of herself and me, and her reply would be to toss up her short frocks, and a complete exposure of her lovely thighs, downy motte, and sweet young slit, which she would insist on my feeling, and which I was too weak to resist doing. It was the torture of Tantalus I was called upon to endure, and the consequence was as much enforced absence as I could keep from the Colonel's house, and the consequent feeling on Fanny's side that my object was to avoid her. I could not tell Fanny the truth, for she would have been madder than ever, to have heard that I had felt Mabel's grotto for the first time immediately after she had told me of the wonderful and delicious dream she had had of my poking her at Nowshera. . . .

'WALTER'
(c1895)

The Girl on the Omnibus

My Secret Life, by 'Walter', was first published in eleven volumes in the
last decade of the nineteenth century. The author describes his continual
pursuit of women between his adolescence and middle-age – if his word is
to be trusted, he made love to fifteen hundred girls and women. He was a
dreadful man: he never shrank from seducing, then rejecting, his friends'
wives or sisters, his servants, or even small children – his horrifying
accounts of his dealings with some of the child prostitutes who crowded
the streets of London in his time are the more horrific because he was only
one of the many men who used them. Buying a little girl from a procuress
in Vauxhall, he casually remarks 'She did not holler at all really.' 'Love' is
not a word in his vocabulary.

Nevertheless, no account of English erotic literature could omit
consideration of this most frank and detailed of all sexual autobiographies
(there are over four thousand pages in the work). Perhaps some of the
incidents are out of his imagination; but his accounts of his seductions are
so vivid and immediate, so urgent (not to say so revealing of his character)
that if they are indeed fiction then 'Walter' was a very considerable
novelist. One of his adventures began on a Charing Cross omnibus, which
he boarded in Cockspur-street. He sat next to a tall, handsome woman,
who immediately responded to his approaches. When they got off the 'bus
in the thick yellow London fog, she agreed to meet him in Trafalgar
Square in two days' time.

On the appointed day, I was by the Nelson column, and saw a well
grown woman walking quickly with her veil down. She walked past
me, I followed not recognising her, but knowing that if she returned
when she got to the end of the square she would be waiting for
someone. She did. I bowed and said 'Kensington?' 'Yes,' said she
lifting her veil with a laugh, and putting her arm at once in mine. In
five minutes we were in my favourite house – she seemed agitated
and kept her veil down, saying 'Let's walk quickly,' which we did.

She threw off her veil and bonnet directly she was in the room. I
kissed her at once. How delicious is the first illicit kiss of a pretty
woman. 'I'm so glad you've come, I half doubted you.' 'Ah, who'd
have thought it,' she replied. Down on the sofa we sat questioning

[141]

each other, mutually curious. I dare say both told lies enough, she more, I expect, from the sequel, than I – having certainly more to hide.

But almost directly, and whilst chatting, her fat thighs offered no obstruction to my fingers, our mouths joined, and we fell silent. She in the voluptuous enjoyment of being felt, I in feeling her.

'Let's do it,' said I rising. At once she began undressing. I did the same, and in shirt and chemise only, in a couple of minutes we mounted the bed.

Tho' there was a large fire, and two gas lamps burning, she wanted to get under the counterpane. I stirred the fire, and moved the cheval glass, so that in two glasses we could see ourselves reflected. We kissed. I lay naked on her. She rubbed her hand over my flesh from my naked rump up to my blade bones. 'What lovely flesh you have,' said she. 'You don't like hairy men, then?' She did not answer, but burst into loud laughter. Then I laid half by her side, half sitting, and she put her tongue to mine, whilst I felt her. But restlessly her eyes first turned to the chimney glass then to the cheval glass, and I saw she was delighted at seeing herself with me naked in the reflection of the glasses.

'Did you never see yourself reflected in a glass naked with a man like this before?' 'Never,' said she, emphatically. 'Do you like it?' 'We look very beautiful, don't we?' she replied. – Then I got up, lifted her limbs, put myself in attitudes for her to see. Again I laid on to the top of her naked, on the sofa. – 'Oh-o,' said she laughing -- 'it's lovely to be naked together.' 'Let's get on the bed, we have more room there.' – She got on the bed quickly, and within the hour I had thrice poked her.

Then we reposed. I got thirsty and suggested wine and other things. No, nothing but gin. A bottle was brought and we drank it with water. It's the only time I have had a lady in a brothel who asked for gin. Then we put on shirt and chemise, and coals on the fire – and in semi-nudity sat again on the sofa, talking and kissing, her eyes fixed on the looking-glass. . . .

It was nearly ten, she said she must think of going, but still we sat half reclining on the sofa, feeling each other and kissing. 'I'll have you before you go.' 'Can you?' 'Come to the bed, no, stop, kneel on the sofa instead, and we can see ourselves.' She was amorous enough for anything. I pushed the cheval glass and sofa about, till with the chimney glass we could see every movement.

Immediately afterwards she poured out a tumbler full of very strong gin and water, and drank it right off. She dressed quickly. Yes, I'll meet you again on Saturday. She did not wish to be seen walking with me; but when quite dusk, she would be near to the end of the street. I was to go to the house when I saw her, she to follow me in a minute. 'And mind I can only stop an hour or so.' She made me promise then not to follow her. At leaving I made some offers. – No, she herself would get a cab directly. No, she had plenty of money to pay for it. Then she took another tumbler of strong gin and water and departed – leaving me very curious, but pleased with her full grown charms, voluptuous libidinosity, and the baudy amusements we had enjoyed.

On the Saturday, it came off exactly as planned. We were shown into a back bedroom without so many glasses. 'It's not such a nice room as the other,' she remarked. I rang. 'The front is engaged, sir, the upper front if you like.' There we went. (Her veil carefully down.) There the glasses were much the same. She began stripping instantly, I followed, and for a minute or two we lay on the sofa, looking and feeling; then she sighed so that at once on the bed we went and her intense enjoyment added greatly to my pleasure. At each succeeding embrace she seemed more and more impassioned. I've never had a woman held me so tightly to her as she did when copulating. In a hurry she went off as before, promising to meet me on the following Thursday, and stop late. The looking-glasses were an exciting novelty to her, as I have found them to other women. She said they excited her and that she had never seen herself fucking in a looking-glass before. . . .

The day came when I was again to meet my unknown. She was such an amorous bedfellow, she so enjoyed my baudy pranks, speechless when doing them with me in her intense enjoyment, that I anticipated the day of meeting with impatience. I usually rode to and from my home and Charing Cross, but it being a clear, bright day, I walked, and near to the place at which the unknown lady had descended from the omnibus on the foggy night, and as I was thinking of the pleasure of the evening to come, I met the lady herself, with a child about seven or eight years old. We were about fifty feet off when we recognised each other. She grasped the child's hand, and ran across the road dragging it with her in the very teeth of the carriage traffic, hurried on, never looked back, got into a cab and drove off rapidly, and before I could make up my mind what to do, the cab was out of sight.

With a presentiment of evil, I went to the appointed spot – walked about for an hour, enquired at the house, went to the Nelson column, thinking I might have made a mistake in the place of meeting, back again to the Haymarket, and did this for three hours in a state of fury with unsatisfied lust, but she never came, and I have never seen her since. At intervals for some days later I walked all about the neighbourhood where I had met her, but never saw her. I had taken a great fancy to the lustful lady and was much mortified. Had my accidental meeting stopped her, or had she ever intended to meet me again. Was she single, wife, or widow? Was her husband abroad, was she a kept woman? That she was not a harlot was the only point about which I could make up my mind, and that she was a voluptuous, libidinous creature was certain. I wonder if a woman with a large clitoris is more lewd than others.

I went home angry and disappointed. Why I did not have the pleasure of a gay lady, I can't tell. I often can't make out my reasons for my behaviour in sexual matters.

ANON
(c1880)

Miss Coote's Methods

The Pearl, a Monthly Journal of Facetiae and Voluptuous Reading, was perhaps the best-known Victorian erotic magazine, though it was short-lived (running only from July 1879 to December 1880). The contents were various: there were bawdy limericks, pornographic poems based on popular songs of the period, and court reports (somewhat imaginatively embellished). But the chief contents were the serials, which included *Sub-Umbra, or Sport Among the She-Noodles* (in which the young narrator tells of his sexual adventures while on a holiday with his cousin Frank and three teen-age girl cousins), *Lady Pokingham; or They All Do It (Giving an Account of her Luxurious Adventures, both before and after her Marriage with Lord Crom-Con*); and, a novel about whipping being absolutely obligatory – flagellism was after all known among the French as 'the English vice' – *Miss Coote's Confession, or the Voluptuous Experience of an Old Maid*, from which the following extract is taken. The novel is in the form of letters to a friend.

My dear Nellie –

In my last letter you had an account of some pretty everyday larceny, but in this you will read about a pretty young lady who was also a thief by nature, not from any necessity, in fact it was a case of what they call in these degenerate days Kleptomania, no wonder when downright thieving is called by such an outlandish name that milk and water people have almost succeeded in abolishing the good old institution of the rod.

Miss Selina Richards was a cousin of Laura Sandon, my old schoolfellow and first bedfellow at Miss Flaybum's; by-the-by, can you explain or did you ever understand how girls can be *fellows*, but I know of no other term which will apply to the relationship in question. Is there no feminine to that word? It certainly is a defect of the English language.

Well, being on a visit to Laura when I was about eighteen, she mentioned the case to me, saying that her cousin Selina was such an inveterate thief her family were positively afraid to let her go anywhere from home for fear she should get into trouble, and that her parents were obliged to confine her to her room when they had any visitors in the house, as the young thief would secrete any trifles, more especially jewellery, she could lay her hands upon, and you know Rosa what an awful disgrace it would be to all the family if she should ever be accused of such a thing.

ROSA – But have they never punished her properly, to try and eradicate the vice?

LAURA – They confine her to her room, and often keep the child on bread and water for a week, but all the starving and lecturing in the world won't do any good.

ROSA – Have they never tried a good whipping?

LAURA – It never seems to have entered the stupid heads of her father and mother, they are too tender-hearted for anything of that kind.

ROSA – Laura, dear, I don't mind confessing to you I should dearly love to birch the little *voleuse*, ever since I left school our last grand *séance* at the breaking-up party has quite fascinated me, when I think it over the beautiful sight of the red bleeding posteriors, the blushes of shame and indignation of the victims, and above all the enjoyment of their distress at being so humiliated and disgraced before others. We often enjoy our old schoolbirchings in private, and a little while ago I administered an awful whipping to our gardener's wife and her two little girls for stealing my fruit etc., and effected quite a cure, they are strictly honest now. You are coming to see us soon, can't you persuade your aunt and uncle to entrust Selina to your care, with the promise that I am to be thoroughly informed of her evil propensity; on second thoughts I think you should say you have told me, and that I offer to try and cure the girl, if they will only give me *carte blanche* to punish her in my own way. You will have a great treat, we shall shock the girl's modesty by stripping and exposing her, you will see how delightful the sight of her pretty form is, added to the distressing sense of humiliation we will make her feel, the real lovers of the birch watch and enjoy all the expressions of the victim's face, and do all they can to increase the sense of degradation, as well as to inflict terrible and prolonged torture by skillful appliance of the rod, and placing the victim in most painful, distended positions to receive her chastisement.

from *The Pearl: Miss Coote's Confession*

[This plan was put into operation, and Selina was caught stealing jewellery. She is told she must be punished.]

By my orders the victim is well stretched out on the ladder, as I generally preferred it to the whipping post, and having armed myself with a very light rod made of fine pieces of whalebone, which would sting awfully without doing serious damage, I went up to the ladder for commencement, but first made them loosen her a bit, and place a thick sofa bolster under her loins, then fasten her tightly again with her bottom well presented, the drawers pinned back on each side, and her chemise rolled up and secured under her arms; poor Selina seemed to know well enough what was coming, it checked her tears, but she begged and screamed piteously for me to forgive and wait and see if she ever stole anything again.

MISS COOTE (laughing) – 'Why, what a little coward you are. I should have thought such a bold thief would have more spirit, and I have hardly touched you yet, you won't be hurt more than you can fairly bear; you would do it again directly if I don't beat it out of you now.'

SELINA – 'My arms and limbs are so dreadfully stretched, and my poor behind still smarts from the three whacks you gave. Oh! Have pity! Have mercy! Dear Miss Coote.'

MISS COOTE – 'I must not listen to such childish nonsense, you're both a thief and a dreadful liar, Miss Selina; will you, will you – do it again?' giving three smart stinging cuts, the whalebone fairly hissing through the air as she flourishes it before each stroke to make it sound more effective.

SELINA – 'Ah! Ah! Ah—r—r—re! I can't bear it, you're thrashing me with wires, the blows are red hot. Oh! Oh! I'll never, never do it again!' Her bottom finely streaked already with thin red lines, the painful agony being greatly increased by the strain on her wrists and ankles and she cannot restrain her writhing at each cut.

MISS COOTE – 'You don't seem to like it, Selina, but indeed it's for your good; how would you like to be branded B.C. with a really red hot iron, you'd sing a different song then; but I'm wasting my time – there – there – there – you've only had six yet, how do you howl you silly girl!'

SELINA – 'Ah—r—r—r—re!' with a prolonged shriek, 'you're

killing me! Oh! I shall die soon!' her bottom redder than ever.

MISS COOTE – 'You'll have a dozen whalebone cuts,' counting and cutting deliberately till she calls twelve, then giving a little pause as if finished, so the victim composes the features with a sigh of relief, and then gives another thundering whack, exclaiming 'Ah! Ha! Ha! you thought I had done, did you, Miss Prig; it was a baker's dozen you were to get. I always give thirteen as twelve for fear of having missed one, and like to give the last just as they think it is all over.'

SELINA – 'I know it's well deserved, but oh! so cruel; you will let me go now; pray forgive me, indeed, you may depend upon me in the future', still sighing and quivering from the effects of the last blow.

MISS COOTE – 'You're not to get off so easily, Miss Prig; your bottom would be all right in a few minutes, and then you would only laugh when you think of it. The real rod is to come: look at this bum-tickler, it's the real birch grown in my own grounds, and well pickled in brine these last two days to be ready for you when caught. It will bring your crime to mind in a more awful light, and leave marks to make you remember it for days to come.'

SELINA – 'Pray let me have a drink, if I must suffer so much more; my tongue is as dry as a board. Miss Coote, you are cruel; I am not old enough to bear such torture.'

MISS COOTE – 'Be quiet. You shall have a drink of champagne. But don't talk about your tender age. That makes your crime still worse, for you have shown such precocious disgusting cunning, far beyond your years.'

She has the refreshing draught, and the rod resumes its sway.

MISS COOTE – 'You bad girl. Your bottom shall be marked for many a day; I'll wager you don't steal as long as the marks remain. Two dozen's the punishment, and then we'll see to your bruises, and put you to bed. One – two – three – four . . .' increasing the force of the blows scientifically with each cut, and soon beginning to draw the skin up into big bursting blood-red weals.

VICTIM – 'Mother! Mother! Ah! Ah—r—r—re! I shall die. Oh! kill me quickly, if you won't have mercy.' She writhes in such agony that her muscles stand out like whipcord, and by their continued quivering straining action, testify to the intensity of her pain.

MISS COOTE – laughing and getting excited – 'That's right, call your Mother, she'll soon help you! Ha! Ha! She didn't think how I should cure you, when your Papa gave his consent for me to punish you as I like. Five, six, seven . . .' she goes on counting and thrashing the poor girl over the back, ribs, loins and thighs, wealing her everywhere, as well as on the posteriors. All the spectators are greatly moved, and seem to enjoy the sight of Selina's blood dripping down, down till her stockings are saturated and it forms little pools beneath her on the floor.

The victim has not sufficient strength to stand this very long; her head droops, and she is too weak to scream, moaning and sighing fainter and fainter, till at last she fairly swoons, and the rod is stopped at the twenty-second stroke.

Miss Coote is quite exhausted with her exertions, and sinking on a sofa, fondly embraces her friend Laura, describing to her all the thrilling sensations she has enjoyed during the operation, which the flushed cheeks and sparkling large blue eyes of Laura show she is beginning duly to appreciate.

FRANK HARRIS
(1856–1931)

A Passionate Adventure in Paris

Frank Harris, successively editor of *The Fortnightly Review*, *The Saturday Review* and *Vanity Fair*, also wrote *The Man Shakespeare*, *The Women of Shakespeare*, and the first important biography of Oscar Wilde. But he is now perhaps chiefly remembered for the immensely long autobiography *My Life and Loves*, distinguished as it is by innumerable romantic anecdotes about the great and famous: Harris was one of the most accomplished and polished liars of his time. It has been suggested that the erotic elements of this book are possibly more accurate than the rest; and certainly many of his sexual adventures have the breathless ring of truth about them. In Chapter XXIII of the second volume of his auto-biography, he writes about *A Passionate Adventure in Paris: A French Mistress*.

I was going once from London to Paris: in the train at Calais there was a young German who asked a French fellow traveller something or another and was snubbed for his pains; the French-man evidently guessed his nationality from his bad accent and faulty French. Resenting the rudeness, I answered the question, and soon the German and myself became almost friends. When we reached Paris, I told him I was going to the Hôtel Meurice, and next day he called on me, lunched with me, and afterwards we drove together to the Bois.

Something ingenuous-youthful in the man interested me: we had hardly got into the Avenue des Acacias when he told me he thought French girls wonderfully attractive. Five minutes afterwards we crossed a victoria in which there was one very pretty girl and an older woman; my German exclaimed that the girl was a beauty and wanted to know if it would be possible to get acquainted with such a star. I told him that nothing was easier: they were a pair of *cocottes*, and if he had a couple of hundred francs to spare he would be well received. I advised him the next time our carriages met to jump into the one with the pretty girl and make hay while the sun shone. He thought this a quite impossible feat, and so the next time we passed, I told him to follow me, and jumped into the carriage.

from *My Life and Loves*

At once the coachman turned down a side road and drove rapidly cityward. I put an arm round each of the women and assured them of our company at the Café Anglais. After a few minutes the pretty one whispered to me pertly 'You must take your choice,' and as I turned to the older woman, she responded 'You won't regret it if you choose me!'

To cut a long story short, we all dined together in a private room and afterwards conducted the women to their home. My German went upstairs with his inamorata and I went into a large apartment on the first floor. Here, to my astonishment, was a young girl of perhaps twelve who had evidently fallen asleep. As soon as the light was turned on, she sprang to her feet, evidently confused, and hurried to the door. 'Don't go,' I said, for she was very pretty, but smiling she hurried out. 'Your child?' I turned to my companion, who nodded, it seemed to me. This occurrence helped to confirm my resolution. 'I'm going to sleep on the sofa,' I said, 'or if you wish it, I'll go to my hôtel and you can have the girl with you.'

'No, no,' replied my companion, whose name was Jeanne d'Alberi. 'She never sleeps here, she has her own room, and I am interested in your talk and not a bit sleepy. The theatre is my passion; you've not given me a single kiss,' she added, coming over to me and holding up her face.

'I'm not much in the humour for kissing,' I said. 'I'm sleepy; I think I've drunk too much; that Musigny was potent.'

'As you please,' she said, and in two minutes had made up a bed for me on the sofa. I pulled off my outer garments, and whilst listening to her splashing in her *cabinet de toilette*, fell fast asleep.

I was awakened suddenly by the acutest pang of pleasure I had ever felt, and found Jeanne on top of me. How she had managed it, I don't know, but the evil was done, if evil there was, and my sensations were too intense to be abandoned. In a moment I had reversed our positions, and was seeking a renewal of the delight, and not in vain: her sex gripped and milked me, with an extraordinary strength and cleverness, such as I had never before imagined possible. Not even with Topsy had I experienced such intensity of pleasure. Taking her in my arms, I kissed her again and again in passionate surprise. 'You can kiss me now,' she said pouting, 'but you didn't believe me when I told you in the victoria to choose me and you would profit by the exchange. My friend has only her pretty face,' she added contemptuously.

'You're a wonder,' I exclaimed, and lifting her up I carried her over to the bed. As I laid her down I lifted her nightie: she was well made from the waist down, but her breasts were flaccid and hung low. Still, one thing was sure. 'That wasn't your daughter,' I said; 'You've never had a child.'

She nodded, smiling. 'I was lonely,' she said simply, 'and Lisette was so pretty and so merry that I adopted her years ago, when she was only a year old. I'm old at the game, you see,' she added quietly. . . .

A day or so afterwards, she said 'I shall have to send Lisette to school unless we go south together; she's getting to be a big girl and is exquisitely pretty. You should see her in her bath.'

'I'd love to,' I said without thinking. The next evening when we came in, Jeanne took me to the next floor and opened the door. There was Lisette in the bath, a model of girlish beauty, astonishingly lithe and lovely. She turned her back on us and snatched a towel hanging near, but Jeanne held it back, saying, 'Don't be silly, child. Frank won't eat you, and I've told him how pretty and well-formed you are.'

At this the girl lifted big inscrutable eyes to her and stood at gaze, a most exquisite picture: the breasts just beginning to be marked, the hips a little fuller than a boy's, the feet and hands smaller – a perfect Tanagra statuette in whitest flesh with a roseate glow on the inside of arms and thighs, while the Mount of Venus was just shadowed with down. She stood there waiting, an entrancing maiden figure. I felt my mouth parching, the pulses in my temples beating. What did it mean? Did Jeanne intend—?

The next moment Jeanne lifted the child out of the bath. Covering her with a towel she said, 'Dry yourself and come down, dear. We're all going to dine soon.'

. . . Before returning to London, I gave a big lunch to people of importance in the theatre and in journalism and invited Jeanne and referred everything to her and drew her out, throning her, and afterwards returned to her house for dinner. While she was changing and titivating, I took Lisette in my arms and kissed her with hot lips again and again while feeling her budding breasts, till she put her arms around my neck and kissed me just as warmly; and then I ventured to touch her little half-fledged sex and caress it, till from *My Life and Loves*

it opened and grew moist and she nestled up to me and she whispered: 'Oh! how you excite me!'

'Have you ever done it to yourself?' I asked. She nodded with bright dancing eyes. 'Often, but I prefer you to touch me.' For the first time I heard the truth from a girl and her courage charmed me. I could not help laying her on the sofa and turning up her clothes; how lovely her limbs were, and how perfect her sex. She was really exquisite, and I took an almost insane pleasure in studying her beauties, and parting the lips of her sex with kisses: in a few minutes she was all trembling and gasping. She put her hand on my head to stop me. When I lifted her up, she kissed me. 'You dear,' she said with a strange earnestness, 'I want you always. You'll stay with us, won't you?' I kissed her for her sweetness.

When Jeanne came out of the cabinet, we all went into the dining-room, and afterwards Lisette went up to her room after kissing me, and I went to bed with Jeanne, who let me excite her for half an hour; and then mounting me milked me with such artistry that in two minutes she brought me to spasms of sensation such as I had never experienced before with any other woman. Jeanne was the most perfect mistress I had met up to that time, and in sheer power of giving pleasure hardly to be surpassed by any of western race.

An unforgettable evening, one of the few evenings in my life when I reached both the intensest pang of pleasure with the even higher aesthetic delight of toying with beautiful limbs and awakening new desires in a lovely body and frank honest spirit.

EDITH WHARTON
(1862–1937)

'My Little Girl . . .'

Edith Wharton was a distinguished American novelist and short-story writer, educated by governesses, who when she was 23 married a husband whom twenty years later she divorced on the grounds of insanity. She started writing short stories for *Scribner's Magazine*, and in 1920 won the Pulitzer Prize for her novel *The Age of Innocence*. Among her papers after her death was discovered the following fragment of a short story entitled *Beatrice Palmato*, which tells of an incestuous relationship between a wealthy and cultured Londoner and his daughter, to whom, as a result, a child is born.

The room was warm, and softly lit by one or two pink-shaded lamps. A little fire sparkled on the hearth, and a lustrous black bear-skin rug, on which a few purple velvet cushions had been flung, was spread out before it.

'And now, darling,' Mr Palmato said, drawing her to the deep divan, 'let me show you what only you and I have the right to show each other.' He caught her wrists as he spoke, and looking straight into her eyes, repeated in a penetrating whisper: 'Only you and I.' But his touch had never been tenderer. Already she felt every fibre vibrating under it, as of old, only now with the more passionate eagerness bred of privation, and of the dull misery of her marriage. She let herself sink backward among the pillows, and already Mr Palmato was on his knees at her side, his face close to hers. Again her burning lips were parted by his tongue, and she felt it insinuate itself between her teeth, and plunge into the depths of her mouth in a long searching caress, while at the same moment his hands softly parted the thin folds of her wrapper.

One by one they gained her bosom, and she felt her two breasts pointing up to them, the nipples hard as coral, but sensitive as lips to his approaching touch. And now his warm palms were holding each breast as in a cup, clasping it, modelling it, softly kneading it, as he whispered to her, 'like the bread of the angels.'

An instant more, and his tongue had left her fainting mouth, and was twisting like a soft pink snake about each breast in turn, passing from one to the other till his lips closed on the nipples, sucking them with a tender gluttony.

Then suddenly he drew back her wrapper entirely, whispered: 'I want you all, so that my eyes can see all that my lips can't cover,' and in a moment she was free, lying before him in her fresh young nakedness, and feeling that indeed his eyes were covering it with fiery kisses. But Mr Palmato was never idle, and while this sensation flashed through her one of his arms had slipped under her back and wound itself around her so that his hand again enclosed her left breast. At the same moment the other hand softly separated her legs, and began to slip up the old path it had so often travelled in darkness. But now it was light, she was uncovered, and looking downward, beyond his dark silver-sprinkled head, she could see her own parted knees, and outstretched ankles and feet. Suddenly she remembered Austin's rough advances, and shuddered.

The mounting hand paused, the dark head was instantly raised. 'What is it, my own?'

'I was—remembering—last week—' she faltered, below her breath.

'Yes, darling. That experience is a cruel one – but it has to come once in all women's lives. Now we shall reap its fruit.'

But she hardly heard him, for the old swooning sweetness was creeping over her. As his hand stole higher she felt the secret bud of her body swelling, yearning, quivering hotly to burst into bloom. Ah, here was his subtle forefinger pressing it, forcing its tight petals softly apart, and laying on their sensitive edges a circular touch so soft and yet so fiery that already lightnings of heat shot from that palpitating centre all over her surrendered body, to the tips of her fingers, and the ends of her loosened hair.

The sensation was so exquisite that she could have asked to have it indefinitely prolonged; but suddenly his head bent lower, and with a deeper thrill she felt his lips pressed upon that quivering invisible bud, and then the delicate firm thrust of his tongue, so full and yet so infinitely subtle, pressing apart the close petals, and forcing itself in deeper and deeper through the passage that glowed and seemed to become illumined at its approach. . . .

'Ah—' she gasped, pressing her hands against her sharp nipples, and flinging her legs apart.

EDITH WHARTON

Instantly one of her hands was caught, and while Mr Palmato, rising, bent over her, his lips on hers again, she felt his fingers pressing into her hand that strong fiery muscle that they used, in their old joke, to call his third hand.

'My little girl,' he breathed, sinking down beside her, his muscular trunk bare, and the third hand quivering and thrusting upward between them, a drop of moisture pearling at its tip.

She instantly understood the reminder that his words conveyed, letting herself downward along the divan until her head was in a line with his middle she flung herself upon the swelling member, and began to caress it insinuatingly with her tongue. It was the first time she had ever seen it actually exposed to her eyes, and her heart swelled excitedly: to have her touch confirmed by sight enriched the sensation that was communicating itself through her ardent twisting tongue. With panting breath she wound her caress deeper and deeper into the thick firm folds, till at length the member, thrusting her lips open, held her gasping, as if at its mercy; then, in a trice, it was withdrawn, her knees were pressed apart, and she saw it before her, above her, like a crimson flash, and at last, sinking backward into new abysses of bliss, felt it descend on her, press open the secret gates, and plunge into the deepest depths of her thirsting body. . . .

'Was it . . . like this . . . last week?' he whispered.

ANON
(c1881)

Love and Fancy

The Amatory Experiences of a Surgeon, published in an edition of 150 by (the fly-leaf assures us) 'the Nihilists, Moscow', records a boy's seduction by his fellows at public school, and his subsequent career as a medical man whose single object in life seems to be the seduction of his patients – a tradition in some medical circles, *cf* the diaries of the Elizabethan astrologer and amateur doctor, Simon Forman. In between vivid descriptions of his activities, the Surgeon found time to consider the part played by the mind in 'the pleasures of Venus', as he and almost every other nineteenth century writer describes them.

Not all the glowing descriptions of amatory writers, not the inspired breath of passion itself, can truly, and in sufficient degree, estimate the force of those desires, and the intoxicating delirium of that enjoyment in which the softer sex plays so important a part, and in the gratification of which she relishes a more than equal degree of pleasure.

Were I to cover these pages with descriptions of the most seductive or lascivious scenes, I should fail to realise its full effect.

Language stops short of the reality. No words, however passionate, however glowing, could transport the bosom, and enthrall the frame, like the one magic soul-dissolving sensation experienced by lovers in the celebration of those mystic rites, but if my readers will follow me while I tell them of some of my amatory experiences, their own feelings may perhaps enable them to sympathise with mine, and thus by analogy enjoy again some of the most sensual and moving incidents in their own careers. . . .

When Sappho loved a fair being of her own sex even to madness, she doubtless found a means to gratify the passion with which she burned, although to us men, and more particularly to medical men, it is surprising how a perfect enjoyment could be arrived at without a penetrating power on either side.

Woman is formed to receive within her the all-important member of the other sex, and if she is deprived of that there is but one substitute to compensate for it, and that is imagination. But the

[157]

inspired poetess possessed imagination in an inordinate degree, and no doubt she brought into play, in those soft encounters of which the old Greek writers tell us, a sufficient amount of that essential to constitute a pleasure no less keen than novel.

And so at the present day what is wanting in absolute reality, is by an imaginative mind supplied by the fancy. When a man gives himself up to the pleasures of self-enjoyment, does not the idea that he is procuring these agreeable sensations by unnatural means tend to heighten his feelings? And does he not try to picture – aye, to a most marvellous exactness – how he would feel were those finishing throbs of ecstasy experienced upon the panting bosom of the lovely being he is lusting for?

Even so, this pleasure, in whatever degree it is experienced, is ever to be increased by the action of the mind.

You are mounted on the body of a woman of pleasure; you imagine, perhaps in ignorance, that you are the first to pluck the maiden flower from a lovely and innocent girl. Have you not precisely the same sensations that would be experienced in the actual deflowering of a maid? Of course you have; and in no case can the adage be more properly applied than when in allusion to such a deception it is remarked, 'Where ignorance is bliss, 'tis folly to be wise.'

The mind has everything to do with the action of the body in matters of this nature, as in all others, and in none in a more direct degree.

It is in the knowledge that you are engaged in an act of the greatest indecency, that you are in fact uniting the most outrageously sensual part of your body to a no less sensual part than the closest recesses of a woman's person; that you have pushed that lascivious instrument of yours to the utmost within her belly, and that you are about to flood her very vitals with a stream of that all-wondrous fluid with which man is endowed. This is what constitutes the zest of enjoyment with a man of sensual mind, and any pictures which add additional piquancy to the act are provocative of increased ardour and enjoyment.

ELINOR GLYN
(1864–1943)

The Tiger Skin

Elinor Glyn had a success with her first novel, *The Visits of Elizabeth* (1900), and went on to become one of the most successful romantic novelists of her time, turning out books which excited and captivated an enormous, predominantly female, audience. *Three Weeks* (1907), the story of a romance between a callow young Englishman and a ravishing and experienced Balkan Queen, caused a sensation, and sold over five million copies. Perhaps its most famous scene is the one which follows: Paul Verdayne, having seen and admired a mysterious fellow-guest in a Swiss hotel – he is on holiday from his *fiancée*, a parson's daughter whose chief recreations are 'games of golf and hockey, or a good run on her feet with the hounds' – scrapes acquaintance with her, and after a tantalising conversation receives a note: 'Paul – I am in the devil's mood today. About 5 o'clock come to me by the terrace steps.' Pausing only to send her a tiger-skin he has bought for her as a present, he comes.

A bright fire burnt in the grate, and some palest orchid-mauve silk curtains were drawn in the lady's room when Paul entered from the terrace. And loveliest sight of all, in front of the fire, stretched at full length, was his tiger – and on him – also at full length – reclined the lady, garbed in some strange clinging garment of heavy purple crêpe, its hem embroidered with gold, one white arm resting on the beast's head, her back supported by a pile of the velvet curtains, and a heap of rarely bound books at her side, while between her red lips was a rose not redder than they – an almost scarlet rose. Paul had never seen one as red before.

The whole picture was barbaric. It might have been some painter's dream of the Favourite in a harem. It was not what one would expect to find in a sedate Swiss hotel.

She did not stir as he stepped in, dropping the heavy curtains after him. She merely raised her eyes, and looked Paul through and through. Her whole expression was changed; it was wicked and dangerous and *provocante*. It seemed quite true, as she had said – she was evidently in the devil's mood.

Paul bounded forward, but she raised one hand to stop him.

'No! you must not come near me, Paul. I am not safe today. Not yet. See, you must sit there and we will talk.'

And she pointed to a great chair of Venetian workmanship and wonderful old velvet which was new to his view.

'I bought that chair in the town this morning at the curiosity shop on the top of Weggisstrasse, which long ago was the home of the Venetian envoy here – and you bought me the tiger, Paul. Ah! that was good! My beautiful tiger!' And she gave a movement like a snake, of joy to feel its fur under her, while she stretched out her hands and caressed the creature where the hair turned white and black at the side, and was deep and soft.

'Beautiful one! beautiful one!' she purred. 'And I know all your feelings and your passions, and now I have got your skin – for the joy of my skin!' And she quivered again with the movements of a snake.

It is not difficult to imagine that Paul felt far from calm during this scene – indeed, he was obliged to hold on to his great chair to prevent himself seizing her in his arms.

'I'm—I'm so glad you like him,' he said in a choked voice. 'I thought perhaps you would. And your own was not worthy of you. I found this by chance. And oh! good God! if you knew how you are making me feel – lying there wasting your caresses upon it!'

She tossed the scarlet rose over to him; it hit his mouth.

'I am not wasting them,' she said, the innocence of a kitten in her strange eyes – their colour impossible to define today. 'Indeed not, Paul! He was my lover in another life – perhaps – who knows?'

'But I,' said Paul, who was now quite mad, 'want to be your lover in this!'

Then he gasped at his own boldness.

With a lightning movement she lay on her face, raised her elbows on the tiger's head, and supported her chin in her hands. Perfectly straight out her body was, the twisted purple drapery outlining her perfect shape, and flowing in graceful lines beyond – like a serpent's tail. The velvet pillows fell scattered at one side.

'Paul – what do you know of lovers – or love?' she said. 'My baby Paul!'

'I know enough to know I know nothing yet which is worth knowing,' he said confusedly. 'But—but—don't you understand, I want you to teach me—'

'You are so sweet, Paul! when you plead like that. I am taking in every bit of you. In your way as perfect as the tiger. But we must talk – oh! such a great, great deal – first.'

A rage of passion was racing through Paul, his incoherent thoughts were that he did not want to talk – only to kiss her – to devour her – to strangle her with love if necessary.

He bit the rose. . . .

'Paul!' she whispered right in his ear, 'am I being wicked for you today? I cannot help it. The devil is in me – and now I must sing.'

'Sing then!' said Paul, maddened with again arising emotion.

She seized a guitar that lay near, and began in a soft voice in some language he knew not – a cadence of melody he had never heard, but one whose notes made strange quivers all up his spine. An exquisite pleasure of sound that was almost pain. And when he felt that he could bear no more, she flung the instrument aside, and leant over his chair again – caressing his curls with her dainty fingers, and purring unknown strange words in his ear.

Paul was young and unlearned in many things. He was completely enthralled and under her dominion – but he was naturally no weakling of body or mind.

'*You* mustn't be teased. My God! it is you who are maddening me!' he cried, his voice hoarse with emotion. 'Do you think I am a statue, or a table, or chair – or inanimate like that tiger there? I am *not* I tell you!' and he seized her in his arms, raining kisses upon her which, whatever they lacked in subtlety, made up for in their passion and strength. 'Some day some man will kill you I suppose, but I shall be your lover – first!'

The lady gasped. She looked up at him in bewildered surprise, as a child might do who sets a light to a whole box of matches in play. What a naughty, naughty toy to burn so quickly for such a little strike!

But Paul's young, strong arms held her close, she could not struggle or move. Then she laughed a laugh of pure glad joy.

'Beautiful, savage Paul,' she whispered. 'Do you love me? Tell me that.'

'Love you!' he said. 'Good God! Love you! Madly, and you know it, darling Queen.'

'Then,' said the lady in a voice in which all the caresses of the world seemed melted, 'then, sweet Paul, I shall teach you many things, and among them I shall teach you how – to – LIVE.'

ANON
(c1900)

The Glass Princess

When newsprint became cheap, there appeared in Paris a great number of low-priced, high-circulation 'newspapers' and magazines, which specialised in the reporting of crime and gossip. In these often appeared *feuilletons*, or short stories, most of them more or less erotic, some more imaginative than others, and a few with real charm. Paul Tabori translated and republished a number of them in 1970 – among them *The Glass Princess*.

Once upon a time there was a Princess and she was quite, quite unapproachable. She lived in a palace of glass which rose upon the summit of a glass mountain. At the foot of the mountain clouds of ravens fluttered over the rotting corpses of her would-be lovers who had tried to climb the sheer cliff-side. Only on the side facing the city where the mountain was the steepest and sheerest were there no bodies – no one had ever dared to make an attempt at this point for it seemed utterly impossible.

The Princess herself, however, was not made of glass but was flesh and blood and this was the greatest torment of her suitors. She was lovelier than all the women of her country. It was impossible to escape the seductive and tantalising sight of her body. And her charms were perfectly and constantly visible in every detail – at the most, there was an occasional, rainbow-hued tiny cloud playing around her ankles or hovering momentarily around her full, pear-shaped breasts, like the spume of a waterfall. The palace, as we said before, was of transparent glass. It is hard to imagine how clear and transparent this glass was – nor to describe the clothes of the Princess which were spun of the lightest gossamer, a masterpiece of the weaver's and dyer's art.

The Princess never removed her clothes – not even when she went to sleep. For they were softer and more resilient than the most delicate spider's web lace. Nor did they leave bare the smallest part of her snow-white body; they were high-necked and closed to her chin, falling over her legs to the ankles of her tiny feet. She was just as chaste as she was beautiful, this virgin Princess. It was a torment

[163]

and a joy at the same time to see her – truly, men suffered the tortures of Tantalus.

The wall of corpses on three sides of the mountain rose higher with every hour, the swarm of the scavenging birds became thicker and thicker.

Like ants the daring suitors toiled with alpenstocks, icepicks and climbing irons – but no ropes for there was no one who would aid his rival – trying to ascend the mirror-smooth chimneys and rock-falls. But all in vain. Sooner or later their strength faltered; some reached only a hundred feet or so, others when they were almost on the top. Then they plummeted into the depths, shattering their bones and smashing their limbs on the jagged glass ridges and ledges which were sharper than well-honed knives and daggers.

But if any of them had succeeded in reaching the summit and stepping on the platform outside the terrace of the palace, he would still have to face the formidable task of winning the favours of the Princess. And that would only be possible for a suitor clad in glass armour, harder than the uniform of the halberdiers who, encased in clinking but unbreakable glass, paraded up and down on proud sentry-go along the parapets. And yet, thus the Princess had stipulated, such armour had to be finer and even more transparent than her own dresses. And this, of course, was totally impossible.

One day, however, a Prince arrived in the capital whose cradle had been rocked in a distant eastern land. In his own way he was just as perfect in beauty as the Princess – but his inclinations were totally different. While she loved unyielding glass above all and in every shape, he was addicted incurably to – softness. Above all in beds. He had a whole collection of them and he used them all in turn to test their consistency and resilience. He possessed beds upon which one drifted like the rosy clouds of the dawn without even being conscious of the mattress; beds that would have made Lucifer comfortable after his fall from Heaven; beds upon which making love was ten thousand times the usual pleasure – for they participated in the lovers' embrace, changing position and shape, rearing and dipping as fancy required. Yet he still sought for something better, more perfect, even more fabulous.

Before he set out to woo the Princess, he proclaimed a competition, promising the most precious jewels of his father's enormous treasury to the person who created the lightest and

from *The Glass Princess*

softest bed in the world. Naturally, old and young hastened to participate in a contest with such glittering prizes. Some shot the ravens croaking over the corpses for they thought their down was airier than the swans'; others journeyed far north to garner the soft fur of polar bears or the feathers of gannets. A woman in childbed twisted the neck of the stork when it brought her baby. But the first prize went to a young boy who plucked the wings of his guardian angel.

After he had presented several consolation prizes, the Prince arranged for the thousands of beds to be set up at the foot of the glass mountain – and on the side where it was the sheerest. Then he started to climb the cliff wall in order to reach the summit. Of course he fell – not once but ten times, a hundred times – and without the soft cushions and mattresses of the beds he would have been killed at the very first occasion. But after he had landed dozens of times, now on his head, now on his princely bottom, to the great amusement of the entire population of the city, he acquired sufficient experience with this strenuous training – and got to the top.

From this spot a back door led into the palace.

No sentry barred his way – they were all posted on the less steep sides of the mountain. And that was very lucky indeed, for the Prince's armour would not have stood up to any blow or thrust. On the other hand he perfectly fulfilled the second condition which the Princess had set; his clothes were so transparent and delicate that even the glass gown of the Princess was a crude, heavy fabric compared to it.

No poet could describe the delight of the Princess when she saw him approach her in this apparel. No painter's brush could depict it. She measured him from head to foot, noticeably pausing about half-way down – and she seemed never to get her fill of the sight. Thinner than a soap-bubble, the garment he wore enveloped his manly limbs – and his manhood rose nobly to the occasion.

And the Princess was even more enchanted when the Prince declared that he had brought her a dress of exactly the same material – so that they could be on an exactly equal footing. Then he opened his arms.

The Princess cast off her glass gown so that it broke, like an eggshell, into a thousand slivers. She had never seen herself naked before. She gazed down her own shimmering beauty, from her neck to her soles, wrapped only in the rosy mist her maiden modesty spread over her face, her breasts, her navel, her thighs.

Lowering her eyes, she asked him for the promised gown.

'Why, you're already wearing it!' laughed the Prince.

And at this moment she realised that he was as bare as the day he was born – and threw herself into his arms.

While the royal guards patrolled outside in their clinking glass armour, protecting three sides of the palace, the lovers left through the back door. For the Princess wanted no part any more of glass palaces and glass uniforms.

They took off down the steep mountainside as if they were diving into a swimming pool. The Prince had taken good care that they should have a soft landing. And when they landed in the softest of all the beds, they were in no hurry to get up again.

.

ANDRÉ GIDE
(1869–1951)

Un Adolescent Merveilleux

Gide, born of strict Calvinist parents, was a courageous bisexual whose marriage was wrecked by his wife's inability to either understand or accept his paganism or homosexuality; she remained the only person he ever really loved. In *Corydon* (1924) he presented in dialogue form a defence of homosexuality. In *Si le grain ne meurt* (1929), an autobiography, he describes a meeting, in Algiers, with Oscar Wilde.

Nothing suggested a café; the door was like all the other doors; it was open, and we did not have to knock. Wilde was well known here – I describe the place in *Amyntas*, for I often returned to it. Several old Arabs sat on mats smoking *kief*, and barely moved as we took our places among them. And at first I did not understand what there was, here, to attract Wilde; but soon I saw, in the shadows by the fireplace, a *caouadji*, very young, preparing two cups of ginger tea for us – Wilde preferred this to coffee. I had let myself sink into the strange torpor of the place when, in the half-open door, appeared the most marvellous boy. He stood for some moments, leaning on the lintel with an elbow, outlined against the darkness. He seemed uncertain whether or not to come in, and I was even afraid he might leave, but at a sign from Wilde he smiled, came towards us, and sat facing us on a stool a little lower than the mats upon which we sat cross-legged, Arab-style. He took a reed flute from his Tunisian waistcoat, and began to play, exquisitely. Wilde told me a little later that he was called Mohammed, and that 'he belonged to Bosie*'; if he had hesitated before coming in, it was because he had not seen Lord Alfred. His fine black eyes had the languorous look of the hashish-smoker; he was olive-skinned; I admired the fineness of his fingers on the flute, the litheness of his adolescent body, the grace of his bare legs, one resting on the knee of the other, under the full white *culottes*. The *caouadji* came and sat beside him, accompanying him on a kind of *darbouka*. Like the flowing of limpid water the

* Wilde's lover, Lord Alfred Douglas

sound of the flute made its way through an extraordinary silence, so that one forgot the time, the place, one's companion, and all the world's troubles. We sat, without moving, for what seemed an infinite time; and I would have stayed even longer if Wilde had not suddenly taken me by the arm, breaking the spell.

'Come,' he said.

We left, walked a little way down the passage, followed by our ugly guide, and I thought the evening was over; but at the first turning Wilde stopped, put his huge hand upon my shoulder – he was taller than me – and said in a low voice:

'Dear, would you like the little flute-player?'

What a dark passage that was! I thought my heart would stop. And what courage it took to answer, in a strangled voice, 'Yes.'

Wilde immediately turned to the guide, who had rejoined us, and whispered something which I did not hear. The guide left, and we walked to the place where we had left the carriage.

We were no sooner in it than Wilde burst out laughing, not so much in pleasure as in triumph; it was an interminable laughter, uncontrollable, insolent; and the more it disconcerted me, the more he laughed. I ought to say that if Wilde had told me the secrets of his life, he knew nothing of mine; I had told him nothing, by word or action. The proposition which he had made was bold; what amused him was that it had been accepted. He laughed like a child, like a devil. The great pleasure of a debauchee is to debauch others. After my adventure at Sousse, the Devil had indeed not much to do to complete his victory; but after all, Wilde did not know this, nor that I had been vanquished in advance – or, if you like (for should one speak of 'defeat' if one is so proud?) that in imagination, in thought, I had already overcome all my scruples. True enough, I did not know this myself; it was, I think, only when I answered 'Yes' that I knew my conscience was vanquished.

From time to time, quelling his laughter, Wilde apologised: 'I'm sorry to laugh so much; but it's too much for me. I just can't keep it in!' And he laughed again.

He still laughed as we arrived at a café, in the Place du Théâtre, where we paid off the carriage.

'It's still too early,' said Wilde. And I did not dare ask what he had arranged with the guide, nor where nor how nor when the little flute-player would come to me. I began to doubt whether the proposition which he had made would come to anything; I was afraid to question him lest I reveal the violence of my lust.

We only waited for a moment at that unpleasant café. I imagine that if Wilde did not go straight to the *petit bar* of the Hôtel de l'Oasis, where we went next, it was because he preferred to keep the Moorish café a secret, and made a short detour to put a little distance between the obvious and the clandestine.

Wilde persuaded me to drink a cocktail, and took several himself. We waited for half an hour. How long it seemed! Wilde laughed still, but not so compulsively, and when we did speak, it was of nothing important. At last he looked at his watch.

'It's time,' he said, getting up.

We walked towards the crowded quarter of the town, down past the great mosque below the hôtel (I have forgotten its name) which one passes on the way to the harbour – an ugly quarter, though once perhaps the most beautiful. Wilde preceded me into a house with double doors, and we had no sooner gone in than through another door appeared two enormous policemen, whose presence terrified me. Wilde smiled at my fear.

'Ah, dear, don't worry; it proves that the hôtel is perfectly safe. They're here to protect foreigners. I know them. Excellent chaps who enjoy my cigarettes. They understand us very well.'

We let the cops go first. They passed the second floor, where we stopped. Wilde took a key from his pocket, and showed me into a tiny flat with two rooms, where, a few moments later, our base guide rejoined us. The two boys followed, each wrapped in a *burnous* which hid his face. The guide left. Wilde showed me into the inner room with little Mohammed and himself stayed in the outer one with the *darbouka* player.

Later, every time I went in search of pleasure, I pursued my memories of that night. After my adventure in Sousse, I had fallen miserably into vice. Lust, if I had snatched at it in passing, had been furtively enjoyed – though deliciously, one evening, in a boat with a young oarsman on Lake Como (before I went to Brévine) when my ecstasy had been wrapped about by moonlight, the misty enchantment of the lake and the soft smells of the banks. Nothing more; nothing but a fearful desert full of unanswered appeals, unfulfilled efforts, uneasiness, struggle, enervating dreams, imaginary triumphs, and abominable depression. At La Rocque, the summer before last, I was afraid of going mad; almost all the time I was there, I was locked in my room, where I should have been working, where I tried to work in vain (I was writing *Le Voyage d'Urien*), obsessed, haunted, hoping perhaps to escape in some excess, to come out into the clear air having exorcised my daemon (I recognised his cunning), but exhausting nothing but myself, exhausting myself maniacally, and to the verge of imbecility, of madness.

Ah! what a hell I lived through! And not a friend to whom I could speak, not a word of advice; I thought compromise impossible, and because I refused to surrender, I was damned. . . . But why should I recall those sad days? Does the memory explain that night's delirium? My efforts with Mériem, the attempt to be 'normal', was unsuccessful because it found no echo in my personality. No constraint now, nothing contrived, nothing doubtful; no ashes in these memories. My rapture was boundless – so much so that I cannot imagine it greater even if I had been in love. What is love, after all? Why shouldn't desire alone rule my heart? My pleasure was without second thoughts, without remorse. But how can I describe my delirium at holding in my naked arms that perfect, savage little brown body, eager, lascivious?

I spent a long time, after Mohammed had left me, in a state of trembling exaltation, and although I had reached the peak of pleasure five times with him, I re-lived my ecstasy again and again, and back in my room at the hôtel prolonged the memories until dawn. At the first pale light I got up; I ran, yes really ran, in sandals, far beyond Mustapha; the night had not in the least tired me – on the contrary a liveliness, a kind of lightness of body and soul did not leave me all day.

SIDONIE-GABRIELLE COLETTE
(1873–1954)

Summer in Normandy

Colette was born in Burgundy, and before she was twenty-one married
Henry Gauthier-Villars, a Paris journalist, critic and novelist. At his
behest she started to write memoirs of her childhood and schooldays,
which became the Claudine books. After she left 'Willy' in 1906 she earned
her living as a dancer and mime in music-hall, but continued to write, and
eventually became one of the most popular and admired of living French
writers. *Chéri*, perhaps her best-known book, was published in 1920. She
wrote magnificently about the life of the senses, and *Chéri* is perhaps the
most vivid account of the classic affair between a very young man and a
middle-aged woman. In the extract that follows, Léa, half-seduced by the
already knowing adolescent boy, has invited him to stay with her in the
country.

When Léa recalled their first summer in Normandy, she would sum
it up impartially: 'I've had other naughty little boys through my
hands, more amusing than Chéri, more likeable, too, and more
intelligent. But all the same, never one to touch him.'

'It's funny,' she confided to the old Baron de Berthellemy,
towards the end of the summer of 1906, 'but sometimes I think I'm
in bed with a Chinese or an African.'

'Have you ever had a Chinaman or a Negro?'

'Never.'

'Well then?'

'I don't know. I can't explain. It's just an impression.'

The impression had grown upon her slowly, also an astonishment she had not always been able to conceal. Her earliest
memories of their idyll were abundantly rich, but only in pictures of
delicious food, superb fruit, and the pleasure of taking pains over
her country larder. She could still see Chéri – paler in the blazing
sunlight – dragging along his exhausted body beneath the lime-tree
tunnels in Normandy, or asleep on the sun-warmed paving beside a
pond.

Léa used to rouse Chéri from sleep to cram him with strawberries
and cream, frothy milk, and corn-fed chicken. With wide, vacant

eyes, as though dazed, he would sit at dinner watching the mazy motions of the moths round the bowl of roses, and then look at his wrist-watch to see whether the time had come to go to bed: while Léa, disappointed but unresentful, pondered over the unfulfilled promises of the kiss at Neuilly and good-naturedly bided her time.

'I'll keep him cooped up in this fattening-pen till the end of August, if need be. Then, back in Paris again – ouf! – I'll pack him off to his precious studies.'

She went to bed mercifully early, so that Chérie – after nuzzling against her till he had hollowed out a selfishly comfortable position – might get some sleep. Sometimes, when the lamp was out, she would watch a pool of moonlight shimmering over the polished floor, or listen, through the chorus of rustling aspens and shrilling crickets, unceasing by night or day, to the deep, retriever-like sighs that rose from Chéri's breast.

'Why can't I go to sleep? Is there something wrong with me?' she vaguely wondered. 'It's not this boy's head on my shoulder – I've held heavier. The weather's wonderful. I've ordered him a good plate of porridge for tomorrow. Already his ribs stick out less. Yes, of course, I remember . . . I'm going to send for Patron, the boxer, to give the boy some training. We've plenty of time between us, Patron and I, to spring a surprise on Madame Peloux.'

She fell asleep, lying stretched out on her back between the cool sheets, the dark head of her naughty little boy resting on her left breast. She fell asleep, to be aroused sometimes – but all too rarely – by a waking desire of Chéri's towards the break of day.

Patron actually arrived after they had been two months in their country retreat, with his suitcase, his small pound-and-a-half dumb-bells, his black tights, his six-ounce gloves, and his leather boxing-boots, laced down to the toe. Patron, with his girlish voice, his long eyelashes, and his splendid tanned skin, as brown as the leather of his luggage – he hardly looked naked when he took off his shirt. And Chéri, by turns peevish, listless, or jealous of Patron's smooth strength, started the slow, oft-repeated movements. They were tiresome, but they did him good.

'One . . . sss . . . two . . . sss . . . I can't hear you breathing . . . three . . . sss . . . Don't think I can't see you cheating there with your knee . . . sss . . .'

An awning of lime foliage filtered the August sunlight. The bare bodies of instructor and pupil were dappled with purple reflections from the thick red carpet spread out upon the gravel. Léa watched the lessons with keen attention. Sometimes during the quarter of an hour's boxing, Chéri, drunk with new-found strength, lost all control and, red-faced with anger, attempted a foul blow. Rock-like, Patron stood up to his swings, and from the height of his Olympian glory let fall oracular words – words of wisdom that packed more weight than his proverbial punch.

'Steady on, now! That left eye's wandering a bit! If I hadn't stopped myself in time, it would have had a nasty taste of the stitches on my right glove.'

'I slipped,' Chéri said, enraged.

'It's not a question of balance,' Patron went on, 'it's a question of morale. You'll never make a boxer.'

'My mother won't let me, isn't that a pity?'

'Whether your mother lets you or not, you'll never make a boxer, because you've got a rotten temper. Rotten tempers and boxing don't go together. Aren't I right, Madame Léa?'

Léa smiled, and revelled in the warm sun, sitting still and watching the bouts between these two men, both young and both stripped. In her mind she kept comparing them. 'How handsome Patron is – as solid as a house! And the boy's shaping well. You don't find knees like his running about the streets every day of the week, or I'm no judge. His back, too, is . . . will be . . . marvellous. Where the devil did Mother Peloux drop her line to fish up a child like that? And the set of his head! quite a statue! But what a little beast he is! When he laughs, you'd swear it's a greyhound snarling!' She felt happy and maternal, bathed in quiet virtue. 'I'd willingly change him for anyone else,' she said to herself, with Chéri naked in the afternoon beside her under the lime-tree bower, or with Chéri naked in the morning on her ermine rug, or Chéri naked in the evening on the edge of the warm fountain. 'Yes, handsome as he is, I'd willingly make a change, if it weren't a question of conscience!'

She confessed her indifference to Patron.

'And yet,' Patron objected, 'the lad's very nicely made. There's muscles on him now such as you don't see on our French lads; his are more like a coloured boy's – though he couldn't look any whiter, I must say. Nice little muscles they are, and not too showy. He'll never have biceps like melons.'

[173]

'I should hope not, Patron! But then, you know, I didn't take him on for his boxing!'

'Of course not,' Patron acquiesced, letting his long lashes droop, 'There's – your feelings to be considered.'

He was always embarrassed by Léa's unveiled allusions to sex, and by her smile – the insistence of the smiling eyes she brought to bear on him whenever she spoke of love.

'Of course,' Patron tried another tack, 'if he's not altogether satisfactory . . .'

Léa laughed. 'Altogether! no . . . but I find being disinterested is its own reward. . . .'

In fact, Léa herself understood precious little about Chéri after three months' intimacy. If she still talked to Patron, who now came only on Sundays, or to Berthellemy, who arrived without being invited but left again two hours later, about 'sending Chéri back to his blessed studies,' it was because the phrase had become a kind of habit, and as though to excuse herself for having kept him there so long. She kept on setting a limit to his stay, and then exceeding it. She was waiting.

'The weather is so lovely. And then his trip to Paris last week tired him. And, besides, it's better for me to get thoroughly sick of him.'

For the first time in her life, she waited in vain for what had never before failed her: complete trust on the part of her young lover, a self-surrender to confessions, candours, endless secrets – those hours in the depths of the night when, in almost filial gratitude, a young man unrestrainedly pours out his tears, his private likes and dislikes, on the kindly bosom of a mature and trusted friend.

'They've always told me everything in the past,' she thought obstinately. 'I've always known just what they were worth – what they were thinking and what they wanted. But this boy, this brat . . . No, that would really be the limit.'

He was now strong, proud of his nineteen years, gay at meals and impatient in bed; even so he gave away nothing but his body, and remained as mysterious as an odalisque. Tender? Yes, if an involuntary cry or an impulsive hug is an indication of tenderness. But the moment he spoke, he was 'spiteful' again, careful to divulge nothing of his true self.

from *Chéri*

How often at dawn had Léa held him in her arms, a lover soothed, relaxed, with half-closed lids! Each morning his eyes and his mouth returned to life more beautiful, as though every waking, every embrace, had fashioned them anew! How often, at such moments, had she indulged her desire to master him, her sensual longing to hear his confession, and pressed her forehead against his, whispering, 'Speak. Say something. Tell me . . .'

But no confession came from those curved lips, scarcely anything but sulky or frenzied phrases woven round 'Nounoune' – the name he had given her when a child and the one he now used in the throes of his pleasure, almost like a cry for help.

'Yes, I assure you, he might be a Chinese or an African,' she declared to Anthime de Berthellemy, and added, 'I can't tell you why.' The impression was strong but confused, and she felt lazily incompetent to find words for the feeling that she and Chéri did not speak the same language.

It was the end of September when they returned to Paris. Chéri went straight to Neuilly, the very first evening, to 'spring a surprise' on Madame Peloux. He brandished chairs, cracked nuts with his fist, leaped on to the billiard-table and played cowboy in the garden at the heels of the terrified watch-dogs.

'Ouf!' Léa sighed, as she entered her house in the Avenue Bugeaud, alone. 'How wonderful! – a bed to myself!'

But at ten o'clock the following night, she was sipping coffee and trying not to find the evening too long or the dining-table too large, when a nervous cry was forced from her lips. Chéri had suddenly appeared, framed in the doorway – Chéri, wafted on silent, winged feet.

He was not speaking or showing any sign of affection, but just running towards her.

'Are you mad?'

Shrugging his shoulders, disdaining all explanations, just running towards her. Never asking, 'Do you love me?' 'Have you already forgotten me?' Running towards her.

A moment later they were lying in the middle of Léa's great brass-encumbered bed. Chéri pretended to be worn out and sleepy. This made it easier to grit his teeth and keep his eyes tight shut, suffering as he was from a furious attack of taciturnity. Yet, through his silence, she was listening as she lay beside him, listening with delight to the distant delicate vibration, to the imprisoned tumult thrumming within a body that sought to conceal its agony, its gratitude and love.

LYTTON STRACHEY
(1880–1932)

The Bow-Wow and the Pussy

Lytton Strachey, the author of *Eminent Victorians* and of a fine biography of Queen Victoria, wrote *Ermyntrude and Esmeralda* in 1913 for the artist Henry Lamb, with whom he was in love. While working on his autobiographical essay on Cardinal Manning, he was also composing this dialogue between two aristocratic seventeen-year-olds, who have agreed to tell each other all they can discover about the mysteries of love. Esmeralda is interested to pass on news of a scandal when her Papa discovers her brother Godfrey in bed with his tutor Mr Mapleton; but Ermyntrude, an MP's daughter, is more fortunate, for she is actually initiated into the pleasures of love by Henry, the family footman. Incidentally, while *pussy* has been a sexual synonym since the seventeenth century, it seems that Strachey was the first writer to complete the joke by using *bow-wow* as a synonym for the penis (though 'to dog' was a nineteenth century term for copulation).

Henry was not like an ordinary footman. He was much better-looking and taller and stronger. He had very black hair that was rather curly, and black eyebrows and dark blue eyes and a straight nose that turned up at the end which made him look impudent, and a small mouth with perfectly white teeth, and a very nice neck indeed. I'm sure if you could have seen him in his dark green livery and silver buttons your pussy would have pouted too – especially if you could have felt what his fingers were like. I didn't tell you, but that time [when their hands had met] I wanted to hug him, and I really think I might have, if the kitten hadn't jumped out of its basket just that instant. Wasn't it an absurd joke that the two pussies should have begun playing pranks at the same time . . .?

At half-past six he came in when I wasn't at all expecting him. He said that a window was broken in the back-stairs and that Jessop [the butler] was out and that my father was out, and would I give the order to have it mended, as last time my father had been very angry at orders being given without his leave. So I said yes, and then he said, 'It's near the top of the backstairs, Miss,' and didn't go away. So I said, 'Is it a large pane?' And he said, 'Not very, Miss, would you like to see it?' So I said 'You'd better show it to me.' I was rather frightened when I said that, but he answered very quickly 'Yes, Miss, I think that would be the best way.' And then he said we'd better have a candle, because it was 'that dark on them stairs', so he lighted one, and off we went – upstairs, and then round along the little landing under the dome, and then through the door to the back stairs, and down them until we came to the window with the broken pane. Henry held up the candle to show it me, and said 'You see, Miss, it ain't a very big hole.' I leant over to look at it better, and put my hair too near the candle, and my hair gave a frizzle, which gave Henry a fright, and he said, 'Oh, take care, Miss! Your hair!' I said, 'Would you mind if I burnt my hair, Henry?' And he said 'Mind, Miss? Why, they might take both my ears off me, that they might, Miss, before I let any manner of harm come to your hair!' So I laughed, and said 'That would be a pity, Henry; you've got such nice ears.' – 'Not as nice as your hair, Miss.' – 'Why do you like my hair so much, Henry?' – 'It's got a colour on it the same as the butter down in our country, Miss – Dorsetshire, that is.' – 'Do you think it feels as nice as it looks, Henry?' – 'That I do, Miss!' – So I laughed again, just a little, and said 'Then why don't you stroke it?' And then he didn't say anything, but put out his hand, and looked at my eyes, and I looked at his eyes, and then – well, it didn't seem to be me any longer, but it was like something else that made me do things, and I put my arm round his neck all of a sudden, and he hugged me so hard that I could only just breathe, and it felt as if he was hugging me with the whole of his body. And then the candle fell over and went out, and it was pitch dark, and after that I hardly know what happened, because it was so very exciting, but somehow I began to half lie down on the stairs, which are quite steep and nothing but wood, and Henry was on the top of me, hugging me just as much as ever, so you can imagine that it wasn't particularly comfortable. I forgot to say that directly he hugged me I felt my pussy pouting so enormously that I didn't know what to do – except hug him back, which seemed only to make it pout more. But when we were lying down it did it even more still. Then Henry began pulling my skirt up and even my petticoat, and I began helping him, and it was very funny – we were both in such a hurry, and his body twisted about so much and he breathed so hard that I half began to feel frightened. But he held me too tightly for

[178]

me to have possibly got away, even if I'd wanted to, and then all of a sudden my pussy began to hurt most horribly, and I very nearly screamed. It was as if something was going right through me, but though it hurt my pussy so, it made it stop pouting at the same time and begin to purr instead, as if it liked it, and I think it did like it better than anything else in the world. I can't understand why pussies should like so much being hurt. And the curious thing was that I suppose I liked it too, because I went on kissing Henry more and more, and although I was so uncomfortable and hot and all squashed-up and disarranged and I believe nearly crying, I didn't at all want it to stop, and I was very sorry when Henry said he would have to go and lay the dinner or Jessop would ask him where he'd been. . . .

I must tell you that Henry told me afterwards that what he'd said about Papa and the orders for the window was a story, and he'd said it to try and make me go there with him, and if I hadn't, he told me that he'd settled to give warning and go away that very night. He said that his bow-wow had begun to pout so much, especially when he was handing me the vegetables, that he couldn't have stood it any longer. But that night, when he handed me the vegetables, it was a great lark, because my pussy was pouting too. After dinner, when I'd gone up to bed, it was still more of a lark. I'd arranged it with Henry. When all the lights were out I opened my door a very little, and then he came in, and after we'd kissed each other a great deal we took off our clothes. I was very excited to see what his bow-wow was like, but I was astonished to see that he hadn't got one, but a very funny big pink thing standing straight up instead. I was rather frightened, because I thought he might be deformed, which wouldn't have been at all nice, so I asked him what it was. Then he laughed so much that I thought everyone would hear, and at last I discovered that it *was* his bow-wow after all, and it turns out that that is what they get like when they pout! I was very pleased indeed, and so was my pussy when his bow-wow went into it, and after that we went to bed. Ever since then he's come every night, and I've enjoyed myself very much. It's a pity I didn't know about it before, because we might have begun doing it directly he came here, and I might have done it before that with the last George but one, who looked quite pretty, but of course not nearly as handsome as Henry.

D. H. LAWRENCE
(1885–1929)

The Lady and the Gamekeeper

Because D. H. Lawrence wrote, or attempted to write, more freely about sex than any other serious novelist of his generation, he became in the mind of the casual or non-reading public very much associated with it; this was partly due to the underground reputation of his novel *Lady Chatterley's Lover*, first published privately in Rome in 1928. In 1960 this book became the subject of a famous prosecution under the Obscene Publications Act when Penguin published in England a paperback edition. A jury found the publishers not guilty, and the book became for the first time available to the general reader. Intent on proving what was true, its importance and seriousness as a work of literature, witnesses perhaps overvalued it; but it remains a vivid, sober and moving account of a love affair. Its eroticism arises naturally out of its plot, and has two aspects – an intense but oblique sexuality exemplified in my first extract, a description of the first sight Lady Chatterley has of Mellors, her husband's gamekeeper; and a more overt, sometimes overblown attempt to describe the fundamentally indescribable, as in my second extract, one of the scenes between the two after they have become lovers.

She stood and listened, and it seemed to her she heard sounds from the back of the cottage. Having failed to make herself heard, her mettle was roused, she would not be defeated.

So she went round the side of the house. At the back of the cottage the land rose steeply, so the back yard was sunken, and enclosed by a low stone wall. She turned the corner of the house and stopped. In the little yard two paces beyond her, the man was washing himself, utterly unaware. He was naked to the hips, his velveteen breeches slipping down over his slender loins. And his white slim back was curved over a big bowl of soapy water, in which he ducked his head, shaking his head with a queer, quick little motion, lifting his slender white arms, and pressing the soapy water from his ears, quick, subtle as a weasel playing with water, and utterly alone. Connie backed away round the corner of the house, and hurried away to the wood. In spite of herself, she had had a shock. After all, merely a man washing himself; commonplace enough, Heaven knows.

from *Lady Chatterley's Lover*

Yet in some curious way it was a visionary experience: it had hit her in the middle of the body. She saw the clumsy breeches slipping down over the pure, delicate, white loins, the bones showing a little, and the sense of aloneness, of a creature purely alone, overwhelmed her. Perfect, white, solitary nudity of a creature that lives alone, and inwardly alone. And beyond that, a certain beauty of a pure creature. Not the stuff of beauty, not even the mode of beauty, but a lambency, the warm, white flame of a single life, revealing itself in contours that one might touch: a body!

He took her in his arms again and drew her to him, and suddenly she became small in his arms, small and nestling. It was gone, the resistance was gone, and she began to melt in a marvellous peace. And as she melted small and wonderful in his arms, she became infinitely desirable to him, all his blood-vessels seemed to scald with intense yet tender desire, for her, for her softness, for the penetrating beauty of her in his arms, passing into his blood. And softly, with that marvellous swoon-like caress of his hand in pure soft desire, softly he stroked the silky slope of her loins, down, down between her soft warm buttocks, coming nearer and nearer to the very quick of her. And she felt him like a flame of desire, yet tender, and she felt herself melting in the flame. She let herself go. She felt his penis risen against her with silent amazing force and assertion and she let herself go to him. She yielded with a quiver that was like death, she went all open to him. And oh, if he were not tender to her now, how cruel, for she was all open to him and helpless!

She quivered again at the potent inexorable entry inside her, so strange and terrible. It might come with the thrust of a sword in her softly-opened body, and that would be death. She clung in a sudden access of terror. But it came with a strange slow thrust of peace, the dark thrust of peace and a ponderous, primordial tenderness, such as made the world in the beginning. And her terror subsided in her breast, her breast dared to be gone in peace, she held nothing. She dared to let go everything, all herself, and be gone in the flood.

And it seemed she was like the sea, nothing but dark waves rising and heaving, heaving with a great swell, so that slowly her whole darkness was in motion, and she was ocean rolling its dark, dumb mass. Oh, and far down inside her the deeps parted and rolled asunder, in long, far-travelling billows, and ever, at the quick of her, the depths parted and rolled asunder, from the centre of soft plunging, as the plunger went deeper and deeper, touching lower, and she was deeper and deeper disclosed, the heavier the billows of her rolled away to some shore, uncovering her, and closer and closer plunged the palpable unknown, and further and further rolled the waves of herself away from herself, leaving her, till suddenly, in a soft, shuddering convulsion, the quick of all her plasm was touched, she knew herself touched, the consummation was upon her, and she was gone. She was gone, she was not, and she was born: a woman.

Ah, too lovely, too lovely! In the ebbing she realised all the loveliness. Now all her body clung with tender love to the unknown man, and blindly to the wilting penis, as it so tenderly, frailly, unknowingly withdrew, after the fierce thrust of its potency. As it drew out and left her body, the secret, sensitive thing, she gave an unconscious cry of pure loss, and she tried to put it back. It had been so perfect! And she loved it so!

And only now she became aware of the small, bud-like reticence and tenderness of the penis, and a little cry of wonder and poignancy escaped her again, her woman's heart crying out over the tender frailty of that which had been the power.

'It was so lovely!' she moaned. 'It was so lovely!' But he said nothing, only softly kissed her, lying still above her. And she moaned with a sort of bliss, as a sacrifice, and a newborn thing.

And now in her heart the queer wonder of him was awakened. A man! The strange potency of manhood upon her! Her hands strayed over him, still a little afraid. Afraid of that strange, hostile, slightly repulsive thing that he had been to her, a man. And now she touched him, and it was the sons of god with the daughters of men. How beautiful he felt, how pure in tissue! How lovely, how lovely, strong, and yet pure and delicate, such stillness of the sensitive body! Such utter stillness of potency and delicate flesh. How beautiful! How beautiful! Her hands came timorously down his back, to the soft, smallish globes of the buttocks. Beauty! What beauty! a sudden little flame of new awareness went through her. How was it possible, this beauty here, where she had previously only been repelled? The unspeakable beauty to the touch of the warm, living buttocks! The life within life, the sheer warm, potent loveliness. And the strange weight of the balls between his legs!

from *Lady Chatterley's Lover*

What a mystery! What a strange heavy weight of mystery, that could lie soft and heavy in one's hand! The roots, root of all that is lovely, the primeval root of all full beauty.

She clung to him, with a hiss of wonder that was almost awe, terror. He held her close, but he said nothing. He would never say anything. She crept nearer to him, nearer, only to be near to the sensual wonder of him. And out of his utter, incomprehensible stillness, she felt again the slow, momentous, surging rise of the phallus again, the other power. And her heart melted out with a kind of awe.

And this time his being within her was all soft and iridescent, purely soft and iridescent, such as no consciousness could seize. Her whole self quivered unconscious and alive, like plasm. She could not know what it was. She could not remember what it had been. Only that it had been more lovely than anything ever could be. Only that. And afterwards she was utterly still, utterly unknowing, she was not aware for how long. And he was still with her, in an unfathomable silence along with her. And of this, they would never speak.

When awareness of the outside began to come back, she clung to his breast, murmuring, 'My love! My love!' And he held her silently. And she curled on his breast, perfect.

HENRY MILLER
(1891–1980)

Never so Happy

Henry Miller, a naïve American novelist, has written so consistently about sex – in, for instance, *Tropic of Cancer* and his trilogy *The Rosy Crucifixion* (of which *Sexus*, 1949, is the first volume) – that he is mistakenly known popularly as a pornographer, whereas his true importance is probably as an autobiographer. His writings about sex are usually brutal, and often seem to degrade women, all of whom he seeks to see solely in sexual roles.

As [Maude] came back I heard her whispering to the girl from upstairs. She tapped lightly on the glass panel. 'Put something on,' she cooed. 'I've got Elsie with me.'

I went into the bathroom and wrapped a towel around my loins. Elsie went into a fit of laughter when she saw me. We hadn't met since the day she found me lying in bed with Mona. She seemed in excellent good humour and not at all embarrassed by the turn of events. They had brought down another bottle of wine and some cognac. And the gramophone and the records.

Elsie was in just the mood to share our little celebration. I had expected Maude to offer her a drink and then get rid of her more or less politely. But no, nothing of the kind. She wasn't at all disturbed by Elsie's presence. She did excuse herself for being half-naked, but with a good-natured laugh, as if it were just one of those things. We put a record on and I danced with Maude. The towel slipped off but neither of us made any attempt to pick it up. When we ungrappled I stood there with my prick standing out like a flagpole and calmly reached for my glass. Elsie gave one startled look and then turned her head away. Maude handed me the towel, or rather slung it over my prick. 'You don't mind, do you, Elsie?' she said. Elsie was terribly quiet – you could hear her temples hammering. Presently she went over to the machine and turned the record over. Then she reached for her glass without looking at us and gulped it down.

'Why don't you dance with her?' said Maude. 'I won't stop you. Go ahead, Elsie, dance with him.'

I went up to Elsie with the towel hanging from my prick. As she

[184]

turned her back to Maude she pulled the towel off and grabbed it with a feverish hand. I felt her whole body shake as though a chill had come over her.

'I'm going to get some candles,' said Maude. 'It's too bright in here.' She disappeared into the next room. Immediately Elsie stopped dancing, put her lips to mine and thrust her tongue down my throat. I put my hand on her cunt and squeezed it. She was still holding my cock. The record stopped. Neither of us pulled away to shut the machine off. I heard Maude coming back. Still I remained locked in Elsie's arms.

This is where the trouble starts, I thought to myself. But Maude seemed to pay no attention. She lit the candles and then turned the electric light off. I was pulling away from Elsie when I felt her standing beside us. 'It's all right', she said. 'I don't mind. Let me join in.' And with that she put her arms around the two of us and we all three began kissing one another.

'Whew! it's hot!' said Elsie, breaking away at last.

'Take your dress off if you like,' said Maude. 'I'm taking this off,' and suiting action to word she slipped out of the wrap and stood naked before us.

The next moment we were all stark naked.

I sat down with Maude on my lap. Her cunt was wet again. Elsie stood beside us with her arm around Maude's neck. She was a little taller than Maude and well built. I rubbed my hand over her belly and twined my fingers in the bush that was almost on the level with my mouth. Maude looked on with a pleasant smile of satisfaction. I leaned forward and kissed Elsie's cunt.

'It's wonderful not to be jealous any more,' said Maude very simply.

Elsie's face was scarlet. She didn't quite know what her role was, how far she dared go. She studied Maude intently, as though not altogether convinced of her sincerity. Now I was kissing Maude passionately, my fingers in Elsie's cunt the while. I felt Elsie pressing closer, moving herself. The juice was pouring over my fingers. At the same time Maude raised herself and, shifting her bottom, adroitly managed to sink down again with my prick neatly fitted inside her. She was facing forward now, her face pressed against Elsie's breasts. She raised her head and took the nipple in her mouth. Elsie gave a shudder and her cunt began to quiver with silken spasms. Now Maude's hand, which had been resting on Elsie's waist, slid down and caressed the smooth cheeks. In another moment it had slipped farther down and encountered mine. I drew my hand away instinctively. Elsie shifted a little and then Maude leaned forward and placed her mouth on Elsie's cunt. At the same time Elsie bent forward, over Maude, and put her lips to mine. The three of us were now quivering as if we had the ague.

As I felt Maude coming I held myself in, determined to save it for Elsie. My prick still taut, I gently raised Maude from my lap and reached for Elsie. She straddled me face forward and with uncontrollable passion she flung her arms around me, glued her lips to mine, and fucked away for dear life. Maude had discreetly gone to the bathroom. When she returned Elsie was sitting in my lap, her arm around my neck, her face on fire. Then Elsie got up and went to the bathroom. I went to the sink and washed myself there.

'I've never been so happy,' said Maude, going to the machine and putting on another record.

VLADIMIR NABOKOV
(1899–1977)

A Restless Night

Lolita was first published in 1950. A cool, cynical look at the passion of a middle-aged man for a pre-adolescent girl – the novel added the word 'nymphet' to the language – it attracted a great deal of vituperation, but also a great deal of critical praise. Philip Toynbee called the book 'pervasively and continuously funny, with a humour which is both savage and farcical.' Lionel Trilling pointed out that the novel 'is about love. Perhaps I shall be better understood if I put the statement in this form: *Lolita* is not about sex, but about love. Almost every page sets forth some explicitly erotic emotion or some overt erotic action and still it is not about sex. It is about love. This makes it unique in my experience of contemporary novels. . . .' It is also true that far from the narrator having seduced his nymphet, the opposite is the case: after marrying her mother in order to be near Lolita, the narrator embarks on a tour of awful American motels, where he books rooms for himself and his 'daughter'. They share, sometimes, a bed; but he carefully keeps his hands off her. Until—

The door of the lighted bathroom stood ajar; in addition to that, a skeleton glow came through the Venetian blind from the outside arclights; these intercrossed rays penetrated the darkness of the bedroom and revealed the following situation.

Clothed in one of her old nightgowns, my Lolita lay on her side with her back to me, in the middle of the bed. Her lightly veiled body and bare limbs formed a Z. She had put both pillows under her dark tousled head; a band of pale light crossed her top vertebrae.

I seemed to have shed my clothes and slipped into pyjamas with the kind of fantastic instantaneousness which is implied when in a cinematograph scene of the process of changing is cut; and I had already placed my knee on the edge of the bed when Lolita turned her head and stared at me through the striped shadows. . . . For at least two minutes I waited and strained on the brink, like that tailor with his home-made parachute forty years ago when about to jump from the Eiffel Tower. Her faint breathing had the rhythm of sleep. Finally I heaved myself on to my narrow margin of bed, stealthily pulled at odds and ends of sheets piled up to the south of my stone-cold heels – and Lolita lifted her head and gaped at me.

As I learned later from a helpful pharmaceutist, the purple pull [I had given her] did not even belong to the big and noble family of barbiturates, and though it might have induced sleep in a neurotic who believed it to be a potent drug, it was too mild a sedative to affect for any length of time a wary, albeit weary, nymphet. Whether the Ramsdale doctor was a charlatan or a shrewd old rogue, does not, and did not, really matter. What mattered, was that I had been deceived. When Lolita opened her eyes again, I realised that, whether or not the drug might work later in the night, the security I had relied upon was a sham one. Slowly her head turned away and dropped on to her unfair amount of pillow. I lay quite still on my brink, peering at her rumpled hair, at the glimmer of nymphet flesh, where half a haunch and half a shoulder dimly showed, and trying to gauge the depth of her slumber by the rate of her respiration. Some time passed, nothing changed, and I decided I might risk getting a little closer to that lovely and maddening glimmer; but hardly had I moved into its warm purlieus than her breathing was suspended, and I had the odious feeling that little Dolores was wide awake and would explode in screams if I touched her with any part of my wretchedness. . . .

And less than six inches from me and my burning life, was nebulous Lolita! After a long, stirless vigil, my tentacles moved towards her again, and this time the creak of the mattress did not wake her. I managed to bring my ravenous bulk so close to her that I felt the aura of her bare shoulder like a warm breath upon my cheek. And then, she sat up, gasped, muttered with insane rapidity something about boats, tugged at the sheets and lapsed back into her rich, dark, young unconsciousness. As she tossed, within that abundant flow of sleep, recently auburn, at present lunar, her arm struck me across the face. For a second I held her. She freed herself from the shadow of my embrace – doing this not consciously, not violently, not with any personal distaste, but with the neutral, plaintive murmur of a child demanding its natural rest. And again the situation remained the same: Lolita with her curved spine to Humbert, Humbert resting his head on his hand and burning with desire and dyspepsia. . . .

Upon hearing her first morning yawn, I feigned handsome

from *Lolita*

profiled sleep. I just did not know what to do. Would she be shocked at finding me by her side, and not in some spare bed? Would she collect her clothes and lock herself up in the bathroom? Would she demand to be taken at once to Ramsdale – to her mother's bedside – back to camp? But my Lo was a sportive Lassie. I felt her eyes on me, and when she uttered at last that beloved chortling note of hers, I knew her eyes had been laughing. She rolled over to my side, and her warm, brown hair came against my collarbone. I gave· a mediocre imitation of waking up. We lay quietly. I gently caressed her hair, and we gently kissed. Her kiss, to my delirious embarrassment, had some rather comical refinements of flutter and probe which made me conclude that she had been coached at an early age by a little Lesbian. No Charlie boy could have taught her *that*. As if to see whether I had my fill and learned the lesson, she drew away and surveyed me. Her cheekbones were flushed, her full underlip glistened, my dissolution was near. All at once, with a burst of rough glee (the sign of the nymphet!) she put her mouth to my ear – but for quite a while my mind could not separate into words the hot thunder of her whisper, and she laughed, and brushed the hair off her face, and tried again, and gradually the odd sense of living in a brand new, made new dream world, where everything was permissible, came over me as I realised what game she and Charlie had played. 'You mean you have never——?' – her features twisted into a stare of disgusted incredulity. 'You have never——' she started again. I took time out by nuzzling her a little. 'Lay off, will you,' she said with a twangy whine, hastily removing her brown shoulder from my lips. (It was very curious the way she considered – and kept doing so for some time – all caresses except kisses on the mouth or the stark act of love either 'romantic slosh' or 'abnormal'.)

'You mean,' she persisted, now kneeling above me, 'you never did it when you were a kid?'

'Never,' I said quite truthfully.

'Okay,' said Lolita, 'here is where we start.'

ANAÏS NIN
(1903–1977)

Saffron

Anaïs Nin, critic, essayist, fiction-writer and (perhaps primarily) diarist, was born in France, but spent most of her later life in America. At one period of her life, with a number of friends, she needed money so badly (as she put it) that she devoted herself entirely to the writing of erotica, and 'became the Madame of an unusual house of literary prostitution.' Her erotic short stories, of which this is one, are accomplished enough to rise considerably above the pornographic.

Fay had been born in New Orleans. When she was sixteen she was courted by a man of forty whom she had always liked for his aristocracy and distinction. Fay was poor. Albert's visits were events to her family. For him their poverty was hastily disguised. He came very much like the liberator, talking about a life Fay had never known, at the other end of the city.

When they were married, Fay was installed like a princess in his house, which was hidden in an immense park. Handsome coloured women waited on her. Albert treated her with extreme delicacy.

The first night he did not take her. He maintained that this was proof of love, not to force oneself upon one's wife, but to woo her slowly and lingeringly, until she was prepared and in the mood to be possessed.

He came to her room and merely caressed her. They lay enveloped in the white mosquito netting as within a bridal veil, lay back in the hot night fondling and kissing. Fay felt languid and drugged. He was giving birth to a new woman with every kiss, exposing a new sensibility. Afterwards, when he left her, she lay tossing and unable to sleep. It was as if he had started tiny fires under her skin, tiny currents which kept her awake.

She was exquisitely tormented in this manner for several nights. Being inexperienced, she did not try to bring about a complete embrace. She yielded to this profusion of kisses in her hair, on her neck, shoulders, arms, back, legs. . . . Albert took delight in kissing her until she moaned, as if he were now sure of having awakened a particular part of her flesh, and then his mouth moved on.

from *Little Birds*

He discovered the trembling sensibility under the arm, at the nascence of the breasts, the vibrations that ran between the nipples and the sex, and between the sex mouth and the lips, all the mysterious links that roused and stirred places other than the one being kissed, currents running from the roots of the hair to the roots of the spine. Each place he kissed he worshipped with adoring words, observing the dimples at the end of her back, the firmness of her buttocks, the extreme arch of her back, which threw her buttocks outwards – 'like a coloured woman's,' he said.

He encircled her ankles with his fingers, lingered over her feet, which were perfect like her hands, stroked over and over again the smooth statuesque lines of her neck, lost himself in her long heavy hair.

Her eyes were long and narrow like those of a Japanese woman, her mouth full, always half-open. Her breasts heaved as he kissed her and marked her shoulder's sloping line with his teeth. And then as she moaned, he left her, closing the white netting around her carefully, encasing her like a treasure, leaving her with the moisture welling up between her legs.

One night, as usual, she could not sleep. She sat up in her clouded bed, naked. As she rose to look for her kimono and slippers a tiny drop of honey fell from her sex, rolled down her leg, stained the white rug. Fay was baffled at Albert's control, his reserve. How could he subdue his desire and sleep after these kisses and caresses? He had not even completely undressed. She had not seen his body.

She decided to leave her room and walk until she could become calm again. Her entire body was throbbing. She walked slowly down the wide staircase and out into the garden. The perfume of the flowers almost stunned her. The branches fell languidly over her and the mossy paths made her footsteps absolutely silent. She had the feeling that she was dreaming. She walked aimlessly for a long while. And then a sound startled her. It was a moan, a rhythmic moan like a woman's complaining. The light from the moon fell there between the branches and exposed a coloured woman lying naked on the moss and Albert over her. Her moans were moans of pleasure. Albert was crouching like a wild animal and pounding against her. He, too, was uttering confused cries; and Fay saw them convulsed under her very eyes by the violent joys.

Neither one saw Fay. She did not cry out. The pain at first

paralysed her. Then she ran back to the house, filled with all the humility of her youth, of her inexperience; she was tortured with doubts of herself. Was it her fault? What had she lacked, what had she failed to do to please Albert? Why had he had to leave her and go to the coloured woman? The savage scene haunted her. She blamed herself for falling under the enchantment of his caresses and perhaps not acting as he wanted her to. She felt condemned by her own femininity.

Albert could have taught her. He had said he was wooing her . . . waiting. He had only to whisper a few words. She was ready to obey. She knew he was older and she innocent. She had expected to be taught.

That night Fay became a woman, making a secret of her pain, intent on saving her happiness with Albert, on showing wisdom and subtlety. When he lay at her side she whispered to him, 'I wish you would take your clothes off.'

He seemed startled, but he consented. Then she saw his youthful, slim body at her side, with his very white hair gleaming, a curious mingling of youth and age. He began to kiss her. As he did so her hand timidly moved towards his body. At first she was frightened. She touched his chest. Then his hips. He continued to kiss her. Her hand reached for his penis, slowly. He made a movement away from it. It was soft. He moved away and began to kiss her between the legs. He was whispering over and over again the same phrase, 'You have the body of an angel. It is impossible that such a body should have a sex. You have the body of an angel.'

Then anger swept over Fay like a fever, an anger at his moving his penis away from her hand. She sat up, her hair wild about her shoulders, and said, 'I am not an angel, Albert. I am a woman. I want you to love me as a woman.'

Then came the saddest night Fay had ever known, because Albert tried to possess her and he couldn't. He led her hands to caress him. His penis would harden, he would begin to place it between her legs, and then it would wilt in her hands.

He was tense, silent. She could see the torment on his face. He tried many times. He would say, 'Just wait a little while, just wait.' He said this so humbly, so gently. Fay lay there, it seemed to her, for the whole of the night, wet, desirous, expectant, and all night he made half finished assaults on her, failing, retreating, kissing her as if in atonement. Then Fay sobbed.

This scene was repeated for two or three nights, and then Albert no longer came to her room.

And almost every day Fay saw shadows in the garden, shadows embracing. She was afraid to move from her room. The house was completely carpeted and noiseless, and as she walked up the stairs once she caught sight of Albert climbing behind one of the coloured girls and running his hand under her voluminous skirt.

Fay became obsessed with the sounds of the moaning. It seemed to her that she heard it continuously. Once she went to the coloured girls' rooms, which were in a separate little house, and listened. She could hear the moans she had heard in the park. She broke into tears. A door opened. It was not Albert who came out but one of the colored gardeners. He found Fay sobbing there.

Eventually Albert took her, under the most unusual circumstances. They were going to give a party for Spanish friends. Although she seldom shopped, Fay went to the city to get a particular saffron for the rice, a very extraordinary brand that had just arrived on a ship from Spain. She enjoyed buying the saffron, freshly unloaded. She had always liked smells, the smells of the wharves, and warehouses. When the little packages of saffron were handed to her, she tucked them in her bag, which she carried against her breast, under her arm. The smell was powerful, it seeped into her clothes, her hands, her very body.

When she arrived home Albert was waiting for her. He came towards the car and lifted her out of it, playfully, laughing. As he did so, she brushed with her full weight against him and he exclaimed, 'You smell of saffron!'

She saw a curious brilliance in his eyes, as he pressed his face against her breasts, smelling her. Then he kissed her. He followed her into her bedroom, where she threw her bag on the bed. The bag opened. The smell of saffron filled the room. Albert made her lie on the bed fully dressed, and without kisses or caresses, took her.

Afterwards he said happily, 'You smell like a coloured woman.' And the spell was broken.

VIOLETTE LEDUC
(1907–1972)

I Can See the World

Violette Leduc was born in Faucon, and was a writer preoccupied largely with physical ugliness, illegitimacy, and sexual nonconformity – all of which were elements of her own life. She was 'discovered' by Simone de Beauvoir, who persuaded Albert Camus to publish her novel *L'Asphyxie*. She was perhaps best known for two autobiographical novels, *La Folie en tête* and *La Bâtarde*, from which the following extract is taken. The scene is a school dormitory.

I reached my muslin curtain, following the nightly routine. An iron hand seized me and led me elsewhere. Isabelle threw me down on to her bed and buried her face in my underclothes.

'Come back when they're asleep,' she said.

She drove me out again, she chained me to her.

I was in love: there was nowhere I could hide. There would be only the respites between our meetings.

Isabelle was coughing as she sat up in bed, Isabelle was ready beneath her shawl of hair. The picture I was going back to paralysed me. I collapsed on to my chair, then on to the rug: the picture followed me everywhere.

I undressed in the half darkness, I pressed my chaste hand against my flesh, I breathed, I recognised my existence, I yielded myself. I piled up the silence at the bottom of my basin, I wrang it out as I wrang out my flannel, I spread it gently over my skin as I wiped myself.

The monitor put out the light in her room. Isabelle coughed again: she was calling to me. I decided that if I didn't close my tin of dentifrice I would remember what everything was like before I went to Isabelle in her room. I was preparing a past for myself.

'Are you ready?' whispered Isabelle on the other side of my curtain.

She was gone again.

I opened the window of my cell. The night and the sky wanted no part of us. To live in the open air meant soiling everything outside. Our absence was necessary for the beauty of the evening trees. I risked my head in the aisle, but the aisle forced me back. Their sleep frightened me: I hadn't the courage to step over the sleeping girls, to walk with my bare feet over their faces. I closed the window again and the curtain shivered, like the leaves outside.

'Are you coming?'

I turned on my torch: her hair was falling as I had imagined it, but I had not foreseen her nightgown swollen with that bold simplicity. Isabelle went away again.

I went into her cubicle with my torch.

'Take off your nightgown and put out the light. . . .'

I put out her hair, her eyes, her hands. I stripped off my nightgown. It was nothing new: I was stripping off the night of every first love.

'What are you doing?' Isabelle asked.

'I'm dawdling.'

She stifled her laughter in the bed as I posed naked in my shyness for the shadows.

'What are you doing, for heaven's sake?'

I slid into the bed. I had been cold, now I would be warm.

I stiffened, I was afraid of brushing against her hair beneath the bed-clothes. She took hold of me, she pulled me on top of her: Isabelle wanted our skins to merge. I chanted with my body over hers, I bathed my belly in the lilies of her belly. I sank into a cloud. She touched me lightly on the buttocks, she sent strange arrows through my flesh. I pulled away, I fell back.

We listened to what was happening inside us, to the emanations from our bodies: we were ringed around with other couples. The bed springs gave a groan.

'Careful!' she said against my mouth.

The monitor had switched on her light. I was kissing a little girl with a mouth that tasted of vanilla. We had become good little girls again.

'Let's squeeze each other,' Isabelle said.

We tightened the girdles that were all we had in the world.

'Crush me. . . .'

She wanted to but she couldn't. She ground my buttocks with her fingers.

'Don't listen to her,' she said.

The monitor was urinating in her toilet pail. Isabelle was rubbing

[195]

her toe against my ankle as a token of friendship.

'She's asleep again,' Isabelle said.

I took Isabelle by the mouth, I was afraid of the monitor, I drank our saliva. It was an orgy of dangers. We had felt the darkness in our mouths and throats, then we had felt peace return.

'Crush me,' she said.

'The bed . . . it will make a noise . . . they'll hear us . . .'

We talked amid the crowding leaves of summer nights.

I was crushing, blotting out, thousands of tiny cells beneath my weight.

'Am I too heavy?'

'You'll never be too heavy. I feel cold,' she said.

My fingers considered her icy shoulders. I flew away, I snatched up in my beak the tufts of wool caught on thorns along the hedgerows and laid them one by one on Isabelle's shoulders. I tapped at her bones with downy hammers, my kisses tumbling one on top of another as I flung myself onward through an avalanche of tenderness. My hands relieved my failing lips; I moulded the sky around her shoulders. Isabelle rose, fell back, and I fell with her into the hollow of her shoulder. My cheek came to rest on a curve.

'My darling.'

I said it over and over.

'Yes,' Isabelle said.

She said: 'Just a minute,' and paused.

'Just a minute,' Isabelle said again.

She was tying back her hair, her elbow fanned my face.

The hand alighted on my neck: a frosty sun whitened my hair. The hand followed my veins, downward. The hand stopped. My blood beat against the mount of Venus on Isabelle's palm. The hand moved up again: it was drawing circles, overflowing into the void, spreading its sweet ripples ever wider around my left shoulder, while the other lay abandoned to the zebra night striped by the breathing of the other girls. I was discovering the velvet of my bones, the glow hidden in my flesh, the infinity of forms I possessed. The hand was trailing a mist of dreams across my skin. The heavens beg when someone strokes your shoulder: the heavens were begging now. The hand moved upward once again, spreading a velvet shawl up to my chin, then down once more, persuasively, heavier now, shaping itself to the curves it pressed upon. Finally there was a squeeze of friendship. I took Isabelle into my arms, gasping with gratitude.

'Can you see me?' Isabelle asked.

'I see you.'

She stopped me from saying more, slid down in the bed, and kissed my curly hairs.

'Listen, horses!' a girl cried nearby.

'Don't be afraid. She's dreaming. Give me your hand,' Isabelle said.

I was weeping for joy.

'Are you crying?' she asked anxiously.

'I love you: I'm not crying.'

I wiped my eyes.

Her hand undressed my arm, halted near the vein in the crook of the elbow, fornicated there among the traceries, moved downward to the wrist, right to the tips of the nails, sheathed my arm once more in a long suède glove, fell from my shoulder like an insect, and hooked itself into the armpit. I was stretching my neck, listening for what answers my arm gave the adventuress. The hand, still seeking to persuade me, was bringing my arm, my armpit, into their real existence. The hand travelled over the chatter of white bushes, over the last frosts on the meadows, over the first buds as they swelled to fullness. Spring that had been chirping with impatience under my skin was now bursting forth into lines, curves, roundnesses. Isabelle, stretched out upon the darkness, was fastening my feet with ribbons, unravelling the swaddling bands of my alarm. With hands laid flat upon the mattress, I was immersed in the self-same magic as she. She was kissing what she had caressed, and then, lightly, her hand ruffled and whisked with the feathers of perversity. The octopus in my entrails quivered. Isabelle was drinking at my breast, the right, the left, and I drank with her, sucking the milk of darkness when her lips had gone. The fingers were returning now, encircling and testing the warm weight of my breast. The fingers were pretending to be waifs in a storm; they were taking shelter inside me. A host of slaves, all with the face of Isabelle, fanned my brow, my hands.

She knelt up in the bed.

'Do you love me?'

I led her hand up to the precious tears of joy.

Her cheek took shelter in the hollow of my groin, I shone the torch on her, and saw her spreading hair, saw my own belly beneath the rain of silk. The torch slipped, Isabelle moved suddenly toward me.

As we melted into one another we were dragged up to the surface by the hooks caught in our flesh, by the hairs we were clutching in our fingers; we were rolling together on a bed of nails. We bit each other and bruised the darkness with our hands.

Slowing down, we trailed back beneath our plumes of smoke, black wings sprouting at our heels. Isabelle leaped out of bed.

I wondered why Isabelle was doing her hair again. With one hand she forced me to lie on my back, with the other, to my distress, she shone the pale yellow beam of the torch on me.

I tried to shield myself with my arms.

'I'm not beautiful. You make me feel ashamed,' I said.

She was looking at our future in my eyes, she was gazing at what was going to happen next, storing it in the currents of her blood.

She got back into bed, she wanted me.

I played with her, preferring failure to the preliminaries she needed. Making love with our mouths was enough for me: I was afraid, but my hands as they signalled for help were helpless stumps. A pair of paint brushes was advancing into the folds of my flesh. My heart was beating under its molehill, my head was crammed with damp earth. Two tormenting fingers were exploring me. How masterly, how inevitable their caress. . . . My closed eyes listened: the finger lightly touched the pearl. I wanted to be wider, to make it easier for her.

The regal, diplomatic finger was moving forward, moving back, making me gasp for breath, beginning to enter, arousing the tentacles in my entrails, parting the secret cloud, pausing, prompting once more. I tightened, I closed over this flesh of my flesh, its softness and its bony core. I sat up, I fell back again. The finger which had not wounded me, the finger, after its grateful exploration, left me. My flesh peeled back from it.

'Do you love me?' I asked.

I wanted to create a diversion.

'You mustn't cry out,' Isabelle said.

I crossed my arms over my face, still listening under my lowered eyelids.

from *La Bâtarde*

Two thieves entered me. They were forcing their way inside, they wanted to go further, but my flesh rebelled.

'My love . . . you're hurting me.'

She put her hand over my mouth.

'I won't make any noise,' I said.

The gag was a humiliation.

'It hurts. But she's got to do it. It hurts.'

I gave myself up to the darkness and without wanting to, I helped. I leaned forward to help tear myself, to come closer to her face, to be nearer my wound: she pushed me back on the pillow.

She was thrusting, thrusting, thrusting. . . . I could hear the smacking noise it made. She was putting out the eye of innocence. It hurt me: I was moving on to my deliverance, but I couldn't see what was happening.

We listened to the sleeping girls around us, we sobbed as we sucked in our breath. A trail of fire still burned inside me.

'Let's rest,' she said.

My memories of the two thieves grew kinder, my wounded flesh began to heal, bubbles of love were rising. But Isabelle returned to her task now, and the thieves were turning faster, ever faster. Where did this great wave come from? Smoothly now, into the depths. The drug flowed down toward my feet, my dreaming flesh lay steeped in visions. I lost myself with Isabelle in our pathetic gymnastics.

A great pleasure seemed to begin. It was only a reflection. Slow fingers left me. I was hungry, avid for her presence.

'Your hand, your face. Come closer.'

'I'm tired.'

Make her come closer, make her give me her shoulder, make her face be close to mine. I must barter my innocence for hers. She is not breathing: she is resting. Isabelle coughed as though she were coughing in a library.

I raised myself up with infinite precautions, I felt new-made. My sex, my clearing, and my bath of dew.

I switched on the torch. I glimpsed the blood, I glimpsed the red hair. I switched it off.

The rustling of the shadows at three in the morning sent a cold shudder through me. The night would pass, the night would soon be nothing but tears.

I shone the torch, I was not afraid of my open eyes.

'I can see the world. It all comes out of you.'

The dawn trailing its shrouds. Isabelle was combing her hair in a limbo of her own, a no-man's land, where her hair was always hanging loose.

'I don't want the day to come,' Isabelle said.

It is coming, it will come. The day will shatter the night beneath its wheels.

'I'm afraid of being away from you,' Isabelle said.

A tear fell in my garden at three in the morning.

I would not let myself think a single thought, so that she could go to sleep in my empty head. The day was advancing through the dark, the day was erasing our wedding night. Isabelle was going to sleep.

'Sleep,' I said beside the flowering hawthorn that had waited for the dawn all night.

Like a traitor, I got out of the bed and went to the window. There had been a battle high up in the sky and its aftermath was chill. The mists were beating a retreat. Aurora was alone, with no one to usher her in. Already there were clusters of birds in a tree, pecking at her first beams . . . I looked out at the half-mourning of the new day, at the tatters of the night, and smiled at them. I smiled at Isabelle and pressed my forehead against hers, pretending we were fighting rams. That way I would forget what I knew was dying. The lyric downpour from the birds as they sang and crystallised the beauty of the morning brought only fatigue: perfection is not of this world even when we meet it here.

'You must go,' Isabelle said.

Leaving her like a pariah, leaving her furtively made me feel sad too. I had iron balls chained to my feet. Isabelle offered me her grief-stricken face. I loved Isabelle without a gesture, without any token of my passion: I offered her my life without a sign.

Isabelle pushed herself up and took me in her arms.

'You'll come every night?'

'Every night.'

JEAN GENET
(1910–   )

Armand and Robert

Genet, born illegitimate in Paris, never knew his parents, and was brought up in a state orphanage. At the age of ten he was first discovered thieving, and for thirty years wandered about Europe, finding himself imprisoned by the police of almost every country he visited. After ten convictions for theft in France, he was sentenced to life imprisonment, and only released after a petition signed by a group of distinguished French writers, led by Jean Cocteau. While in prison, he wrote his novel *Our Lady of the Flowers*; he also wrote three wellknown plays, *The Maids*, *The Blacks* and *The Balcony*. The following extract is from *The Thief's Journal*, first published in France in 1949.

I saw [Armand] in Sylvia's room. When I entered, Stilitano told him at once that I was French and that we had met in Spain. Armand was standing up. He did not offer me his hand, but he looked at me. I remained near the window without seeming to pay any attention to them. When they decided to go to the bar, Stilitano said to me, 'Are you coming, Jean?'

Before I had a chance to answer, Armand asked, 'Do you usually take him along?'

Stilitano laughed and said, 'If it bothers you, we can leave him.'

'Oh, bring him along.'

I followed them. After having a drink, they separated, and Armand did not shake my hand. Stilitano said not a word about him to me. A few days later, when I met him near the docks, Armand ordered me to follow him. Almost without speaking he took me to his room. With the same apparent scorn, he subjected me to his pleasure.

Dominated by his strength and age, I gave the work my utmost care. Crushed by that mass of flesh, which was devoid of the slightest spirituality, I experienced the giddiness of finally meeting the perfect brute, indifferent to my happiness. I discovered the sweetness that could be contained in a thick fleece on torso, belly and thighs and what force it could transmit. I finally let myself be buried in that stormy night. Out of gratitude or fear I placed a kiss

[201]

on Armand's hairy arm.

'What's eating you? Are you nuts or something?'

'I didn't do any harm.'

I remained at his side in order to serve his nocturnal pleasure. When he went to bed, Armand whipped his leather belt from the loops of his trousers and made it snap. It was flogging an invisible victim, a shape of transparent flesh. The air bled. If he frightened me then, it was because of his powerlessness to be the Armand I see, who is heavy and mean. The snapping accompanied and supported him. His rage and despair at not being *him* made him tremble like a horse subdued by darkness, made him tremble *more and more*. He would not, however, have tolerated my living idly. He advised me to prowl around the station or the zoo and pick up customers. Knowing the terror inspired in me by his person, he didn't deign to keep an eye on me. The money I earned I brought back intact. He himself operated in the bars. He carried on various kinds of traffic with the dockers and seamen, who respected him. Like all the local pimps and hoodlums of the time, he wore sneakers. Being silent, his footstep was heavier and more elastic. Often he wore a pair of blue woollen sailor trousers, the flap of which was never completely buttoned, so that a triangle would hang down in front of him, or sometimes it was a slightly rolled pocket that he wore on his belly. No one had such a sinuous walk as he. I think that he slid along that way in order to recapture the memory of the body he had had as a twenty-year-old hoodlum, pimp and sailor. He was faithful to it, as one is to the fashions of one's youth. But, himself a figure of the most provocative eroticism, he wished also to express it by language and gesture. Accustomed to Stilitano's modesty and to the crudeness of the dockers in their bars, I was the witness of, often the pretext for proceedings which were the height of audacity. In front of anybody Armand would grow lyrical over his member. No one interrupted him. Unless some tough, annoyed by his tone and remarks, retorted.

'My cock,' he once said, 'is worth its weight in gold.'

'It's not heavy,' said a seaman.

'Heavier than that beer-mug you've got in your hand!'

'I doubt it.'

'You want to weigh them?'

'O.K.'

Bets were quickly laid, and Armand, who was already unbuttoned and had a stiff hard-on, put his prick on the seaman's flat
palm.

'The beer-mug,' he said.

At times, with his hand in his pocket, he would stroke himself as
he stood drinking at the bar. He would boast at other times that he
could lift a heavy man on the end of his cock. Not knowing what this
obsession with his member and strength corresponded to, I
admired him. In the street, though he would draw me to him with
his arm as if to embrace me, a brutal push of the same arm would
thrust me aside. Since I knew nothing about his life, except that he
had been around the world and that he was Flemish, I tried to
distinguish the signs of the penal colony from which he must have
escaped, bringing back with him that cropped skull, those heavy
muscles, his hypocrisy, his violence, his fierceness.

Meeting Armand was such a cataclysm that though I continued
to see Stilitano often, he seemed to move off from me in time and
space. It was long ago and far away that I had wedded this
youngster whose toughness, with its veil of irony, had suddenly
been transformed into a delicious gentleness. Never, during all the
time I lived with Armand, did Stilitano joke about us. His
discretion became delicately painful to me. He soon came to
represent Bygone Days.

Unlike Stilitano, Armand was not a coward. Not only did he not
refuse single combat, but he accepted dangerous jobs involving
force. He even dared conceive them and work out the details. A
week after our meeting, he told me that he would be gone for a while
and that I was to wait for him to return. He asked me to take care of
his belongings, a suitcase containing some linen, and he left. For a
few days I felt lighter, I no longer carried the weight of fear.
Stilitano and I went out together several times.

Had he not spat into his hands to turn a crank, I would not have
noticed a boy of my own age. This typical workman's gesture made
me so dizzy that I thought I was falling straight down to a period –
or region of myself – long since forgotten. My heart awoke, and at
once my body thawed. With wild speed and precision the boy
registered on me: his gestures, his hair, the jerk of his hips, the curve
of his back, the merry-go-round on which he was working, the
movement of the horses, the music, the fair-ground, the city of

Antwerp containing them, the Earth cautiously turning, the Universe protecting so precious a burden, and I standing there, frightened at possessing the world and at knowing I possessed it.

I did not see the spit on his hands: I recognised the puckering of the cheek and the tip of the tongue between his teeth. I again saw the boy rubbing his tough, black palms. As he bent down to grab the handle, I noticed his crackled, but thick leather belt. A belt of that kind could not be an ornament like the one that holds up the trousers of a man of fashion. By its material and thickness it was penetrated with the following function: holding up the most obvious sign of masculinity which, without the strap, would be nothing, would no longer contain, would no longer guard its manly treasure but would tumble down on the heels of a shackled male. The boy was wearing a windbreaker, between which and the trousers could be seen his skin. As the belt was not inserted into loops, at every movement it rose a bit as the trousers slid down. I stared at the belt, spellbound. I saw it operating surely. At the sixth jerk of the hips, it girdled – except at the fly where the two ends were buckled – the chap's bare back and waist.

'It's nice to see, huh?' said Stilitano.

Watching me watch, he spoke not of the merry-go-round but of its guardian spirit.

'Go tell him you like him. Go on.'

'Don't kid around.'

'I'm talking seriously.'

He was smiling. As neither my age nor bearing would have permitted me to approach or observe him with the light or amused arrogance assumed by distinguished-looking gentlemen, I wanted to go away. Stilitano grabbed me by the sleeve.

'Come on.'

I shook him off.

'Let me alone,' I said.

'I can see that you like him.'

'What of it?'

'What of it? Invite him for a drink.'

He smiled again, and said, 'Are you scared of Armand?'

'You're crazy.'

'Well? You want me to go up to him?'

Just at that moment, the boy stood upright, his face flushed and gleaming: he was a congested prick. As he adjusted his belt, he approached us. We were on the pavement and he was standing on the baseboards of the merry-go-round. Since we were looking at him, he smiled and said, 'That's a real workout.'

'It must make you thirsty,' said Stilitano. And turning to me he added, 'You going to treat us to a drink?'

Robert went with us to a café. The joyousness of the event and its simplicity set my head spinning. I was no longer at Robert's side, nor even at Stilitano's. I was scattering myself to all the corners of the world and I was registering a hundred details which burst into light stars, I no longer know which. . . .

DENTON WELCH
(1915–1948)

Animal Magic

Denton Welch was an art student when, at the age of twenty, he had an accident which made him an invalid for the rest of his life. His first publication, an autobiographical novel, *Maiden Voyage*, showed great promise, which to some extent was fulfilled in his short stories; tragically, his illness and early death precluded any real development of his talent, but his published work remains remarkable, and not least remarkable are his journals, a selection from which was published in 1952, and one entry from which follows.

14 December 1942, Monday

Suddenly I remember that afternoon by the river near Henfield. It must have been in the summer of 1933 when I was in a sort of disgrace with my aunt and grandfather because I had left China to go to an art school and *would not* 'settle down.' My aunt had said, 'If you want to study art, why don't you do some work? You should be sketching every day; instead of that, you wander in the fields doing nothing at all from morning till night.'

I left the house and wandered again as she had described, only this time I wandered on my bicycle and got as far as the river. It is a forgotten place, because the road-bridge was washed away a hundred years ago and now there is only a footbridge and a track across the fields.

I threw my bicycle into the hedge and started off across the tufty grass. In the winter, I thought, this will all be flooded. Now it was hot and heavenly with the scented, dried-up grass and a loneliness almost piercing.

I sat down on the bank where I had sometimes seen small boys bathing. The river was wide and deeper there and one could dive from the bridge.

I sat there nursing my solitude yet longing for somebody to talk to. And as I longed, I saw approaching from the old farm-house on the opposite bank, a brown figure – almost the colour of the landscape – that sort of worn, lichen, olive green-brown.

It crossed the bridge and walked along the bank in my direction. While he was still some way off I saw that his hair was of that pale, 'washed' gold, because it suddenly glinted in the sun as if it were metal.

He came up to me coolly, with the loose, bent-kneed stride of someone used to walking over rough fields.

'Thinking of going in?' he said pleasantly and in an unexpectedly 'educated' voice.

I was so pleased at this sudden appearance and so curious that I looked him straight in the face and smiled. He smiled back.

I saw the gold hair, untidy and rough, gold eyebrows too, sunburnt chestnut skin and the vivid brick-dust cheeks and lips which framed the almond-white teeth. Not distinguished or handsome – the ears were thick, all the details unfinished, yet the skin, the teeth, the eyes, the hair had that wonderful, shorter-than-springtime, polished, shining look as of some liquid or varnish of life spread over the whole body. The shirt and the breeches were the colour of the mud and the cow-dung caked on them. By their dullness and drabness they stimulated one's imagination so that one could almost feel the tingling fire and coolness of the body they sheathed.

'Lusty' and 'rough' were the words that flooded through me as I looked at him. In their right sense they fitted him perfectly. As you can see I was extremely impressed by him. He must have been a few years older than I was and my capacity for hero-worship was enormous at that time. It still is. He was all that I was not – stalwart, confident and settled into a 'manly' life.

The only thing I could not quite understand was the 'educated' voice. It struck a slightly jarring note, yet made communication much easier and more 'natural'. I started the eternal game of placing people and fitting them into their right pigeon-hole. He could not be ordinary 'gentry'. Nobody would wear quite such dirty clothes or such hob-nailed boots unless they were *really* working. Besides, he had come, as if from home, from that ancient farmhouse which, by its untouched appearance where no single beam was exposed, proved that no 'improver' had been near it since the eighteenth century.

On the other hand he could not be an ordinary farm-hand. I was just deciding that perhaps he was the farmer's ambitiously educated son, when he stopped all my dreary surmises by saying that he was down here learning farming – at least I think he said this, but I am not absolutely sure for at that moment he started undressing.

With the words, 'If there are any women round here they'll get an eyeful!' he started to pull his shirt over his head. I was shocked at the whiteness of the skin on his chest and upper arms when he stood up in only his trousers. They were junket-white, but matt, as if powdered with oatmeal. The long gloves of his burnt arms and hands and the bronze helmet of his face and neck joining this whiteness, did something curious to me. I could only gape and wonder as he stripped his wonderful body. He unlaced his boots and kicked them off, then peeled down his thick and sweat-sticky stockings. The breeches he pulled off roughly, and stood revealed with the gold hair glinting on his body as well as on his head.

As I say, I could only watch. This was not just an ordinary man taking off his clothes for a swim – and yet it was. It was this prosaic, mundane quality and the bubbling-up spring of some poetry which held me enthralled.

He flung back his hair with the gesture which is considered girlish when used by effeminate men. (When used by others it has, of course, a quite different effect.) Then he dived into the muddy water and came up spitting and laughing. 'Bloody filthy water,' he shouted, and spluttered, 'bloody filthy water, but it's lovely.'

He stood up near the bank, so that the water gartered his legs round the middle of his calves. The hairs on his body and legs dripped like sparkles of water. He looked like a truncated statue fixed to a base in the bowl of a fountain.

He whirled his arms round, dived, and swam about for some time; then he crawled up the bank and lay down beside me on the grass. As he lay with his face to the sky and his eyes shut I watched the rivulets coursing off his body. The main stream flowed down his chest, between the hard pectorals, over the mushroom-smooth belly, to be lost in curly gold hair. I could just descry the quicksilver drops weaving a painful way through the golden bush.

He opened his eyes and saw me staring at him; he didn't seem to mind. He sat up and started to rub his arms and chest brutally with a dirty towel.

'I'm working down here at the moment. What do you do?' he asked, abruptly but without giving offence.

[208]

'I, I'm at an art school,' I got out with difficulty. The shame and fear of sinking in his estimation were very real.

'Oh – my sister's a very clever artist, too,' he said confidently. 'She's been studying for some time and has got a scholarship. She's going abroad.'

He continued talking about his sister and his family. I got the impression, perhaps wrongly, that he was a little in disgrace too. This thrilled me. I felt I had found a brother. When he talked of being drunk and brawling, I was tremendously impressed and horrified – to be so cool and casual about it all! Then I had the fear that the beer would decay his teeth or that they would be knocked out in the fights. This caused me the sort of pain one feels when some beautifully-made and intricate thing is threatened.

He asked me what I had been doing all my holidays and I told him that I had been for one walking tour down to Devonshire and would soon be going for another, as my aunt obviously did not want me at my grandfather's.

'I'd like to do that too,' he said decisively. 'I'd like to go abroad, walking and paying my way wherever I went. My parents wouldn't give me anything, you see,' he added in explanation.

'I wouldn't like to go alone, though,' he mused.

Thoughts, hopes, fears were all seething together in my head. The idea was too exciting to be considered seriously. Here, I longed to step in and say that I would go with him whenever he wanted to go, but I was much too clearsighted not to see the difficulties of money and also of temperament. I felt that I would fall short of his daring and careless sense of power. When I would be tired or timid, he would be vigorous and scornful, and when he would be drunken and brawling I would be frankly alarmed and irritated.

'I'd like to do that too,' I said. 'Fine if we could go together some time,' I added boldly.

If there had been the slightest reluctance I would have been ashamed, but he took me perfectly seriously, saying:

'I wonder if we could ever fix it up.'

We exchanged names. He pulled on his khaki shirt and caked breeches and lost some of his magic, thus becoming more comfortable.

I knew that I would never go with him. I felt cowardly for not *making* it happen in some way.

He held out his hand and I shook it, wondering as I felt the horn on his palm.

'You can always get hold of me there,' he said, pointing to the farm-house; then he turned and walked back along the banks.

I watched him the whole way. The legs and the shoulders and the dirty towel swung in rhythm until he passed through the little gate into the garden.

At the last sight of him I felt unbearably angry and frustrated. I jumped up and ran over the tussocks. I jerked my bicycle out of the hedge and pedalled viciously, cursing God and everybody, pouring scorn and pity in a deluge all over myself.

Now stranger, whose name I have quite forgotten – where are you now? Even if you are not dead in battle, that 'You' is dead and nowhere, for at most it could only have lasted a year or two – that animal magic.

'PAULINE RÉAGE'

Ownership

When *Story of O* first began to circulate as an underground book in Paris in 1954, it was realised that Pauline Réage was a pseudonym. The true authorship of what has been called the best modern pornographic novel remains one of the best-kept of all literary secrets. A chorus of praise greeted its official publication in the relaxed era of the 1970s. It is a work of the utmost violence, and in its intense descriptions of the sadistic and masochistic elements in men, and to even a greater extent in women, has the air of a fable. In the scene which follows, Sir Stephen, the English peer to whom O's *fiancé* has 'given' her, takes her to a cottage on the edge of the forest of Fontainebleau, where his friend Anne-Marie has been entrusted with the task of performing certain operations upon her.

Three other girls lived in the house, each of them had a room on the second floor; the one O was assigned to was on the ground floor, next to Anne-Marie's. Anne-Marie called to the girls, shouting to them to come down to the garden. All three, like O, were naked. In this house of women, carefully hidden by the high walls of the park, and on the side facing a dirt lane by shuttered windows, only Anne-Marie and her servants wore clothing: a cook and two housemaids, older than Anne-Marie, severe in their black alpaca skirts and starched aprons. 'Her name is O,' said Anne-Marie, who had resumed her place on the couch. 'Bring her here, I want to have a closer look at her.' Two of the girls – both brunettes, their hair as dark as the fleece on their sexes, their nipples long and almost violet – helped O to her feet. The other girl was small, chubby, had red hair, and below the almost chalky skin on her chest showed a frightful network of greenish veins. The two girls pushed O almost on top of Anne-Marie who pointed a finger at the three dark zig-zagging stripes on the front of her thighs, welts which were repeated on her buttocks. 'Who whipped you?' she asked. 'Sir Stephen?' 'Yes,' said O. 'With what and when?' 'Three days ago, with a crop.' 'Beginning tomorrow, you'll not be whipped for a month. But you will be today, to designate your arrival, and as soon as I've finished examining you. Sir Stephen has never whipped the inside of your thighs, your legs spread wide apart? No? I dare say not. Men never know. Well, we'll attend to all that in due time. Now show me your waist. Ah, that's better, isn't it?' Anne-Marie kneaded O's smooth waist, pressed with her thumbs, then she sent the little red-head to fetch another corset, and then had it put on O. It too was made of black nylon, so stoutly whaleboned and so narrow that one would have called it a wide leather belt. No garter straps were attached to it. One of the dark-haired girls laced it, and Anne-Marie ordered her to draw it as tight as she possibly could. 'This is terrible,' O said, 'it hurts terribly.' 'Exactly,' said Anne-Marie, 'and that is why you are much more lovely now. But you didn't tighten yours enough. From now on you'll wear this one this way, every day. Tell me now how Sir Stephen preferred to use you. I need to know.' She had gripped the fingers of one hand in O's womb, and O could not reply. Two of the girls had seated themselves on the ground, the third girl, one of the dark-haired ones, at the foot of Anne-Marie's chaise-longue. 'You,' she said, 'turn her around, let me see her behind.' O was turned around, her behind was presented to Anne-Marie, and the two girls pried it open. 'Of course,' Anne-Marie said, 'You've no need to reply. You'll have to be marked there, on the buttocks. Get up. We'll put on your bracelets. Colette will bring the box, we'll draw lots to see who's to do the whipping; Colette, go get the box and bring the disks. Then we'll go into the music room.' Colette was the taller of the two brunettes, the other was named Claire, the little red-head Yvonne. O had not hitherto noticed that they all three wore, as at Roissy, a leather collar and wristbands, and, as well, similar bands at the ankles. When Yvonne had selected suitable bracelets for O and put them on her, Anne-Marie handed O four numbered metal disks, inviting her not to look at the numbers and to give one to each of them without looking at the numbers. O distributed the disks. Each of the three girls looked at her, no one spoke, waiting for Anne-Marie to speak. 'I have two,' said Anne-Marie; 'who has one?' Colette had one. 'Take O away, she's yours.' Colette seized O's arms, brought her hands round behind her back, fastened the two wristbands together, and pushed her ahead of her. At the threshold of a French door which opened into a little wing forming an L with the main part of the building, Yvonne, who was preceding them, removed O's sandals. The French window admitted light into a room which, at the back, was a raised rotunda;

the ceiling, a shallow cupola, was supported, at the entrance to the
apse-like circular niche, by two slender columns spaced about two
yards apart. On the floor of the niche was a platform, four steps led
up to it, and like the rest of the room, it was covered with red felt
carpeting. The walls were white, the French door curtains red, the
curved divans rimming the inside of the niche were upholstered in
the same red felt on the floor. In the rectangular part of the room,
which was wider than it was deep, there was a fireplace and opposite
this a large cabinet radio phonograph; to left and right, arranged in
shelves, was a record library. By a door near the fireplace it
communicated directly with Anne-Marie's bedroom. The sym-
metrical door, being unframed, resembled the door to a closet.
Except for the divans and the radio phonograph, the room was bare
of furniture. While Colette had O sit down on the edge of the
platform – which, at the centre, was more similar to a stage, the
steps being to right and left of the columns – the two other girls
closed the French door after having drawn the curtains about a
third of the way. Surprised, O then noticed that it was a double door
and Anne-Marie, who was laughing, said: 'Why, by all means,
there's no reason to let the whole neighbourhood hear your
screams. The walls, you will observe, are padded – nothing of what
goes on here can be heard outside. Lie down.' She grasped her
shoulders, thrust her down upon the red felt, then drew her a little
way forward; O's hands clawed at the edge of the stage – she was
about to fall – Yvonne fastened each of them to a ring, and her flanks
were thus suspended over space. Anne-Marie made her double her
knees up against her chest, then O felt her legs put under a sudden
tension and drawn in the same direction: straps had been slipped
through the eyes in her ankle-bands and hooked to other eyes half-
way up the columns, she was drawn somewhat in the air and
exposed in such a manner that the only visible parts of her were the
cracks in her belly and behind, drawn violently open. Anne-Marie
caressed the inside of her thighs. 'This is the part of the body where
the skin is softest,' she said, 'don't spoil it, Colette. Go easy.' Colette
was standing, straddling her waist, and through the bridge formed
by her sunburned legs O saw the cords of the whip she was holding.
At the first strokes, which burned her belly, O moaned. Colette,
after striking to the right, shifted to the left, stopped, began again. O
struggled with all her might, she believed that the straps were going

to cut through her skin. She did not want to plead, she did not want to beg to be spared. But Anne-Marie intended to drive her to that, to begging and pleading. 'Faster,' she told Colette, 'and harder.' O's body stiffened, she braced herself, but in vain. A minute later she gave way to tears and screams, while Anne-Marie caressed her face. 'Just a little more,' she said, 'and then it will be all over. Just five minutes more. You can scream for five minutes, can't you? Surely. It's twenty-five past. Colette, you'll stop at half-past, when I tell you.' But O screamed no, no, for God's sake no, she couldn't bear it any longer, no, she couldn't stand this another second. However, she did have to stand it until the end and, at half-past, Anne-Marie smiled at her. Colette left the stage. 'Thank me,' Anne-Marie said to O, and O thanked her. She knew very well why Anne-Marie had judged it above all else necessary to have her whipped. That a woman was so cruel, and more implacable than a man, O had never once doubted. But O had thought that Anne-Marie was seeking less to manifest her power than to establish a complicity between O and herself. O had never understood, but had finally come to recognise as an undeniable and very meaningful truth, the contradictory but constant entanglement of her feelings and attitudes: she liked the idea of torture, when she underwent it she would have seen the earth go up in fire and smoke to escape it, when it was over with she was happy to have undergone it, and all the happier the crueller and more prolonged it had been. Anne-Marie had correctly calculated upon O's acquiescence and revolt, and knew very well that her pleadings for mercy had been genuine and her final thanks authentic. There was a third reason for what she had done, and she explained it to O. She felt it important to make each girl who entered her house and who thus entered an entirely feminine society, sense that her condition as a woman would not lose its importance from the fact that, here, her only contacts would be with other women, but to the contrary, would be increased, heightened, intensified. It was for this reason she required the girls to be naked at all times; the manner in which O had been flogged, as well as the position in which she had been tied, had the same purpose. Today, it would be O who would remain for the rest of the afternoon – for three more hours – with her legs spread and raised, exposed upon the platform and facing the garden. She would have the incessant desire to close her legs; it would be thwarted. Tomorrow, it would be Claire and Colette, or again Yvonne, whom from *Story of O*

O would watch in her turn. The process was far too gradual, far too minute (as, likewise, this manner of applying the whip), to be used at Roissy. But O would discover how effective it was. Apart from the rings and the insignia she would wear, upon her departure, and restored to Sir Stephen, she would find herself much more openly and profoundly a slave than she could imagine possible.

'JEAN DE BERG'

The Photographs

'Jean de Berg' published *The Image* in Paris in 1956, and dedicated it to 'Pauline Réage', the author of the most famous modern pornographic novel, *Story of O*. Mlle Réage, in a Foreword, speculated on the author's possible identity: it might be, she thought, that he was male, though the fact that the narrator of the story is a man might also conceal the fact that the author was a woman, for the book seemed to her to have a basically feminine drive: 'Even chained, down on her knees, begging for mercy, it is the woman, finally, who is in command.' The story is of a man who is introduced by a friend, Claire, to a young model, Anne, who he finds pleasure in subjugating. In the following extract he describes the photographs of Anne which Claire shows him.

In the first one, Anne is wearing a short black slip with nothing underneath but her stockings and a simple garter belt like the one I already admired in the Bagatelle Gardens. But these stockings do not have embroidered tops.

She is standing next to a column . . . and instead of the dress she only has the slip whose thin material she is holding up with both hands, exposing the half-opened thighs and the triangle of her fleece. One leg is straight, the other slightly bent at the knee, the foot only half resting on the floor.

A lace inset decorates the top of the slip, but one can't really make it out because it is pulled to one side, the right shoulder strap not being on at all and the left one having fallen off the shoulder. The black lingerie is thus twisted around, covering half of one breast, and freeing the other breast almost entirely. The breasts are perfect, not too full, far enough apart, with the brown halo that encircles the nipple clearly marked but not too large. The arms are well-rounded and gracefully curved.

The face, under the loose curls, is a real triumph: the eyes consenting, the lips parted, a mingled look of ingénue charm and submissiveness.

The lighting, while accentuating the shadows, softens the lines as it defines them. The light is coming from a Gothic window with austere vertical bars, a part of which can be seen in the background at the edge of the picture. The column in the foreground is of stone, as is the window frame, and is about the same width as the girl's hips next to it. Beyond it, at the other edge of the picture, one can see the edge of an iron bed. The floor is a checkerboard pattern of very large black and white squares.

The second picture, taken closer up, encompasses the bed. It is a single iron bed painted black, stripped of blankets. The sheets are in a state of great disorder. The ironwork of the two upright posts, at the head and foot, is ornate and oldfashioned: metal stems curving and twisting in spirals held together by lighter-coloured rings, probably gilded.

The girl is in the same costume lying across the bed on the rumpled sheets. She is flat on her stomach but turned a little, one hip higher than the other. Her face is buried in the pillows, her dishevelled hair spread over it; her right arm, bent upward, frames her head; the left arm, at an angle to her body, extends in the direction of the wall. On this side, without the shoulder strap, one can just see the beginning of a breast under the armpit.

The slip is again amply pulled up, this time in the back, needless to say. The buttocks are rounded and full, highly evocative. Their firm shape points up some pretty dimples brought into play by the asymmetry of her position. The thighs are opened to a hollow of darkness. The left knee, bent way up, disappears under a fold of the sheets while the foot touches the extended right leg.

The picture is taken from fairly high up so as to display the buttocks in the most accomodating position.

In the next one the girl is entirely naked, hands chained behind her back, kneeling on the black and white checkerboard floor. The picture is taken in profile and also from above. One sees nothing but the girl, kneeling naked on the floor, and the whip.

Her head is lowered. Her hair falls on either side of her face, hiding it, exposing her neck which is bent down as far as it will go. The tip of one breast appears below the shoulder. The thighs are together, leaning backward, and the trunk is bent forward in a way that makes the buttocks protrude most fetchingly as they await their punishment. The wrists are bound together at the back, at waist height, by a slender chain of shiny material.

A similar chain ties the ankles one against the other. The whip is resting on the squares of the floor not far from the little upturned feet, the soles of which one can see.

The whip is of braided leather like those that are used on dogs. From the thin, supple tip it becomes progressively thicker and harder up to the part that one holds in one's hand, which is almost rigid, forming a sort of very short handle. The lash, motionless on the floor, delineates an S whose narrowest tip curves back on itself.

The girl is still naked and on her knees, chained now to the foot of the bed. One sees her from the rear. The ankles are closely bound together but crossed, one foot over the other, which forces the knees wide apart.

The distance between the two hands is much greater, however, on either side of the blond head and at the same level. The arms are held almost horizontally, the elbows bent at a right angle towards the front. The wrists, still with the same metal chains, are attached to either end of the top bar of the iron bedstead.

The trunk and the thighs are held straight without the least bending of the hips. But the whole body is twisted to one side, due to the fatigue caused by this position. The head hangs forward and to the right, almost touching the shoulder.

The buttocks are marked in every direction by deep lines, very clear and distinct, which crisscross the central crack, more or less stressed according to how hard the whip fell.

This picture of little Anne chained to her bed, on her knees in a most uncomfortable position, is obviously more moving because of the cruel evidence of the torture she has undergone. The black ironwork forms a pattern of elegant arabesques behind her.

WILLIAM BURROUGHS
(1914–   )

a. j.'s annual party

William Burroughs was born in St Louis, and was part of the Beat
movement which began in San Francisco in the 1950s. His first book,
Junkie, was an account of his experiences as a drug addict – he had been
addicted to heroin, and lived a rough life in New Orleans and Mexico,
where he shot his wife by accident. After apomorphine treatment in 1957,
he rejected drugs as a way of life, and subsequently in *The Naked Lunch*
(1959), *The Soft Machine* (1961) and *Nova Express* (1964) produced a series
of books in experimental formats. *The Naked Lunch,* from which the
following extract is taken, is a 'realistic' account of a junkie's life, with all
the horrors of the dreamlike – nightmare-like – experiences of a drug state
heavily emphasised. His chief obsessions are sexual.

On Screen. Red-haired, green-eyed boy, white skin with a few
freckles . . . kissing a thin brunette girl in slacks. Clothes and hair-
do suggest existentialist bars of all the world cities. They are seated
on a low bed covered in white silk. The girl opens his pants with
gentle fingers and pulls out his cock which is small and very hard. A
drop of lubricant gleams at its tip like a pearl. She caresses the
crown gently: 'Strip, Johnny.' He takes off his clothes with swift
sure movements and stands naked before her, his cock pulsing. She
makes a motion for him to turn around and he pirouettes across the
floor parodying a model, hand on hip. She takes off her shirt. Her
breasts are high and small with erect nipples. She slips off her
underpants. Her pubic hairs are black and shiny. He sits down
beside her and reaches for her breast. She stops his hands.
    'Darling, I want to rim you,' she whispers.
    'No. Not now.'
    'Please, I want to.'
    'Well, all right. I'll go wash my ass.'
    'No, I'll wash it.'
    'Aw shucks now, it ain't dirty.'
    'Yes it is. Come on now, Johnny boy.'
    She leads him to the bathroom. 'All right, get down.' He gets
down on his knees and leans forward, with his chin on the bath mat.

'Allah,' he says. He looks back and grins at her. She washes his ass with soap and hot water sticking her finger up it.

'Does that hurt?'

'Noooooooooooooo.'

'Come along, baby.' She leads the way into the bedroom. He lies down on his back and throws his legs back over his head, clasping elbows behind his knees. She kneel down and caress the backs of his thighs, his balls, running her fingers down the perennial divide. She push his cheeks apart, lean down and begin licking the anus, moving her head in a slow circle. She push at the sides of the asshole, licking deeper and deeper. He close his eyes and squirm. She lick up the perennial divide. His small, tight balls. . . . A great pearl stands out on the tip of his circumcised cock. Her mouth closes over the crown. She sucks rhythmically up and down, pausing on the up stroke and moving her head around in a circle. Her hand plays gently with his balls, slide down and middle finger up his ass. As she suck down toward the root of his cock she tickles his prostate mockingly. He grin and fart. She is sucking his cock now in a frenzy. His body begins to contract, pulling up toward his chin. Each time the contraction is longer. 'Wheeeeeee!' the boy yell, every muscle tense, his whole body strain to empty through his cock. She drinks his jissom which fills her mouth in great hot spurts. He lets his feet flop back onto the bed. He arches his back and yawns.

Mary is strapping on a rubber penis. 'Steely Dan III from Yokohama,' she says, caressing the shaft. Milk spurts across the room.

'Be sure that milk is pasteurized. Don't go giving me some kinda awful cow disease like anthrax or glanders or aftosa. . . .'

'When I was a transvestite Liz in Chi used to work as an exterminator. Make advances to pretty boys for the thrill of being beaten as a man. Later I catch this one kid, overpower him with supersonic judo I learned from an old Lesbian Zen monk. I tie him up, strip off his clothes with a razor, and fuck him with Steely Dan I. He is so relieved I don't castrate him literal he come all over my bed-bug spray.'

'He was torn in two by a bull dyke. Most terrific vaginal grip I ever experienced. She could cave in a lead pipe. It was one of her parlor tricks.'

from *The Naked Lunch*

'And Steely Dan II?'

'Chewed to bits by a famished candiru in the Upper Baboonasshole. And don't say "Wheeeeee!" this time.'

'Why not? It's real boyish.'

'Barefoot boy, check thy bullheads with the madame.'

He looks at the ceiling, hands behind his head, cock pulsing. 'So what shall I do? Can't shit with that dingus up me. I wonder is it possible to laugh and come at the same time? I recall, during the war, at the Jockey Club in Cairo, me and my asshole buddy, Lu, both gentlemen by act of Congress . . . nothing else could have done such a thing to either of us. . . . So we got laughing so hard we piss all over ourselves and the waiter say: "You bloody hash-heads, get out of here!" I mean, if I can laugh the piss out of me I should be able to laugh out jissom. So tell me something real funny when I start coming. You can tell by certain premonitory quiverings of the prostate gland. . . .'

She puts on a record, metallic cocaine be-bop. She greases the dingus, shoves the boy's legs over his head and works it up his ass with a series of corkscrew movements of her fluid hips. She moves in a slow circle, revolving on the axis of the shaft. She rubs her hard nipples across his chest. She kisses him on the neck and chin and eyes. He runs his hands down her back to her buttocks, pulling her into his ass. She revolves faster, faster. His body jerks and writhes in convulsive spasms. 'Hurry up, please,' she says, 'The milk is getting cold.' He does not hear. She presses her mouth against his. His sperm hits her breast with light, hard licks.

Mark is standing in the doorway. He wears a turtleneck black sweater. Cold, handsome, narcissistic face. Green eyes and black hair. He looks at Johnny with a slight sneer, his head on one side, hands on his jacket pockets, a graceful hoodlum ballet. He jerk his head and Johnny walk ahead of him into the bedroom. Mary follow. 'All right, boys,' she says, sitting down naked on a pink silk dais overlooking the bed. 'Get with it!'

Mark begin to undress with fluid movements, hip rolls, squirm out of his turtleneck sweater revealing his beautiful white torso in a mocking belly dance. Johnny, deadpan, face frozen, breath quick, lips dry, remove his clothes and drop them on the floor. Mark lets his shorts fall on one foot. He kick like a chorus-girl, sending the shorts across the room. Now he stand naked, his cock stiff, straining up and out. He runs slow eyes over Johnny's body. He smile and lick his lips.

Mark drop on one knee, pulling Johnny across his back by one arm. He stand up and throw him six feet onto the bed. Johnny land on his back and bounce. Mark jump up and grab Johnny's ankles, throws his legs over his head. Mark's lips are drawn back in a tight snarl. 'All right, Johnny boy.' He contracts his body, slow and steady as an oiled machine, push his cock up Johnny's ass. Johnny gives a great sigh, squirming in ecstasy. Mark hitches his hands behind Johnny's shoulders, pulling him down onto his cock which is buried to the hilt in Johnny's ass. Great whistles through his teeth. Johnny screams like a bird. Mark is rubbing his face against Johnny's, snarl gone, face innocent and boyish as his whole liquid being spurt into Johnny's quivering body.

A train roar through him whistle blowing . . . boat whistle, foghorn, sky rocket burst over oily lagoons . . . penny arcade open into a maze of dirty pictures . . . ceremonial cannon boom in the harbor . . . a scream shoots down a white hospital corridor . . . out along a wide dusty street between palm trees, whistles out across the desert like a bullet (vulture wings husk in the dry air), a thousand boys come at once in out-houses, bleak public school toilets, attics, basements, treehouses, Ferris wheels, deserted houses, limestone caves, rowboats, garages, barns, rubbly wind city outskirts behind mud walls (smell of dried excrement) . . . black dust blowing over lean copper bodies . . . ragged pants dropped to cracked bleeding bare feet . . . (place where vultures fight over fish heads) . . . by jungle lagoons, vicious fish snap at white sperm floating on black water, sand flies bite the copper ass, howler monkeys like wind in the trees (a land of great brown rivers where whole trees float, bright coloured snakes in the branches, pensive lemurs watch the shore with sad eyes), a red plane traces arabesques in blue substance of sky, a rattlesnake strike, a cobra rear, spread, spit white venom, pearl and opal chips fall in a slow silent rain through air clear as glycerine. . . .

TERRY SOUTHERN
(1924–   )

Tantalisation Time

Candy, which Terry Southern wrote with Mason Hoffenberg, was hailed as the best farcical sex novel of its time; later, in *Blue Movie* (1970) Southern started out to write a comic novel in which there should not only be satire but eroticism. In the latter novel, he succeeded brilliantly; while the comedy is less pointed than in *Candy*, the later novel, a satire on the making of the ultimate hard-core porno movie, has some highly erotic passages which it can be argued point up the good and bad aspects of sex as a saleable commodity. In the following scene, Dave and Debbie, brother and sister film-stars who have previously appeared only in the most clean-living outdoor all-American sagas, are persuaded to take part in the *Blue Movie*.

It was not until about an hour before wrap time – after a great deal of hemming and hawing (and then only because she couldn't bear being thought of as 'square') – that Debbie had finally agreed to try the love scene with Dave, or at least had agreed that they would get under the blankets together, naked, and hold each other close . . . which they did, and after a bit of nervous giggling, tickling one another, and kidding in general, they had just about settled down enough to try a take.

'Well, Dave,' Boris asked, 'how does it feel?'

'Groovy,' said Dave.

'Debbie?'

'It feels *nice*,' she said, 'nice and warm,' and she snuggled up a little closer.

'Well, I think the way it should happen,' Boris went on, 'is that after you lie there for a minute, embraced, and you're no longer cold, you begin to feel, you know, sexually aware of each other's presence – and so, Dave, you slowly take the blanket off, to look at Debbie's body, which you've never really done before – I mean like *deliberately*.'

'But isn't it supposed to be *cold* in the room?' the girl wanted to know, instinctively grasping at straws.

'Not any more. Remember, the scene opens with you both

[223]

asleep, under separate blankets . . . the fire is very low, the room is cold – Dave wakes up, shivers, puts some more wood on the fire, sits in front of it, huddled in his blanket.. . . then *you* wake and ask him what's wrong. "I'm freezing," he says. "So am I," you say. He moves closer, still shivering, a genuine chill, teeth chattering, that kind of thing, so you say "Maybe we should get under *both* blankets . . . until the room is warmer." And that's what you do. I know it may be cheating a little, timewise, but we've got to lose blankets – I mean, we can't put the camera *under* the blankets. Dig?'

'Dig,' said Dave, and then to Debbie, 'Okay, Sis?'

'Well, gosh . . .' she sighed, 'I guess so.'

'Everything's cool, Sis,' he went on, 'just stay loose,' and then to Boris, 'About how slow with the blanket, B.— like this?' And he moved it down, gradually uncovering her. '*Wow*, Sis,' he admitted softly, 'that *is* a pretty wild body you've got going. Yeah, I think I'm going to dig this.'

She giggled, grasping the top of the blanket just as it passed her navel. 'Well, you don't have to pull it down all the way *now*! I mean, they're not even shooting.'

'That's perfect, Dave,' said Boris, 'just take it a fraction slower – we'll get a little *tantalisation time* going for us.'

'Dig,' said the young man . . .

'Listen, B.,' said Tony, 'we worked out a great scene. We actually ran through it – well, right up to the nitty-gritty part, and it's beautiful. Dig this: first, he uncovers her, looks at her body, then he touches it – you know, like "wondrously", first face, then slowly moves his hand down . . . over her throat, her shoulder, her breast, the curve of her waist, her hip, along her thigh, moving to the back of it, behind the knee, along the calf . . . then slowly up again, stopping on cooze, and at the same time bringing his lips forward to her breast. Right? Okay, meanwhile *she's* started moving *her* hand over *him*, beginning the same way, but beginning *after* he did, so by the time he gets back up to the cooze, she's arriving at his – pardon the expression, Debbie – *cock*, which by now, needless to say, is plenty erect.'

'You ain't just a-jivin'!' Dave interjected, and Debbie giggled and squirmed in her blanket.

'Now, dig,' Tony continued to Boris, 'all this is happening with

[224]

from *Blue Movie*

no dialogue . . . just exploring each other's body, with an innocent
sense of wonder, not even kissing . . . I think if we save the kiss for
the climax – save the kiss until they're actually *coming* . . . *together*
. . . it could be *fantastic* – it would really be a *kiss* then, wouldn't it?
I mean, they've never *kissed* before – except, you know, brother and
sister style, on the cheek, or lightly on the lips – so that when they
finally do this full-on, open-mouth, lots-of-tongue, hot, wet soul
kiss, while they're *coming* . . . well, *that* will be like the real taboo-
breaker, the *kiss*, even more than the fuck. Dig?' He looked from
one to the other.

'Gosh,' said Debbie.

'Heavy,' said Dave.

'Let's shoot it,' said Boris.

What had ensued was quite remarkable. Apparently, Tony's
fantasy as to the intense sexual potential between siblings was not
without certain psychological basis. The relationship (and the
action) between Dave and Debbie progressed almost exactly as he
had always dreamed (and then written) it might. It was as though
they were filming at the Masters-Johnson Clinic – that is to say, an
authentic love-making couple . . . but, instead of *clinical*, it was
beautiful – beautiful *people*, beautiful *lighting*, beautiful *photography*
. . . only the credibility of the sexual experience was the same –
except, with Dave and Debbie, it had an *intensity* quite beyond
anything previously documented.

For Dave, aside from whatever extraordinary psychic impact the
relationship itself ('fucking his sister,' so to speak) may have had,
the pure *sexual fact* of it – for someone coming off an extensive
drug-and-celibacy trip, – was like a child's rediscovery of a
forgotten toy.

The first time he *came*, even though it was very dramatic, and
obviously complete, he continued, hungrily, compulsively striving,
as though he could never possibly get enough of it – while the
fabulous Debbie held on, it seemed, for dear life – great eyes closed,
wet mouth open, not moaning or sighing, just sort of gulping and
swallowing, as though coming with each breath – these being about
one-eighth of a second apart – with her perfect 'Miss All-American
Teen' face transfixed by an unaltering expression of *nirvana toto*
. . .

'Hey, did you dig I came *twice*?'

[225]

'It was beautiful,' said Boris.

'It was *fantastic*,' said Dave, with near manic enthusiasm, then looking at Debbie, 'Wasn't it *fantastic*, Sis?' while she, averting her eyes, blushing like a virgin bride, nodded happily.

'Uh, what would you think . . .' Boris began, by way of getting the show on the road – seeing as how they were set up, ready to shoot, and about thirty-two people standing around waiting – 'what would you think of Debbie being on top for this one?'

Dave wagged and nodded his head, brows arching. 'Outta sight, man . . . wow, yeah, that would be a . . . groove, ha-ha, I almost said "ball",' he nudged Debbie, 'get it, Sis?'

'You *nut*,' she giggled.

'Yeah, man,' Dave went on to Boris, 'I mean, like I'm hip it would be a boss trip . . . and let's get a *mirror*, I really groove on a mirror with the chick on top – and so do a lot of chicks . . . I mean, it's like *narcissus-ville*, you dig?' He turned to Debbie again, 'How about it, Sis, is that part of your bag – I mean, like can you *come* on top?'

She smirked self-consciously and gave him a playful elbow-jab to the ribs. 'You silly-billy,' she chided in her anomalous 'Barbie' manner, '*I* can come on *card tricks!*'

'Too *much*, man,' said Dave, shaking his head and glowing with admiration. 'Where have you been all my life?'

'Beautiful,' said Boris, 'let's, uh, shoot it.'

GORE VIDAL
(1925–)

The Examination

Gore Vidal, an American novelist of some distinction, wrote in *Myra Breckinridge* (1968) a satire on the 'true confession' which attacked various targets with unnerving accuracy – among them the sexual fantasies of Hollywood gossip-writers. Myra, a spectacularly well-built lady (who, it is as well to know, turns out once to have been a man) takes a job as coach at the West Coast drama academy run by Buck Loner, the ex-radio and film Singin' Shootin' Cowboy. In the following scene she conducts a physical examination of the unwilling Rusty Godowsky, a student on whose sexual humiliation she is intent. His posture is bad, perhaps because of an injury to the spine.

I was brusque. 'Let me see your back. Take your shirt off.'

He was startled. 'But there's nothing to see . . . I mean the ribs are all inside me that was broken.'

'I know *where* the ribs are, Rusty.' I was patient. 'But I have to see the exact point where the muscle begins to pull you to one side.'

There was no answer to this. He started to say something but decided not to. Slowly he unfastened his belt and unhooked the top button of the blue jeans. Then he unbuttoned his shirt and took it off. The T-shirt was soaked at the armpits, the result of the strenuous impromptu dance and, perhaps (do I project?), of terror.

For the first time I saw his bare arms. The skin was very white (no one out here goes to the beach in January even though it is quite sunny), with biceps clearly marked though not overdeveloped; large veins ran the length of the forearms to the hands, always an excellent sign, and not unattractive since the veins were not blue but white, indicating skin of unusual thickness, again a good sign. On the forearms coppery straight hairs grew. He paused as though not certain what to do next. I was helpful. 'The T-shirt, too. I haven't got X-ray eyes.'

Glumly he pulled the T-shirt over his head. I watched, fascinated by each revelation of his body. First the navel came into view, small and protruding. Just beneath it a line of dark slightly curly hairs disappeared inside the Jockey shorts which were now visible above the loosened belt. The shirt rose higher. About two inches above the navel, more hairs began (I had seen the topmost branches of this tree of life at the pot party, now I saw the narrow roots slowly widening as the tree made its way to his neck). When the chest was entirely bared, his face was momentarily hidden in the folds of the damp T-shirt, and so I was able to study, unobserved, the small rose-brown breasts, at the moment concave and un-aroused. Then the T-shirt was wadded up and dropped onto the floor.

Aware of my interested gaze, he blushed. Beginning at the base of the thick neck, the lovely colour rose to the level of his eyes. Like so many male narcissists, he is, paradoxically, modest: he enjoys revealing himself but only on his own terms.

A remark about his appearance was obviously called for and I made it. 'You seem in very good condition . . .'

'Well, I work out some, not like I ought to . . . used to . . .' He hooked long thumbs into his belt, causing the smooth pectorals to twitch ever so slightly, revealing the absence of any fat or loosening of skin.

'Now will you please face the wall, arms at your side, with your palms pressed against the wall as hard as you can.'

Without a word, he did as he was told. The back was as pleasing as the front (no hairs on the shoulder, unlike poor Myron, who was forced to remove his with electrolysis). The blue jeans had begun to sag and now hung several inches below the waistline, revealing frayed Jockey shorts. Aware that the trousers were slipping, he tried to pull them up with one hand but I put a stop to that. 'Hands flat against the wall!' I ordered in a sharp voice that would not take no for an answer.

'But, Miss Myra . . .' and his voice was suddenly no longer deep but a boy's voice, plaintive and frightened: the young Lon McCallister.

'Do as I say!'

He muttered something that I could not hear and did as he was told. In the process, the blue jeans cleared the curve of his buttocks and now clung perilously to the upper thighs of which a good two inches were in plain view. It was a moment to cherish, to exult in, to give a life for. His embarrassment was palpable, charging the situation with true drama since from the very beginning it has been quite plain to me that *in no way do I interest him sexually*. Since he detests me, my ultimate victory is bound to be all the more glorious and significant.

I studied my captive for some moments (the spine did indeed make an S-like curve and the thick white trapezoidal ligament was twisted to one side). Of greater interest to me, however, were the Jockey shorts and what they contained. But now I knew that I would have to proceed with some delicacy. I crossed to where he stood. I was so close to him that I could smell the horselike odour men exude when they are either frightened or in a state of rut. In this case it was fright.

Delicately I ran my hand down his spine. He shuddered at my touch but said nothing. Meanwhile I spoke to him calmly, easily, the way one does in order to soothe a nervous animal. 'Yes, I can see the trouble now. It's right here, under the shoulder blade.' I kneaded the warm smooth skin, and again he winced but said nothing while I continued to give my 'analysis' of his condition. 'Perhaps a brace in this area would help.'

Now my hands were at the narrow waist. He was breathing hoarsely, arms pressed so hard against the wall that the triceps stood out like white snakes intertwined, ready to strike.

I felt something warm on the back of one hand: a drop of sweat from his left armpit. 'But perhaps the trouble is lower down. Around the small of the back. Yes, of course! The lumbar region – that's just where it is!'

As I spoke, evenly, hypnotically, I gently inserted my thumbs beneath the worn elastic band of his shorts and before he was aware of what was happening, I had pulled them down to his knees. He gave a strangled cry, looked back over his shoulder at me, face scarlet, mouth open, but no words came. He started to pull away from me, then stopped, recalling that he was for all practical purposes nude. He clung now to the wall, the last protector of his modesty.

Meanwhile I continued to chat. 'Yes, we can start the brace right here.' I touched the end of the spine, a rather protuberant bony tip set between the high curve of buttocks now revealed to me in all their splendour. . . and splendour is the only word to describe them! Smooth, white, hairless except just beneath the spinal tip where a number of dark coppery hairs began, only to disappear from view.

Casually I ran my hand over the smooth slightly damp cheeks. To the touch they were like highly polished marble warmed by the sun of some perfect Mediterranean day. I even allowed my forefinger the indiscretion of fingering the coppery wires not only at the tip of the spine but also the thicker growth at the back of his thighs. Like so many young males, he has a relatively hairless torso with heavily furred legs. Myron was the same. With age, however, the legs lose much of this adolescent growth while the torso's pelt grows heavier.

I had now gone almost as far as I could go with my inspection. After all, I have not yet established total mastery. But I have made a good beginning: half of the mystery has now been revealed, the rest must wait for a more propitious time. And so, after one last kneading of the buttocks, I said, 'That will do for now, Rusty. I think we've almost got to the root of the problem.'

He leaned rigidly, all of a piece, to one side and grabbed the fallen trousers. He kept his legs as much together as possible, pulling on clothes with astonishing speed, the only lapse occurring when something in front was caught by the ascending shorts, causing him to grunt and fumble. But then all was in order and when he finally turned around, the belt buckle had been firmly fastened. He was satisfyingly pale and alarmed-looking.

ROBERT GOVER
(1929–   )

The Ten-Dollah Gun

In *One Hundred Dollar Misunderstanding* (1961) Robert Gover wrote an
hilarious novel told, in alternate chapters, by a WASP American boy,
utterly naïve and self-regarding, and a young black whore called Kitten.
The following extract tells of their first encounter at a 'Negro house of ill-
repute' which James Cartright Holland has decided to inspect, just out of
interest. Kitten tells the story.

I say, Baby you wanna keep yer clothes on?
   He say, No! He say, Course he don' wanna keep his clothes on.
Ooh-wee!
   I say, Honey you don' wanna keep 'em on, thing t'do is take 'em
off!
   He say, Yeah sure yeah! An he start in.
   An he got a long way t'go. Kee-ryees!
   But I say t'myself, I say. Hol' yer ass, Girl. This mothah kin be
jes's dum's he wanna be, he got him that much mazoola.
   He fold his clothes over the chair real careful. I ack like I'm
daydreamin, he do that. He so dum he might git t'thinkin I wanna
rob him. He ack a wee bit mistrussful anyhow. He ack that way, I
ack like I'm the dummes' lil Pickaninny livin.
   I gotta long wait till he finish undressin, he got so much on.
   I wash him real nice an soff, count him bein so awful
tickledingus, and then I gits t'work. Time I start in, I got me so
many worryful considerins t'do, I can't hardly pay no mind
t'techneek. Workin an considerin, an wonnerin does this dum
Whiteboy know what t'do wiff that thing fer the other haff o'his haff
and haff, I find I done me too dam much considerin.
   Nex, I ain been at him a minit, an pop, off he go!
   Kee-ryees!
   An then – I git up an go over t'the basin – this Whiteboy, he sit up
like a mothahjumpin jack-in-a-box an he start lookin at me like I
done somethin wrong.
   Gee-zuz! All that Jack an I can' make nothin go right, he so
fuggin dum. Come in here all loaded up like that an I don' even git a

chance t'show him how good I kin do. Naecher done mess me up at the most baddest time.

An he still lookin, Gee-zuz!

Then he say, That all?

Yeah! He say that! He say that like he think I sposed t'do a lil dance for him nex. Kee-ryees!

I say, Yeah Baby, tha's all. Dam shame, too.

He say, Yeah it's a shame. He say, One ain never enuff fer *him*!

I feel like sayin, Baby way you go off, you musta been savin that *one* fer a mothahlumpin lifetime. On'y you ask me my phone. I fix you up fer the rest o'yer lifetime, long's you want. You ask me my phone, you ain never gonna go so long wiffout pussy you gits *that* trigger-happy agen.

But I don' say nothin an he don' ask me my phone. Can' blame him. I don' even git me a chance t'show my stuff. *Poof*! Invessment gone.

I start in t'git dress' agen, feelin real blue, an he jes still layin there lookin real surprise, like I ain doin right.

I say, Come on, Baby, we gotta git outta here.

He say, Le's go nother one.

I say, Can'. Ain allowed, man. You gotta –

An then I cork ass an start in considerin all over agen. Hell! He done pay ten fer haff an haff an don' even git him one haff. But Kee-ryees! We been up here so mothah-fuggin long now, Madam gonna send for the firetruck, we don' git ass back downstairs. I say t'myself, Gee-zuz Girl! You jes can' go breakin rules fer no trick too dum t'ask you yer phone and git him a lil o'yer ass on the side.

But I can' help tryin one more fishline. I say, Baby ain you got you no sweet lil chick fer that pritty cock?

An she-it! Seem like I jes can' say the right thing roun this dum mothah. He wrinkle up an he start in tryin t'tell me he got him plenty.

I bout t'give him up fer lost. I say t'myseff, This daddio so dum, he gonna end up comin backwar's. Yeah, he gonna end up backfirin. He soun like he is backfirin right now.

Then he quit jawin that crap an he say, Come on, le's go jes one more real quick.

Real quick, he say. Hee hee! His lil ol genrill still up an lookin peppy. Madam say, trick wanna go agen, he pay up right now, else he start in from downstairs all over agen. But this poor mothah done pay fer haff an haff an don' even git haff, and I is out one big fat invessment chance. Ge-zuz! This ain right!

So I say, Now?

He say, yeah now. Real quick, real quick.

Las' trick say that make me break the rule too, an he pay agen then he turn out so fuggin slow on the secen', he dam near wear my ass clean out. Course, that weren't the same. That one, he don' give me no insprashun. This one, he the biggest invessment chance I ever seen in this cathouse. He hum, yeah! But crap, he can' help *that*!

I say t'myseff, I say, Ain no good leavin him go downstairs an pick him out some new cat an give her chance t'make invessment when I got him up here wiff me right now.

Piss on Madam an her git an git!

I say, Baby you promise t'be real quick an don' never tell nobody I do it?

He say, Yeah yeah yeah!

I say, Sure you kin go agen so quick?

He say, Sure sure sure!

I tease a lil more. I say, An you ain gonna tell nobody?

He say, no no no, he ain gonna tell.

I say, But Sugar, I better not. I say, We been up here too long already. I say, Go on, git! Go git you nother girl.

He look real sad, I say that. He look like he gonna go an find him nother girl. Fer real!

Gee-zuz! Ain nothin gonna go right fer me t'night?

I say – real fast – I say, Whoa Baby! I laugh. I say, I'm on'y teasin.

An I outta my clothes agen an on that bed so fast he don' know which end is up. I say, Shove over, Lover. I say, Honeydripper, make room for this Honeydripper!

He do.

Nex, he no sooner in the saddle an we is jes bout ready t'raise hell when—

Gee-zuz Kee-ryess! The godam Francine pop in. Yeah! Loud's a fart in a empty tincan.

She say, Kitten yer in *my* room.

I say, Francine godam yer crazy ass, git outta here!

I kin see my trick gittin all jittery all over agen.

Francine, she say, Don' you know by this time, this *my* room?

I kin feel his ol soljer jes a-wiltin an wiltin.

I say, Come on Baby, don' pay no nevermind t'her.

But he jes too fuss up. Counta Francine bein there.

I say, Francine up yers wiff a lawnmower, you git yer greezy hair the hell outta here.

An she say, Girl who you think yer talkin to?

An I say, You you cottonpickin crab nabber.

An she say, Don you talk t'me like that, you lil bitch, or I'll ruin you.

An I say, Francine can' you see I'm busy jes now? Now how come you don' git?

An she say, No. She say I gotta git, go find nother room.

I say, Francine yer flippin yer lid! You git right now or I'm gonna call fer Madam.

She say, like hell I'm gonna call fer Madam. She tell me *she* is gonna call fer Madam, I don't git. She say, I'm goin right downstairs right now an tell Madam yer in my room an yer takin all fuggin night for one lousy trick.

So I say, Okay Francine, go on, tell Madam.

She ain gonna tell Madam nothin. She do, Madam kick her ass right out! Francine, she don' belong in no cathouse nohow. She don' git along wiff nobody, hardly. She ack like hers don't stink. It do.

Time she git her crazy ass the hell outa there, my poor lil ol Joe College done wilt like somebody bust his balloon, an I gotta start in all the everlovin over agen. Kee-ryess!

I ain never been nobody fer fightin, but Gee-zuz! I fraid I was bigger, I'd lose my blackass Pickaninny head fer considerin an jes take an kick livin hell outta that Francine.

I gotta work real fast now. We was late fore she come in an we ain getting no sooner.

I start in playin nice's I kin unner the circumstances but I gotta start in from scratch. Kee-ryess! I'm talkin pritty's ever I kin, an playin nice's I know how, an he comin along okay.

An nex, Gee-zuz! I git me more trouble!

This muddlehead pull up an look down on me real sad – real, real sad – an he start in talkin sad too. Steada hoppin back in the saddle

[234]

on goin, he is gonna try some make believe sweet talkin. He start in
ackin like he's playin him some dum movie scene. Yeah! He talk sad
an then he look at me like I'm sposed t'talk sad back.

Ooh-wee! He lose me!

I don' know what t'do. I considerin that jack he got an I
considerin how long we been up here an I hearin more tricks jes
streaming in that mothahless front door downstairs, an I jes *know*
Madam gonna wonner what the hell happen t'me.

I say, Sweetheart Lover, we ain got *time* fer that *now*! I say, You
tol' me you gonna be quick. Here you go pissin round like you think
I got all fuggin night! I say, Gee-zuz Baby, Madam gonna think yer
eatin my ass, steada—

Now godam, come on, Baby. Giddy up!

I say all that nice's I kin at that time, an I make him smile. He do
that, I hope t'toot an back he git the idea t'ask me my phone, but he
don' git that idea a-tall! No!

Nex thing I know – jes bout the time we startin t'go good an I gits
movin okay an I goin fine's I ever do go, an I snappin the whip an
punchin the apple, an I wonnerin is my invessment ever gonna
come thru an ask me my phone – an I rollin ass east an rollin ass
wes', an breakin my poor ol Pickaninny back fer this dum mothah –
nex think I know, he git him one more dee-diddly-dum idea, an fore
I know what he is tryin t'do, he got my ass hung up clear off that
bed!

Yeah!

I say, Hol' it, Baby! What the fug you doin?

She-it! I open my big mouff and that son-a-bitch jes stop, plop,
an lay deadweight. Seem every cottonpickin thing I do jes backfire.
I git me nothin but trouble trouble trouble.

He say, He don' know wha's the matter. He say, Seem like *I* is
doin all the *work*!

Yeah! He say *I* is doing the work!

I bout flip my lid right here. I say, Gee-zuz, Sweetie! An I try bes
I kin t'talk nice. I say, Course *I* is doin the work. What the hell you
think? I say, *I* is the *cat*, you is the *trick*! Unnerstan? I say, Now
come on, Lover, giddy up oncet agen an le's git the hell outta here. I
keep tryin t'tell you, we ain got no *time* right *now* – fer talkin.

I say – an alla time tryin t'soun nice – I say, Giddy the sweet
everlovin horsey ass up oncet agen, please!

[235]

Well, she-it! He start in goin, yeah! Sep, this time he got him nother fancy fug idea, an he start in wham jammin me like he's choppin rock. Yeah! He jes a-gruntin an rammin away like he's mad at the whole mothahhumpin worl'.

Course, I know better'n t'open my big mouff *this* time. I keep tryin t'do my stuff best I kin unner the new circumstances, but it ain easy.

Meantime, I'm thinking we jes gotta make it this time an he can' git him nohow no more new dum ideas – an he git him nother one. Yeah! He do!

Gee-zuz! I don' know how one dum Whiteboy kin behave so mean! This time, he curl my blackass right up double an he piledrive like he is tryin' t'stan me on my poor ol Pickaninny head an bump me straight down t'hell!

Yeah! He do that! I don' know what he is tryin t'prove, but I ain bout t'ask no more queshuns.

On'y thing I try, I try a lil reverse English. I say, Tha's-a-way, Baby! Hit it, Sweetheart! Go go go!

He go! And he git him his dee-diddly-godam ten-dollah gun. At las'.

I up outa that bed and doosh on the run an dress – right now! I even fergit all bout that invessment idea, I so scared my ass gonna be mud, time I git back downstairs.

I say, Hey Lover, how come you wanna ack like that? You think pussy made o'steel?

I laugh when I say that. It ain easy, but I do.

He laugh too, dum she-it.

Good thing I laugh.

PHILIP ROTH
(1933–   )

Okay, That's It

Portnoy's Complaint (1969) was the first novel to have masturbation as its
central theme. A black comedy dealing also with the perennial theme of the
Jewish boy and his relationship with his mother, it is perhaps a series of
anecdotes rather than a true novel; but it is consistently and brilliantly
funny. In the following scene the narrator and his adolescent friends at last
manage to persuade a prostitute to relieve them of their virginity. But . . .

Smolka comes back into the kitchen and tells us she doesn't want to
do it.

'But you said we were going to get laid!' cried Mandel. 'You said
we were going to get blowed! Reamed, steamed, and dry-cleaned,
that's what you *said*!'

'Fuck it,' I say, 'if she doesn't want to do it, who needs her, let's
go—'

'But I've been pounding off over this for a week! I ain't going
anywhere! What kind of shit *is* this, Smolka? Won't she even beat
my *meat*?'

Me, with my refrain: 'Ah, look, if she doesn't want to do it, let's
go—'

Mandel: 'Who the fuck is she that she won't even give a guy a
hand-job? A measly hand-job. Is that the world to ask of her? I ain't
leaving till she either sucks it or pulls it – one or the other! It's up to
her, the fucking whore!'

So Smolka goes back in for a second conference, and returns
nearly half an hour later with the news that the girl has changed her
mind: she will jerk off one guy, but only with his pants on, and that's
all. We flip a coin – and I win the right to get the syph! Mandel
claims the coin grazed the ceiling, and is ready to murder me – he is
still screaming foul play when I enter the living room to reap my
reward.

She sits in her slip on the sofa at the other end of the linoleum
floor, weighing a hundred and seventy pounds and growing a
moustache. Anthony Peruta, that's my name for when she asks. But
she doesn't. 'Look,' says Bubbles, 'let's get it straight – you're the

only one I'm doing it to. You, and that's it.'

'It's entirely up to you,' I say politely.

'All right, take it out of your pants, *but don't take them down*. You hear me, because I told him, I'm not doing anything to anybody's balls.'

'Fine, fine. Whatever you say.'

'And don't try to touch me either.'

'Look, if you want me to go, I'll go.'

'Just take it out.'

'Sure, if that's what you want, here . . . here,' I say, but prematurely. 'I-just-have-to-get-it—' Where *is* that thing? In the classroom I sometimes set myself consciously to thinking about DEATH and HOSPITALS and HORRIBLE AUTOMOBILE ACCIDENTS in the hope that such grave thoughts will cause my 'boner' to recede before the bell rings and I have to stand. It seems that I can't go up to the blackboard in school, or try to get off a bus, without its jumping up and saying, 'Hi! look at me!' to everyone in sight – and now it is nowhere to be found.

'Here!' I finally cry.

'Is that it?'

'Well,' I answer, turning colours, 'it gets bigger when it gets harder . . .'

'Well, I ain't got all night, you know.'

Nicely: 'Oh, I don't think it'll be all *night*—'

'Lay down!'

Bubbles, not wholly content, lowers herself into a straight chair, while I stretch out beside her on the sofa – and suddenly she has hold of it, and it's as though my poor cock has got caught in some kind of machine. Vigorously, to put it mildly, the ordeal begins. But it is like trying to jerk off a jellyfish.

'What's a matter?' she finally says. 'Can't you come?'

'Usually, yes, I can.'

Then stop holding it back on me.'

'I'm not. I am trying, Bubbles—'

'Cause I'm going to count to fifty, and if you don't do it by then, that ain't my fault.'

Fifty? I'll be lucky if it is still attached to my body by fifty. *Take it easy*, I want to scream. *Not so rough around the edges, please!* – 'eleven, twelve, thirteen' – and I think to myself, *Thank God, soon it'll be over – hang on, only another forty seconds to go* – but simultaneous with the relief comes, of course, the disappointment, and it is keen: this only happens to be what I have been dreaming about night and day since I am thirteen. At long last, not a cored apple, not an empty milk bottle greased with vaseline, but a girl in a slip, with two tits and a cunt – and a moustache, but who am I to be picky? This is what I have been imagining for myself. . . .

Which is how it occurs to me what to do. I will forget that the fist tearing away at me belongs to Bubbles – I'll pretend it's my own! So, fixedly I stare at the dark ceiling, and instead of making believe that I am getting laid, as I ordinarily do while jerking off, I make believe that I am jerking off.

And it begins instantly to take effect. Unfortunately, however, I get just about where I want to be when Bubbles' workday comes to an end.

'Okay, that's it,' she says, 'fifty,' *and stops*!

'No!' I cry. 'More!'

'Look, I already ironed two hours, you know, before you guys even got here—'

'JUST ONE MORE! I BEG OF YOU! TWO MORE! PLEASE!'

'N-O!'

Whereupon, unable (as always!) to stand the frustration – the deprivation and disappointment – I reach down, I grab it, and POW!

Only right in my eye. With a single whiplike stroke of the master's own hand, the lather comes rising out of me. I ask you, who jerks me off as well as I do it myself? Only, reclining as I am, the jet leaves my joint on the horizontal, rides back the length of my torso, and lands with a thick wet burning splash right in my own eye.

'Son of a bitch kike!' Bubbles screams. 'You got gissum all over the couch! And the walls! And the lamp!'

'I got it in my eye! And don't you say kike to me, you!'

'You *are* a kike, Kike! You got it all over everything, you mocky son of a bitch! Look at the doilies!'

ARMAND COPPENS

Maurice's Party

The Memoirs of an Erotic Bookseller is a strange publication which appeared in several European countries simultaneously in 1969. Clearly pseudonymous, its author purports to be an elderly antiquarian bookseller whose professional life has largely consisted of obtaining erotic books for a limited number of wealthy collectors. In doing so, he has come into contact with a number of strange people with bizarre sexual tastes, of whom he writes with enthusiastic wit. In the following extract he describes a party given by a publisher friend, Maurice, to celebrate his birthday. Among Coppens' fellow-guests were 'three erotic dealers, also a marvellous old roué, Henry, and his over-ripe mistress, a lady of some seventy years, not to mention the dignified Consul-General and the very pompous Mayor of the village in which Maurice's bungalow was situated.' Maurice presents an ancient Japanese silk scroll painted with erotic scenes. The Mayor objects.

'You surely don't expect us to believe you, sir, when you claim that these scrolls can be bought at public auctions?' he blustered indignantly. 'I can assure you that I would never tolerate the public display of such a thing in my town. I have no doubt that it has great artistic value, but it is certainly something which should be kept privately in one's own home. Sex, after all, is not a public matter.'

'What you say may be true today,' I said cautiously, anxious to avoid a row at Maurice's party, 'but it has not always been so. Take Athens, for example, where girls regularly showed their bare behinds in public so that the populace could choose which was the nicest. And what about the triumphal entries of the Dukes of Burgundy, the Kings of France and even the Emperor Charles the Fifth? On these occasions, hundreds of naked women and girls posed for allegorical tableaux without the slightest shame or hesitation at displaying their nude bodies. They even fought each other to take part.'

'That's all very well, Mr Coppens,' he interrupted impatiently. 'But what you're citing are no more than old-fashioned beauty contests. This scroll shows people having sexual intercourse and I assure you that my wife . . .'

'Even your wife, sir,' I countered, 'would copulate in public if the occasion were to include or demand some sexual activity. No one can resist or act contrary to the collective wish of a crowd. The moment a crowd begins to generate a mood, no matter what it is, blood-lust, anger or sex, the individual cannot act independently of that crowd. But that's beside the point. These scrolls were seldom intended for public display. Their prime source of origin was for the instruction of daughters. A father, wishing to arrange an advantageous marriage for his daughter, would commission one of these scrolls for his child's instruction so that he could guarantee that she would know how to satisfy her husband sexually.'

I picked up the scroll and draped it over my arm to show Maurice's guests one of the first pictures, which showed a girl tenderly toying with her husband's testicles. This delightful water-colour was devoid of that burlesque element which later crept into the art. It was refined, delicate and tasteful. But it was also thoroughly convincing, so persuasively erotic, in fact, that I was sexually aroused by it.

'Please close your eyes very slightly,' I instructed the guests around the table, 'and concentrate on the picture. Look at the delicacy and finesse with which the girl is caressing her lover's genitals. Now imagine that you are either performing or experiencing the same act. Now, who among the men has not got an erection?'

Shouts of laughter filled the room. But the little Mayor immediately remonstrated with me.

'You're going beyond the bounds of decency, Coppens,' he exclaimed.

'That's not the point, Jean,' Karin said. 'The point is the erotic effectiveness of the picture. I bet you were as excited as Maurice. Look, he still is.'

Everyone immediately turned to Maurice whose excitement was proudly visible beneath his close-fitting tights. The sight was greeted by an uproar. I immediately adjusted the scroll to display another plate for the guests' inspection. This one showed a girl passionately performing *fellatio* on her partner. A wave of excitement swept through the guests. I drew attention to a third picture, one which showed the girl performing a sort of belly-dance whilst being watched by her visibly excited partner. There was total silence now. Each of the guests was caught by the spell of the drawings. But the spell was shattered suddenly, by Mrs Falcon.

'That reminds me of when I was touring through Russia with a troupe of dancers. Every night, after the performance, we were invited to supper by princes, dukes and army officials. During the meal, a few of us used to perform a belly-dance on the table, among the bottles and plates and serving dishes. One girl, a little Indonesian, used to be able to make her belly and bottom jump in such a lascivious way that none of the men were ever able to control themselves while she performed. They would tear off their uniforms and pursue us around the room. Apart from the fun of it all, we used to make a lot of money out of those after-dinner guests,' she concluded a little sadly.

'What a remarkable memory you have, Mrs Falcon!' a young girl said bitchily.

'I've never had to worry about that, my dear,' cooed Mrs Falcon icily. 'But then I've got something to remember. I doubt very much that you will have when you get to my age.'

The girl was engaged at that time to Henry von A's son. Mrs Falcon indicated the ring which encircled the girl's finger.

'In a couple of years you'll probably have children. Life will be so dull and boring that you'll pray for loss of memory. Why, I bet I could teach you a few things and win more applause, even at my age.'

Having issued her challenge, Mrs Falcon stepped nimbly up on to a chair and then on to the table.

'You take the right and I'll take the left. We'll dance all around the edge of this table until we reach the spot where we began.'

Then, seeing the girl's hesitation, she added sweetly:

'Surely you're not afraid to take me on? A woman of my age?'

The girl still made no move. She obviously did not want to be a wet blanket, but her position was such, as Mrs Falcon well knew, that she could scarcely refuse to take part in the competition without seeming to be a spoilsport. At last, she climbed on to the table and stood forlornly opposite her opponent. Mrs Falcon calmly unbuttoned her blouse, stepped out of her skirt and tossed both garments into the room. It was almost impossible to believe that this woman was nearly seventy. Her body, though a little thick, was still firm and vigorous. Even the vulnerable flesh between the breasts and at the top of the thighs did not appear to have sagged.

'What are you waiting for, dear,' she taunted. 'You surely don't expect the applause without any effort, do you?'

'Come on, Mila. You're not that shy,' shouted her fiancé, from the crowd around the table.

Stung, the girl immediately unzipped her flaming-red dress and slipped out of it. She tossed it, together with her *jupon*, in the general direction of her boy-friend.

'You're going to lose your monopoly,' she called, reaching behind her to unclasp her brassière. Then she slipped out of her panties and handed both articles, with a little bow, to old Henry von A.

'Just look after these for a moment,' she said. 'I'm afraid your son would only lose them. Ready, Mrs Falcon?'

'Certainly,' replied the old woman, quite unruffled. 'I only want to ask the gentlemen to show their appreciation, if any, in the old Russian style. When we danced during those suppers I was telling you about, the men always took out their penises and banged them on the table to indicate their approval. Any girl who failed to please was squirted with soda-water or drenched in champagne. Don't misunderstand me. I'm not asking you to do this in order to be provocative but simply for sentimental reasons.'

During this speech, Mrs Falcon had stripped completely. Now the table was surrounded by excited, shouting men. I shall never forget the sight of Karin determinedly playing with old Henry in a vain attempt to enable him to hit the table with a little vigour.

'Come on, Henry,' she giggled. 'Those four inches won't make a sound. And it's not very complimentary to your hostess.'

Standing provocatively before him, she pulled off her sweater. With her bare breasts and tight, golden trousers, she looked absolutely stunning. But her efforts were wasted on Henry. Perceiving this, Karin said:

'Sorry, Henry. I must go and put some music on. But don't give up hope. It'll all happen one day.'

Karin was shaking with laughter when I joined her at the record player.

'What do you suggest,' she asked. 'How about the Bolero?'

'For God's sake, no. It's much too slow,' I replied.

'Well, the old girl's not so young, you know,' Karin argued.

'Maybe not. But I bet she'll win.'

'You really think so?'

'I'll stake my life on it. Now come on, hurry it up. People are getting restless. Put on a rumba. An LP if possible.'

Karin found a record and dropped it on to the turntable. The music flooded into the room. With my arm round Karin's waist, we strolled back to the table where Mrs Falcon and Mila had already begun to dance. It was already obvious that Mila was being out-danced. Her belly-wriggling was hopeless and, to make matters worse, she moved very stiffly, holding her body quite erect as she edged round the table. Mrs Falcon, on the other hand, was dancing with her back bent right over, her head almost touching the table-top, her abdomen towards the crowd. When she straightened up she contracted her belly with expertise, making it jump, then she pirouetted gracefully in time to the music, and lasciviously waggled her bottom at the audience. The men were overjoyed and banged the table, as requested, with the exuberant abandon of a tribe of savages. Aware that victory was already assured, Mrs Falcon snaked her way towards Mila and began to dance round her. She seemed propelled by the insistent beat of the music. Un-doubtedly she was trying to revenge herself for the girl's initial jibe but there was nothing bitchily calculated about her dance. In a few moments, Mila began to look like an automaton, one of those expressionless *Folies Bergères* girls, whilst Mrs Falcon was lust incarnate. Once again she moved along the edge of the table, her head bent back towards the audience this time. Her hands swayed gently, hovered over, sometimes brushed against the penises which had so recently applauded her performance.

The moment the music stopped, pandemonium broke out. The old woman was lifted down from the table and was surrounded by cheering men, many of whom vied with each other to kiss and fondle her. My attention was caught by the Mayor who had protested so violently against the public performance of sexual acts.

'Shameful, shameful,' he cried, 'but quite marvellous. Dear lady, you ought to be honoured.'

He pulled one of the ribbons from his dinner jacket and with an absurdly gallant gesture, placed it on Mrs Falcon's *mons veneris.*

from *The Memoirs of an Erotic Bookseller*

'Henceforth, Madame, you are a member of the Order of St Brigitte,' he declared. 'And I dare say this is the first time in history that the order has been fastened to the appropriate spot.'

XAVIERA HOLLANDER
(? ——)

The Classy Hooker and How to Find Her

Xaviera Hollander in *The Happy Hooker* (1972) told, with the help of two ghost-writers, the story of her life as an enthusiastic amateur and then an accomplished professional prostitute. This and her subsequent books are a mixture of frank and (as as one might expect) convincing pornography, and sensible advice on a multitude of sexual hang-ups. In her first book she describes, among other things, how to set up and run a high-class brothel – and how to acquire a good group of girls for it.

Believe it or not, honest, hard-working hookers are hard to find. There were girls around who worked the cheap houses, but they were mostly hardened creatures, and I would not then, nor will I now, ever use a girl who has no class. I don't want street hookers, because their mentality is too cheap. I have a classy clientele who pay high prices for class. If a man would never pick up a girl in the street, why should I expect him to go with a street hooker?

At one point I hired a girl who had worked in a cheap house, and as a result, got exactly what I should have expected. Cheap behaviour. In this case I relaxed my policy because the girl, Misty, was outwardly attractive. But when she undressed, there were stretch marks all over her body from children she gave birth to when she was fourteen and fifteen. At nineteen, when she came to me, she was already used up. And I soon found out her niceness was a very thin veneer.

As is my practice with new girls, I gave Misty a pleasant, attractive man as her first customer. The man, a stockbroker, was slightly drunk, but the easy-to-handle type.

Misty retired to the bedroom with him, but within five minutes dramatically reappeared, charging stark naked into the living room, cursing and swearing.

So I went inside and walked into a screaming match between the customer and Misty. 'Listen,' I cried, taking the customer's side, 'you're not working in a twenty-five-dollar whorehouse, so don't behave like a whore.'

'Goddamnit!' she screamed. 'I've already taken care of that

bastard, and now he wants some more.'

It is my philosophy that a man is entitled to more than five minutes of a girl's time, and even if he climaxes quickly, he can expect to be treated warmly and even babied and washed up, if that's what he wants.

Misty quietened down and promised to co-operate, but her background was too strong, and twice next day I had complaints that she was a hard, cold bitch. So I had to dismiss her. . . .

Different madams have different methods of finding girls to work for them, and on a couple of occasions I tried to follow their examples.

A lesbian madam named Janet cruises the gay-girl bars like Cookies, the Three, and Harry's Back East to find working girls. She finds some little dyke, seduces her, invites her to live in her apartment for a few days, then persuades her to go into the game. This isn't too difficult with lesbians, because basically they hate men and enjoy taking their money in exchange for sex.

I tried Janet's approach one night in Maxwell's Plum. I struck up a conversation with a gorgeous little gray-eyed straight girl in the powder-room.

'You're a very lovely-looking girl,' I said. 'Are you by any chance a model?'

The girl stopped applying her lipstick. 'Oh, no, I'm a legal secretary.'

'How come you dress so beautifully on a secretary's salary?' I asked. 'Do you have a rich fiancé?'

'Heavens, no,' she laughed. 'I wish I did, then I wouldn't have to spend every cent I earn on clothes.'

'A girl like you should not have to work, you should have men spending money on you,' I told her. She was so delicious I would have liked to make love to her myself.

'Where can I find that?' she asked, showing casual but genuine interest.

'I know lots of rich men who would like to spoil you. Are you interested?'

'Oh, sure, I'm interested,' she said earnestly. 'As long as there's no sex involved.'

One of my first and most successful girls was a stewardess from El Al airlines, who was very popular until she got rerouted and we lost her. Stewardesses often drift easily into the professional life as a supplemental income, starting out with having flings with married men from the first-class cabin, then asking themselves why do this for free. After a while they do regular stints in houses from Hong Kong to Helsinki, and London to Los Angeles.

Among my early girls was also a young Englishwoman, a former stewardess, recently separated from her violent American husband and just wanting to make enough money to support herself and pay for her divorce action.

How many times I wished my business were legal so I could, indeed, advertise in the employment columns of the newspapers: good pay, flexible hours, opportunity to meet lots of men.

Another madam I knew recruited her staff entirely from among bored Westchester housewives, and her house flourishes in Manhattan on a modest scale to this day. Inés was a Cuban girl who married an American, went to live in Westchester, and spent her days sitting around with other neglected wives listening to them talk about how they screwed the window-washer, the gardener, the delivery man, and anything moving slower than three miles an hour.

'Listen,' she said to them, 'if you like screwing so much, why don't you come down to Manhattan with me and make money out of it?'

Inés herself got divorced and devoted her time to running the brothel in a midtown apartment, and the girls worked for her in rotating shifts. But she had her staff problems, too, because married women are always taking time off to go on vacation with their husbands or to have babies and hysterectomies.

I started hiring girls who had daytime jobs as secretaries and salesgirls and wanted to make some money on the side. I found they were less jaded and more enthusiastic than a 'working' girl who's been screwing her brains out ten times a day in another house. Many high-class call-girls, on the other hand, are also known to be cold and businesslike.

The next step was promotion. A high-class house advertises strictly by word of mouth of satisfied customers, and never goes out soliciting.

Other areas of prostitution go to any lengths to solicit business, like the semi-legit massage parlors that even put cute little girls on

Lexington Avenue these days posing as poll-takers. The only answers they want are the man's opinion of 'special massage', his name, and office telephone number.

Others, as we all know, openly harass people in the streets and hotels and even sometimes savagely attack them.

An operation like mine never approaches people, but waits for the customers to come because they're interested. In other words, it's a supply situation strictly catering to a demand. And as long as there is such a thing as male libido, the ostrich-like law notwithstanding, there will always be a demand for a high-class brothel.

ERICA JONG
(1942–   )

The Zipless Fuck

Erica Jong's novel *Fear of Flying* (1973) is an hilarious account of a bored married woman's search for sexual liberation, which never comes as easily as she hopes. Extremely funny and acute in its examination of a liberated woman's failure to find sexual freedom as satisfying as is generally supposed, the book is also poignant and in essence deeply serious. Early in it, Ms Jong offers her definition of an entirely satisfactory casual encounter.

The zipless fuck was more than a fuck. It was a platonic ideal. Zipless because when you came together zippers fell away like rose petals, underwear blew off in one breath like dandelion fluff. Tongues intertwined and turned liquid. Your whole soul flowed out through your tongue and into the mouth of your lover.

For the true, ultimate zipless A-1 fuck, it was necessary that you never get to know the man very well. I had noticed, for example, how all my infatuations dissolved as soon as I really became friends with a man, became sympathetic to his problems, listened to him *kvetch* about his wife, or ex-wives, his mother, his children. After that I would like him, perhaps even love him – but without passion. And it was passion that I wanted. I had also learned that a sure way to exorcise an infatuation was to write about someone, to observe his tics and twitches, to anatomise his personality in type. After that he was an insect on a pin, a newspaper clipping laminated in plastic. I might enjoy his company, even admire him at moments, but he no longer had the power to make me wake up trembling in the middle of the night. I no longer dreamed about him. He had a face.

So another condition for the zipless fuck was brevity. And anonymity made it even better.

During the time I lived in Heidelberg I commuted to Frankfurt four times a week to see my analyst. The ride took an hour each way and trains became an important part of my fantasy life. I kept meeting beautiful men on the train, men who scarcely spoke English, men whose clichés and banalities were hidden by my ignorance of French, or Italian, or even German. Much as I hate to from *Fear of Flying*

admit it, there are *some* beautiful men in Germany.

One scenario of the zipless fuck was perhaps inspired by an Italian movie I saw years ago. As time went by, I embellished it to suit my head. It used to play over and over again as I shuttled back and forth from Heidelberg to Frankfurt to Heidelberg:

A grimy European train compartment (Second Class). The seats are leatherette and hard. There is a sliding door to the corridor outside. Olive trees rush by the window. Two Sicilian peasant women sit together on one side with a child between them. They appear to be mother and grandmother and grand-daughter. Both women vie with each other to stuff the little girl's mouth with food. Across the way (in the window seat) is a pretty young widow in a heavy black veil and tight black dress which reveals her voluptuous figure. She is sweating profusely and her eyes are puffy. The middle seat is empty. The corridor seat is occupied by an enormously fat woman with a moustache. Her huge haunches cause her to occupy almost half of the vacant centre seat. She is reading a pulp romance in which the characters are photo-graphed models and the dialogue appears in little puffs of smoke above their heads.

This fivesome bounces along for a while, the widow and the fat woman keeping silent, the mother and the grandmother talking to the child and each other about the food. And then the train screeches to a halt in a town called (perhaps) CORLEONE. A tall languid-looking soldier, unshaven, but with a beautiful mop of hair, a cleft chin, and somewhat devilish, lazy eyes, enters the compartment, looks insolently around, sees the empty half-seat between the fat woman and the widow, and, with many flirtatious apologies, sits down. He is sweaty and dishevelled but basically a gorgeous hunk of flesh, only slightly rancid from the heat. The train screeches out of the station.

Then we become aware only of the bouncing of the train and the rhythmic way the soldier's thighs are rubbing against the thighs of the widow. Of course, he is also rubbing against the haunches of the fat lady – and she is trying to move away from him – which is quite unnecessary because he is unaware of her haunches. He is watching the large gold cross between the widow's breasts swing back and forth in her deep cleavage.

Bump. Pause. Bump. It hits one moist breast and then the other. It seems to hesitate in between as if paralysed between two repelling magnets. The pit and the pendulum. He is hypnotised. She stares out of the window, looking at each olive tree as if she had never seen olive trees before. He rises awkwardly, half-bows to the ladies, and struggles to open the window. When he sits down again his arm accidentally grazes the widow's belly. She appears not to notice. He rests his left hand on the seat between his thigh and hers and begins to wind rubber fingers around and under the soft flesh of her thigh. She continues staring at each olive tree as if she were God and had just made them and were wondering what to call them.

Meanwhile the enormously fat lady is packing away her pulp romances in an iridescent green plastic string bag full of smelly cheeses and blackening bananas. And the grandmother is rolling ends of salami in greasy newspaper. The mother is putting on the little girl's sweater and wiping her face with a handkerchief, lovingly moistened with maternal spittle. The train screeches to a stop in a town called (perhaps) PRIZZI, and the fat lady, the mother, the grandmother, and the little girl leave the compartment. Then the train begins to move again. The gold cross begins to bump, pause, bump between the widow's moist breasts, the fingers begin to curl under the widow's thighs, the widow continues to stare at the olive trees. Then the fingers are sliding between her thighs and they are parting her thighs, and they are moving upward into the fleshy gap between her heavy black stockings and her garters, and they are sliding up under her garters into the damp unpantied place between her legs.

The train enters a *galleria*, or tunnel, and in the semi-darkness the symbolism is consummated.

There is the soldier's boot in the air and the dark walls of the tunnel and the hypnotic rocking of the train and the long high whistle as it finally emerges.

Wordlessly, she gets off at a town called, perhaps, BIVONA. She crosses the tracks, stepping carefully over them in her narrow black shoes and heavy black stockings. He stares after her as if he were Adam wondering what to name her. Then he jumps up and dashes out of the train in pursuit of her. At that very instant a long freight train pulls through the parallel track obscuring his view and blocking his way. Twenty-five freight cars later, she has vanished for ever.

One scenario of the zipless fuck.

Zipless, you see, *not* because European men have button-flies rather than zipper-flies, and not because the participants are so devastatingly attractive, but because the incident has all the swift compression of a dream and is seemingly free of all remorse and guilt; because there is no talk of her late husband or of his fiancée; because there is no rationalising; because there is no talk at *all*. The zipless fuck is absolutely pure. It is free of ulterior motives. There is no power game. The man is not 'taking' and the woman is not 'giving'. No one is attempting to cuckold a husband or humiliate a wife. No one is trying to prove anything or get anything out of anyone. The zipless fuck is the purest thing there is. And it is rarer than the unicorn. And I have never had one.

INDEX TO AUTHORS

INDEX TO SOURCES